FOOL'S PUZZLE

FOOL'S PUZZLE

EARLENE FOWLER

BERKLEY PRIME CRIME, NEW YORK

FOOL'S PUZZLE

A Berkley Prime Crime Book
Published by The Berkley Publishing Group
200 Madison Avenue, New York, New York 10016

Quilt designs by Pepper Cory. Printed in *Happy Trails: Variations on the Classic Drunkard's Path Pattern*, published by C&T Publishing, P.O. Box 1456, Lafayette, California 94549.

First edition: May 1994

Library of Congress Cataloguing-in-Publication Data
Fowler, Earlene.
  Fool's puzzle / Earlene Fowler. —1st ed.
    p. cm. — (A Benni Harper mystery)
  ISBN 0-425-14041-5
  I. Title. II. Series.
PS3558.0929F66 1994   93-32322
813'.54—dc20   CIP

Printed in the United States of America

10 9 8 7 6 5 4 3 2 1

For my husband, Allen—
Without a doubt, I'd choose you again

and

For Mary Edith, sister, friend and
"partner in crime" since
the day I was born

ACKNOWLEDGMENTS

As with most endeavors there are always people to thank.

First, I'd like to thank God for grace and blessings I did nothing to deserve.

I'd also like to thank my parents, family and friends for their support, the Fountain Valley Police Department, the staffs at the Huntington Beach and Newport Beach Public Libraries, Steve Bradley for expert gun advice, Darwin Sainz for sharing his knowledge on cattle, my agent, Deborah Schneider, for her hard work and for taking a chance on a new writer, my editor, Laurie Bernstein, for her expert advice and for never failing to make me feel like a million bucks and to Ann Lee, poet and friend, for her unwavering faith in my ability.

And finally, to Jo-Ann Mapson, writer, critic, friend and cowgirl extraordinaire. If there was a silver belt buckle awarded for teaching, you'd be wearing it.

FOOL'S PUZZLE:

A popular traditional quilt pattern best made
with two contrasting colors. It is easily
cut, but very confusing to set together.
The overall pattern is not apparent from
a single block but must be viewed as a whole.
Also known as "Drunkard's Path," "Falling
Timbers," and "Country Husband."

FOOL'S PUZZLE

1

MY DAY DIDN'T start with murder, although the thought crossed my mind.

"Save me," the voice on the phone whispered.

I jerked the instrument underneath the down comforter. Perfect temperature control was shattered, causing me to growl at my caller. "Go away."

"You're my last chance." It was a harsh, old voice, as ratchety as a Las Vegas Wheel of Fortune.

I laughed in derision. "Tough luck." It was cruel perhaps, but not without justification. I'd been burned by this voice before.

"I won't be held responsible for what I do!"

There was, I noted with satisfaction, a hint of panic.

"You know you'll pay if you try anything rash," I cautioned. "I wouldn't mess with her if I were you."

"But I can't take it anymore."

"She's *your* sister, Gramma."

I glanced at the clock-radio on the nightstand next to my bed—seven A.M.—and on a day I didn't need to be at the Folk Art Museum until ten o'clock. We'd been officially closed for the last week as we set up our new exhibit, a collection of antique quilts owned by residents of San Celina County.

A blast of rain rattled the windows of my small Spanish-style house. The Pacific storm that had been camping for days off California's Central Coast had attacked San Celina during the night. While little mouse soldiers marched double time on the roof, I tried to remember whether I'd closed the windows in my truck.

"She's driving me crazy," Gramma Dove complained. "She's waxed all the floors twice. Follows me everywhere. Keeps rearranging my pots and pans."

Now Dove's voice took on her normal loud tone. Aunt Garnet must have left the room. "She's trimmed all my plants down to nubs with those nasty little embroidery scissors of hers. Benni, she's been eyeing my hair real strange."

Dove's long white braid had tempted her younger sister for years.

"She hasn't seen your house yet. She loves craft festivals."

"No way. I've got too much to do this week with the Folk Art Festival. I can't babysit Aunt Garnet." I struggled up, tucked the covers around me, and waited for the attack to begin. I didn't have to wait long.

"Who bought you your first brassiere, young lady? Waste of money that it was. Who taught you all you know about poker? Who changed your dirty diapers?"

"You didn't come to live with us until I was six," I pointed out.

Another blast of rain slapped the bedroom window. I sank down under the covers and prayed the storm wasn't as bad as it sounded.

She tried blackmail. "I never told your daddy what time you and Jack really came in after the senior prom."

She paused for emphasis. "Yet."

I laughed, imagining her scheming look. "Dove, that was seventeen years ago. My virtue hasn't worried Daddy for a long time."

She went for the throat. "Your mama, God rest her soul, would have wanted you to help your defenseless old granny." Her voice cracked dramatically.

"Mama would have been hiding over here with me. And you're about as defenseless as a wolverine."

I shifted the phone to the other ear.

"Who would have thought a son of mine would raise up such a coldhearted daughter?"

"Seems to me I recall spending most of my childhood tagging after you."

"It's a dollar a chip on Thursday," she said, changing the subject once she knew she wasn't getting her way.

"High stakes this year. Who's coming?"

"Everyone but Clarence. He's got some fevered bulls."

Every year at Thanksgiving, Gramma Dove's children, four sons and two daughters and their families, came from all over the country to meet at my dad's ranch outside San Celina. Everyone wore their best boots and brought a hundred bucks for our no-holds-barred-kick-em-in-the-nuts-when-they're-down poker tournament.

"What time are you going to be here?" she asked.

"I don't know," I said, my mind drifting back nine months to the last time most of the family was together at Jack's funeral. I'd sidestepped an invitation to my in-laws' ranch too; after fifteen years of shuffling back and forth between the Harper and Ramsey ranches, the thought of going either place this year made me feel melancholy and a bit queasy.

Dove's voice softened. A rarity for her. "Come up, honeybun. It'll do you good."

"I have a lot of work to get done before Saturday."

She *tsked* under her breath but didn't press it. "You seen Rita lately?"

"Not since she left here a couple of weeks ago."

"Garnet's chewing nails because she hasn't called."

Aunt Garnet's twenty-one-year-old granddaughter, my cousin Rita, moved out from Arkansas two months ago with vague plans of attending college and starting a new life. On the spur of the moment and to everyone's consternation, she broke a two-year engagement with a wonderfully suitable—Southern for wealthy—man. With a certain amount of doubt and apprehension, I was persuaded into letting her live with me. Aunt Garnet, Daddy and even Dove were convinced the company would do me good.

The Oreo crumbs all over the house I tolerated; even the long, sniffly phone calls to her girlfriends in Pine Bluff only raised my blood pressure a few manageable notches, but the morning I wandered into my own kitchen wearing nothing but a pink tee shirt and a pair of Jack's old hunting socks and encountered a sloe-eyed, bare-chested cowboy in a dirty white Stetson, sipping a mug of my chocolate amaretto coffee, I'd had enough.

"Rita'll be back in a minute," he'd said, appraising me from droopy socks to tangled hair, his left hand disappearing behind a silver belt buckle the size of a pie pan. "Went for doughnuts."

I played with the phone cord as Dove continued to complain.

"I could tell Rita was going to be trouble from the day she was born," she said. "She had shifty eyes even then. Where is she?"

"As far as I know she's still working at Trigger's out by the interstate. She's renting a room from a bartender there. A girl named Marla who belongs to the co-op. I guess it's working out okay."

4

"Two of a kind," Dove pronounced. "Probably bringing home a different fella every night of the week."

I made a noncommittal sound.

"You just get ahold of her and tell her to call Garnet. And you'd better be here on Thursday."

"I'll think about it."

"As long as you're thinking, think of some way to get rid of Garnet. Something that won't throw any suspicion on me."

I couldn't help giggling. Dove and her love-hate relationship with her only sister always raised my spirits. "Chin up, old woman. When does she fly back to Arkansas?"

"Three weeks, hallelujah. You're sure that . . . ?"

"Busy, busy, busy."

"Stubborn brat."

"I understand short hair is much easier to take care of."

She snorted and hung up, as usual, before I could beat her to it. The woman had the reflexes of an eighteen-year-old.

I burrowed back under the covers and tried not to think about what the rain would do to the flimsy canvas tents we'd rented for the Folk Art Festival the co-op was sponsoring this weekend. As curator of the Josiah Sinclair Folk Art Museum and chairman of the Artists' Co-op affiliated with it, it was up to me to figure out what to do, and at that moment all I felt capable of was turning over and going back to sleep.

Formerly a morning person, I'd come to dread them since Jack died. There were times, in that moment between sleep and wakefulness, when I'd hear his voice call my name as clear as if he were bending over me, and I would jerk up, my heart beating like a puppy's, to confront an empty room. But in the last month or two,

I'd become wise to my mind's tricks, and though I still heard his voice, I'd bury my head in my pillow, refusing to be fooled, except for my heart.

I crawled out of bed and padded into the kitchen. A gust of wind and rain sprayed the windows again, giving me the feeling of being trapped inside a giant car wash. After putting on the coffee and feeding some bread to the toaster, I lifted the shade over the sink and studied my reflection in the dark window. I undid my braid and pulled my fingers through the tangled curls. If Dove succeeded in pawning Aunt Garnet off on me, it'd be *my* hair as well as my social life she'd be after. Though she'd long ago given up on Dove and Daddy, Rita and I gave her fresh fodder for her self-acclaimed matchmaking abilities. I felt a brief flash of sympathy for my young cousin. Rita was no match for Aunt Garnet's Noah's-Ark mentality.

Flipping on the radio to KCOW, I commiserated with Patsy Cline as she fell to pieces. Brahma Bob gave his usual highly professional and scientific meteorological report—"Rain, rain, rain, as far as this cowboy can see."

After burning my throat with the first cup of coffee, I carried the second into the bedroom to root around for something to wear. Yesterday's jeans hung on the post of my brass bed and looked clean enough for one more day. I grabbed one of Jack's faded flannel shirts, tucked it into my jeans and rolled up the sleeves. Except for his old Colt .45 pistol, they were the only things of his I hadn't packed away. I'd followed the advice of friends and family and started a new life, but as I rubbed the soft, frayed collar of Jack's shirt against my cheek, I couldn't help but wonder what I would do when they all wore out.

Pulling on one brown boot, I limped around searching for the other. It still amazed me how disorganized I'd become since living alone. Though I'd maintained the Harper Ranch books for ten years, in the three months since I'd moved to town I'd had two warnings from the electric company, spent more time than seemed possible searching for my truck keys, and had once squeezed Ben-Gay on my toothbrush.

After a few minutes of half-hearted searching, I gave up and settled for a pair of white hightop Reeboks and quickly rebraided my hair.

The rain peppered my face with icy needles as I dashed out to the red Chevy pickup truck Jack and I bought the first year we were married. Driving south down University Avenue toward the museum, I became ensnarled in a traffic jam of ranchers' trucks, students late for class and senior citizens trying to make that last breakfast-special. It was the first storm of the season, and San Celina, like all California towns south of San Francisco, was unprepared for its intensity. A pink-haired old lady in a tan Gremlin shot me the bird when I accidentally cut in front of her. I laughed when she ignored my palm-up apology and sped past me. I guess senior citizens in a college town had to get tough or move on.

The old Sinclair Hacienda, once so isolated it took a day on horseback to reach the nearest neighbor, now shared its little piece of commercially zoned real estate with the huge Coastal Valley Farm Supply, San Celina Feed and Grain Co-op and a dozen or so small businesses housed in metal prefab buildings. The rain had washed the off-white adobe walls of the two-story hacienda clean of its usual dust, and the building's normally dull, red-tiled roof glistened.

I parked my truck beneath the initial-scarred oak tree at the back of the lot and squeezed through the small pickups and Japanese imports of the artists, managing to avoid all but one puddle.

Trudging through the lobby, my now piebald shoes squeaking like rubber cat toys, I inspected what Eric, the museum's alleged maintenance man, had accomplished.

In the main hall, the floor was a mine field of tools; wooden quilt hangers languished against the adobe walls, and stacks of quilts lay wrapped in tissue and old sheets I'd scrounged from friends, family and members of the co-op. Plastic would have been easier to get and kept the quilts cleaner, but the book on old quilts I'd almost memorized while getting the exhibit put together said it would rot the delicate cotton fibers.

A portable stereo with tiny speakers blasted Van Halen while a leak from the ceiling into a tin saucepan added a percussive zing every few seconds. Silence answered me when I called Eric's name.

Eric Griffin, part-time handyman and full-time goof-off, had been hired by Constance Sinclair, zealous patron of Central California arts and richest lady in the county. The Josiah Sinclair Folk Art Museum, named for her great-grandfather, was currently one of her favorite projects. Eric, the footloose son of some acquaintance of hers, was another.

She felt all he needed to discover what he should do with his life was the encouragement of an older, wiser person and the structure of a regular job. It was my opinion that at twenty-four he was already *doing* his life, but maybe that was jealousy talking.

Until three months ago, my last official employment had been fifteen years before, serving the graveyard shift at Hogie's Truckstop Cafe out on old Highway One. I'd had to compete with five people for the job as curator, and though low-paying and possessing no benefits except the freedom of flexible hours and dressing as I pleased, I was proud of it. Although my fossilized degree in American History was a rather dubious qualification, it was something.

Eric, on the other hand, was one of those people who tripped through life letting others clear the path for him, and with his dark, Lord Byron looks and bad-boy smile, he always had someone, usually female, willing to Teflon the way.

Flipping off the radio, I walked across the red-brick patio in back to the hacienda's old stables, now the co-op studios and museum offices. In the main studio, the activity of the artists reflected the weather, dark and frenzied.

"Benni, when is the other kiln going to be fixed?" called one of the potters, a thin, nervous man whose slick, clay-covered hands deftly pulled an elegant vase skyward from a greenish mass of porcelain. "And the other wheel? There's a lot of people waiting. And what are you going to do if the rain doesn't stop?"

"I've called three repairmen in Santa Barbara," I said. "The cheapest wants a hundred bucks just to drive up and look at them. We can't afford it until we bring in some money."

His dark, goateed face frowned. "People are depending on this. Can't you get Constance to spring for it?"

"You know the co-op is supposed to be self-supporting. I can't go running to Constance every time something breaks."

He grunted, eyed the vase with a scowl and turned off the wheel.

"I'll try again," I said. "And I'm working on the rain angle. Has anyone seen Eric?"

"Last I saw, he was heading toward the woodshop or your office," a woman at one of the quilt frames said.

"Thanks," I said and leaned over to inspect the quilt they were working on. "Robbing Peter to Pay Paul?"

The quilters laughed. "Right again," one of them said.

It was a game we had going the three months I'd worked here. I prided myself on my ability to recognize almost any traditional quilt pattern. It was knowledge I'd picked up from the infamous Aunt Garnet on visits with Dove to Arkansas when I was growing up. I walked down the hallway past the rows of workrooms, stopping briefly to peek into the woodshop. Inhaling the sweet, pine-scented air, I smiled at the rows of primary-colored rocking horses lined up and ready for their future owners, and waved at Ray, the only occupant this early. A big-shouldered man with a red walrus mustache, he was a talented carver of duck decoys and one of the most genial members of the co-op. He waved back and gave me a bushy grin.

Opening the door to my small office, I caught my quarry enthusiastically pounding away on my word processor. His latest venture, a university extension course in writing romance novels, had caused problems between us before.

"Eric," I said, "we have to get those quilts hung today. You know the pre-showing is Friday night. Can't you do that on your own time?"

He looked up at me with sleepy, thick-lashed, brown eyes even I had to admit were sexy. "Tell me what you think. 'Dack's tongue thrust into her ear like a dental probe. Cassandra melted like fresh butter from her father's dairy farm into helpless desire. When he pressed his throbbing sword of manhood . . .'"

"That's terrible," I said, groaning. "I can't believe you actually read that out loud to a classroom of strangers."

"It must be good," he said, grinning his two-hundred-watt smile. "Three women have asked me out for coffee after class. I think I've found my calling."

"You're despicable," I said, laughing in spite of myself. "You're just taking that class to hit on women."

"Nah." He grinned and winked. "Really, there's a lot of money in this stuff. Women buy these books like candy. It's a gold mine." He went back to tapping. "Sybillia says I have real potential. She's helping me."

"Who?"

"My teacher."

"Her name sounds like a social disease. Anyway, you have a job to do. You can get back to your throbbing swords later."

"One sword, Benni. He only has one. How long has it been for you, anyway?" He waved me away as if I were a pesky horsefly. "One more page."

I walked across the room to the outlet. "File it now or I pull the plug on Dack and Cassandra."

"Just a minute."

"Now." I reached for the plug.

"Oh, all right." He punched the file key on the word processor with a flip of his hand. "If you were nicer to me, I might have considered dedicating the book to you. But now . . ." He heaved an exaggerated sigh.

"I'll try and live with the disappointment. I need you to hang those quilts. Constance will kill us, or rather me, if things aren't perfect on Friday night."

He slipped the data disk into the black plastic file on my desk. "Mine has the red label," he said. "Please don't read it without my permission."

"Out." I pointed toward the museum. "Work."

"Slave driver," he said.

"Reprobate."

His dark eyebrows wrinkled in confusion.

"You want to be a writer," I said. "Get a dictionary."

He tossed his head and marched, in what I assumed was an artistic snit, through the door, slamming it with a bang.

I sat down at my desk and contemplated what I should do next. Knowing Dove would ask the next time she called, I made an attempt to locate my cousin Rita. After calling her house without luck, and trying Trigger's Saloon, where her boss said he hadn't seen her since night before last, I left it at that, figuring I'd made a semi-valiant effort. She'd wander back around eventually, probably when she needed money.

The door of my office flew open.

"Help me," Marla Chenier demanded. She slammed a large foam cup and white paper bag down on my desk, then collapsed in the black-and-chrome office chair across from me.

I reached for the cup. "How?"

"That's a bribe," she said. "I'm in desperate need." She shook her curly black hair, spraying fine droplets of water across my desk blotter, then crossed her long, boot-clad legs. At almost six feet tall with strong, even features and a figure that sent most men into adolescent stuttering, she looked anything but desperate.

"Need is such a relative word," I said, opening the cup lid and taking a quick sip of coffee. "What do we really *need*? Water, air, food . . ."

"Sex." She gave a low growl of a laugh that probably doubled her tips at Trigger's.

"What is it with people today? Everyone's mind is in the gutter. Besides, from a scientific point of view that's not a need. That's a want."

"And where did you hear that lie?"

I looked in the bag and pulled out a large jelly doughnut. "I'd rather have money, but this'll do." I took a bite. "Tell me your needs. Your artistic ones, that is."

"Well, if you can't get me a good man, I'll take the next best thing, time at the wheel." She ran long, jagged-nailed fingers through her wet hair. "I've been behind in my pots since I got walking pneumonia last month."

"Let me look at the schedule." I reached over, pulled out a battered notebook with a tooth-marked pencil attached and flipped through. "One of the wheels is down and we don't have money to pay a repairman." I showed her the filled pages. "Sorry, it's booked solid for five days."

"What am I going to do?" She frowned as she twisted a strand of hair around her finger. "My car insurance is due and my mom's got a thousand-dollar medical bill she needs to pay or the doctor won't see her again." She groaned and shook her hair again. "And I've got tons of people who have ordered pots for delivery by Christmas. I'd hate to get a flaky reputation. My pottery is the *only* good thing I have in my life right now."

I chewed on the pencil and studied the filled pages. I wished she'd told me she needed more time sooner, but one of the earliest lessons I'd learned on this job was that failing to plan ahead was a foible of most creative people.

"You can use it after closing hours," I said, making a quick executive decision I hoped I wouldn't regret. "But only if you can find someone to stay up here with you. I don't want you here alone. It's against the rules, but we didn't count on one of the wheels being down so long."

Her face brightened. "Great! Why don't you stay with me? We'll dish the dirt on the other co-op members. The things I could tell you . . ."

"Sounds tempting but I can't. I have to be at Elvia's bookstore at seven-thirty tonight for an author's talk."

"Anybody I'd know?"

"Not unless you're a bird fancier. Elvia's booked some guy who's written about vultures or condors or some bird.

13

According to Elvia, he's very respected in his field, but she's afraid no one will show up. She's a real softie about her authors."

"So why are you going? Are you into birds?"

I grinned, pulled some three-by-five cards out of my top drawer and waved them. "I'm a shill."

"Like in Vegas?" She chuckled. "What are those?"

"My spontaneous questions."

"You're a better friend than me, Benni." Shaking her head, she stood up. "I'll check around and see if any of the others want to stick around tonight."

"I'd rather you didn't," I said, walking her to the door. "I'm breaking the rules letting you come up here after scheduled hours so we'd better not make it too obvious. Can you get someone outside the co-op to come with you?"

"I'll see what Rita's doing," she said. "I think she's off tonight."

"That reminds me. Where is my dear cousin anyway? Her grandmother is in town and wants to see her."

Marla dug into her large canvas bag, found a rubber band and pulled her hair back into a thick ponytail. "You know Rita, here and there. Our shifts haven't overlapped for a week. She hasn't been home for a couple of days, so I assume she found herself a cowboy and is shacking up for a while."

"That's what I was afraid of."

"Don't worry, I'll hunt her down and tell her to give you a call."

"Thanks." I stood up and walked over to the door. "I don't know how you stand living with her. It about drove me nuts."

Marla pointed a long finger at me. "You got to live and let live, Benni. You were an old married lady for too long. Forgot what it was like to go weak in the knees at the sight of a man in a pair of tight jeans."

Shaking my head, I gave my office door a push as someone from the other side pulled. I fell into a pair of strong, tanned arms.

"Whoa, darlin'," a deep, raspy voice drawled. "Always knew you'd eventually fall for me." I smiled up into amused brown eyes, blue-shadowed with fatigue. Though five years older, two inches taller and twenty pounds heavier, my brother-in-law, Wade, reminded me enough of Jack to make my heart beat faster.

"Hey, Marla." He ran a calloused hand through his gray-streaked chestnut hair. "Lookin' good."

Her face stiffened as she squeezed past him. "You smell like a cattle lot."

"That's the smell of money, darlin'."

She frowned and turned to me. "Thanks for letting me come in tonight. I owe you."

"You find Rita and we're even," I said. I gestured for Wade to come into my office. He pulled off his wet jacket and flopped down in my chair, propping his dirty boots on my desk. I smacked the side of his jean-clad legs. "That better just be mud on those boots." I sat down across from him.

"Take a whiff," he said, winking. "I'm not sure."

"What's going on with you and Marla?"

He crossed his legs and shrugged. "Nothing. I'm always giving her a hard time over at Trigger's." He laughed and locked his fingers behind his head. "Don't worry about it."

"How can you still go there?" I asked.

"I've been going to Trigger's for twenty years. Jack and I had some good times there."

I stared at the floor.

"I did go after him," Wade said bitterly. "I can't help it if he left before I got there. He shoulda never got in that jeep after drinking that much."

"I know," I said with a sigh. "You and Jack argued a dozen times a week. He was a big boy. No one made him go to town."

I said the words he expected, but part of me did blame him for causing Jack to go to Trigger's as well as everyone who let Jack drive away. Maybe most of all, I blamed Jack himself, for not calling me at my dad's ranch to pick him up.

He cleared his throat and looked around. "You got a cup?"

"That's a disgusting habit." I took a last gulp of coffee and poured the rest into my fern before handing him the empty cup. "Have you ever seen a picture of someone who has cancer of the mouth?"

He spit a brown stream of tobacco juice into the cup and pulled at his droopy mustache. "I love ya, Benni, but I believe I got myself a wife already."

"All right." I held up my hands. "It's just that I worry about you. How's everyone doing?"

"We're all fine," he said. "That's why I came by. Brought you those baby quilts Ma made for this shindig you're putting on. And she sent Grandma's old quilt. Rings or something."

"The Wedding Ring quilt," I said. "Great! It'll be a perfect addition to the exhibit. Tell her I'll take good care of it. Is she coming to the festival?"

He picked up my brass letter opener and started flipping it up and catching it by the handle. "Who knows? Since Jack . . . well, you know she's been kinda down. Sandra and the kids are coming, though."

"Tell Mom I'll come out when the festival's over and bring her the money for the baby quilts. They'll sell like crazy the first day, I'm sure. Seems like everywhere I look there's a pregnant woman waddling around."

He threw the letter opener up again, missed, and it clattered down on the desk.

I reached over and grabbed it. "You're worse than one of your kids."

"That's what Sandra's always saying," he said, grinning. He spit in the cup again, then tossed it into my trash can.

I wrinkled my nose, thankful I'd put a plastic liner in the can earlier.

"How's she doing with the computer?" I asked.

"Fine," he said, too quickly.

"Is she having problems with the calf weights again? I could give her a hand when I come out next week."

He ignored my offer, pulled out a small pocket knife and started cleaning his nails.

I pointed the letter opener at him. "You know, it wouldn't hurt you to learn to use it."

"Far as I'm concerned, writing stuff down in Dad's old record books is good enough. That computer business was purely Jack's doing." He wiped the blade of the knife on his jeans.

"Computers are here to stay whether you like it or not. Jack proved you saved money using the PC."

"About enough to pay off his college loans," he snapped. Deep lines of resentment bracketed his lips. He swung his legs down and worked damp jeans back over his boots.

I didn't answer, not wanting to go into the subject that Jack and Wade had argued about since their father died twenty years ago. Anger and frustration over Wade's refusal to acknowledge the changes in ranch management and his stubbornness against trying new methods was what drove Jack into town that night nine months ago.

He stood for a moment glaring at me; then his face softened. "Ma wanted me to check on you and tell her

17

how you're doing. What do you want me to tell her?" he asked in a subdued voice. Like all the Harper men, his temper erupted as unpredictably as a teenage boy's, and dissipated just as quickly.

I stood up and slipped an arm around his slightly thickening waist. "Well, how do I look to you?"

He tugged on my braid and smiled. "You look just fine, blondie." My throat constricted at Jack's old nickname for me.

"You get some rest, Wade."

"I'm okay," he said. "Wish you'd come out and visit more often. Ma and Sandra really miss you."

I studied the tiled floor. "It's hard, Wade."

"I know." His hand rubbed a small circle on my back, the roughness catching on the nubby flannel of his brother's shirt. "Sorry to bring it up, but I promised Ma I'd ask."

"Tell her I'll be out to visit next week."

"Sure thing. Want me to throw that out for you?" He gestured at the trash can.

"A true Western gentleman," I teased. "Don't worry about it. You just watch your back."

"Only way to live," he said, pulling on his jacket.

After he left, I sat at my desk for a long time staring at the keyboard of my word processor. I had plenty of work to do—quilt histories to type and frame, grant applications to fill out, Elvia's condor questions to study, but Wade's visit left me unsettled and fidgety.

I picked up the index cards with the condor questions and shuffled them in irritation. Memorizing things had never been my strong suit, so I tossed them down and decided to live dangerously and fake it. What I needed was to do something physical, something that took no thought. Eric certainly needed the help and he seemed to get more done when I worked with him, so I went out to the main hall of the museum.

When I walked in, Eric and Marla were deep in conversation. He stared at the ground while she poked his shoulder with her forefinger.

"That's all you're getting," she said, her voice tight with anger. "And stay out of it."

"What's going on?" I asked. Startled by my voice, she jerked her head around.

"Nothing," she said, with an impatient wave of her hand. Eric continued studying the floor with a nervous smile on his face. Tossing an irritated glance at him, she pushed through the heavy Spanish door, slamming it behind her.

"What did you do?" I asked as he strapped a worn leather tool belt around his slim hips.

"Could you hand me that box of nails?" he asked, climbing the aluminum ladder. I slapped the box in his outstretched hand.

"You haven't conned money out of her for one of your schemes, have you? I've told you I don't want you asking any of the co-op members for money." Eric's get-rich-quick schemes and the money he'd talked various members of the co-op into "investing" in them were another bone of contention between us.

"It's nothing. Don't worry." He pulled a hammer from his belt and started banging a nail into the wall.

"Marla wouldn't be that mad over nothing. What did you do?"

He climbed down the ladder, walked over to the radio and flipped it on. A rock-and-roll scream exploded from the crackly speakers.

"Eric," I said in my most strident tone.

He ignored me and twisted the dial on the radio.

"This had better be done today," I snapped when I realized he wasn't going to tell me anything. Maybe I'd ask Marla the next time I saw her, if she was in a better mood. Then again, maybe it wasn't any of my business.

I chewed on my bottom lip as I walked back to my office. Sometimes the juggling of the personalities in the co-op, as well as the day-to-day problems of just keeping our head above water financially, seemed like it was more trouble than it was worth. I'd convinced Constance when I applied for the job that looking after a bunch of artists couldn't be any more difficult than seeing to a herd of cattle, something I could do blindfolded. I'd discovered in the last three months that not only were cattle more predictable, they were also more cooperative, even on their worst days.

This was the first time in my life I'd been on my own, and for some reason, it seemed important to make it, even if I wasn't quite sure what that meant. There were times, though I never voiced them to anyone, when I'd contemplated going back to the Harper Ranch; it had been my life for fifteen years. I missed the rhythm of animal time, the repetitive pace of life ruled by their needs and the capriciousness of weather. Though I went home tired from the museum every night, it wasn't the heavy, satisfying tiredness that soaked my shoulders and back after long hours doing calf checks or fixing fence.

But I couldn't get past the feeling that it wasn't right to move back; technically, I wasn't family anymore, and though Daddy would love it, going back to live with him and Dove at the Ramsey Ranch seemed like going backwards.

Throw yourself a pity-party and you'll be the only guest is what Dove would say and she'd be right. I was relatively young, healthy and had an interesting, although low-paying, job. What more could a person ask for these days? With that echoing in my mind, I buckled down and cranked out paperwork the rest of the day, arranging for the use of the San Celina High School gym in case of rain and trying to convince the one repairman who would hear me out to fix our kiln and wheel, then bill us. The minute he heard we were an artists co-op, he made a rude remark somewhere between "Right" and a grunt before he hung up.

At six-thirty, my best friend, Elvia, called.

"You're still coming, aren't you?" she asked.

"Wouldn't miss it," I said. "Is the birdman there yet?"

"No smart remarks tonight, Benni. He's very serious about his work."

Elvia managed Blind Harry's Bookstore and Coffee House for the absentee owner, a shadowy Scottish man who owned three casinos in Reno. He bought it five years ago as a tax write-off and expected to keep it as such. He underestimated Elvia. The first year, she finagled funds out of him to make the store's inventory the largest in the county. The second year, she converted the basement storage area to a coffeehouse with round oak tables that seated six, and walls lined with used books that were borrowed and replenished on a regular basis by customers. Serving the best espresso and cheesecake in town, it became the favorite hangout for college kids as well as a growing literary crowd moving in from L.A. and San Francisco.

"I'll be good," I said. "Is there going to be any food at this thing? All I've had to eat today was a jelly doughnut and I'm starving."

"Don't worry," she said. "I'll see that you're fed. Do you look presentable?"

I inspected my mottled Reeboks and brushed at the dried mud. "Reasonably so."

"What are you wearing?" she asked. Since she'd taken charge of the bookstore, her personal shopping habits had caused Anne Klein stock to rise twenty points.

"Who are you, my mother? Don't worry. I look exactly like someone who slogs through marshes looking at birds."

"Condors are not waterfowl," she said. "Didn't you read the cards I gave you?"

I decided silence was the safest response.

"Benni!" she wailed. "You promised."

"I'll be fine, Elvia. I'll memorize them on the way over. Have I ever let you down before?"

She groaned and hung up.

When I walked through the main hall, Eric was, as I'd expected, nowhere to be found. There was evidence that he'd worked, but not enough to convict him. My stomach fluttered in panic, a feeling I attempted to reason away. Not counting Thanksgiving, we still had a day and a half until the pre-showing and auction on Friday night. Plenty of time.

"Honey," Jack used to say when he'd walk in the door, dusty and tired after a long day, and I'd hit him with a list of chores, "I'd be happy to do whatever you need doing, but I can only do one thing at a time."

In the last nine months, his words came back to me whenever I thought I wouldn't make it through another day, another new problem. One thing at a time. And the one thing I needed to do at that particular moment was go see a man about some birds.

2

IT TOOK ME twenty minutes to get a space in the crowded municipal parking lot on Lopez Street. San Celina's
downtown merchants had started their tussle for holiday
dollars the week before with implausible window displays
of a Willie Nelson Santa bulldogging Rudolph, lavender
Christmas trees with power tool ornaments, and pop art
ski wear designed for bodies that could never possibly
have experienced the joy of a McDonald's sundae with
double fudge.

In the last hour, the rain had stopped, but the
infamous, jacket-piercing San Celina wind stung my
cheeks as I stepped down from the truck. I shoved
my hands deep into the pockets of my sheepskin coat.
As I walked toward Blind Harry's, uneasy feelings about
the approaching holiday surrounded me like a mulish
tule fog.

I'd traveled this route with Jack hundreds of times.
The malted milk scent of baking waffle cones, the monkey chatter of skittish teenagers, the wrought-iron street
lamps, draped with fake evergreen and twinkly lights,
were like a favorite old movie. Only the distance felt

different. The three long blocks to the bookstore seemed to stretch the length of my life.

"Where have you been?" Elvia asked. She stood tapping her foot at the top of the scuffed wooden stairs leading to the coffeehouse. "Professor Murphy's talk starts in ten minutes." She searched my face with black, vigilant eyes. "Oh, *amiga*, are you all right?"

"Nice hairdo." I pretended not to hear her question as we walked down the stairs. There's just no way to explain despair without sounding melodramatic. "Isn't that a French twist? Looks very . . . French."

She touched her glossy hair self-consciously and tried not to appear flattered. Elvia's great disappointment in life, to the irritation of her six brothers and bewilderment of her native Mexican parents, was to have been born an American rather than a European.

"Sit there." She pointed to a round table in front of an antique wooden pulpit where a short, rabbit-nosed man in an olive-green corduroy jacket muttered to himself while shuffling through a stack of papers. "Did you look at my questions?"

"Yes," I said. I had indeed looked at the questions. Just hadn't read them. I pulled the cards out of my pocket and waved them at her.

"Don't be so obvious." She pushed me down in one of the oakwood ladderback chairs she'd purchased when the city built the new public library last year.

"You're so bossy."

"Look through his book," she whispered. She shoved a heavy coffee table book in front of me. The cover featured a picture of the ugliest bird I'd ever seen. "Take it up to be signed after his talk."

"Do I get to keep it?" Though in my estimation, a jumbo-sized book on the California condor was not adequate compensation for my trouble, it would make a fine Christmas gift for Dove, one she could complain about for months.

"Yes, yes." She fluttered the air around her with slender fingers and hurried to the back of the room to supervise the buffet of finger sandwiches, pastries and horrible French roast coffee she always served at her literary events.

I tucked the book under my arm and moved to a side table. If forced into asking fabricated questions, I preferred not sitting front-and-center while doing it.

To my surprise, the birdman's talk proved interesting and amusing. With his soft-spoken, slightly batty sense of humor, he seduced the audience of mostly senior citizens attending for the free food into sympathetic support for the almost extinct California condor. As he explained in elaborate, somewhat graphic detail how condors mated, I felt a sharp thwack on the back of my head.

"Hey, cut it out," I said. "Those nails of yours ought to be registered as lethal weapons."

"How condors mate was *not* one of the questions I gave you." Elvia set a steaming white mug in front of me. Her Chanel red lips curved upward, softening her reprimand.

"He seems to be enjoying himself." I held my face over the *café au lait* and inhaled the aroma before taking a sip. She offered a plate of tiny sandwiches. I popped one of the crustless triangles in my mouth, then grimaced. "What is this?"

"Watercress and parsley," she said. "The professor's a vegetarian."

"I must be starving." I grabbed another. "They're awful."

"What's awful?" said a voice behind us.

"Hey, Marla," I said. "What are you doing here?"

25

"I'm double-parked. We need a key." She pushed a long strand of dark hair behind her ear and adjusted her red baseball cap.

"I guess it was too much to expect Eric to be there working. Shoot, the spare keys are in my desk."

"I've got Eric with me, but he doesn't have his keys."

"If I ever figure out why Constance keeps him on, I'll give myself a raise." I pulled my key ring out of my purse and twisted the museum keys off. "I'll need them to open up in the morning, so I'll come by later. That is, unless you want to be up there bright and early."

"Sorry, I'm an artist. I don't do mornings."

"I should be so lucky. How long are you staying tonight?"

"Three, maybe four hours." She pocketed the keys and started up the stairs.

"Wait, I'll go with you. It'll be wasted breath, but I need to talk to Rita and Eric." I grabbed another green-filled triangle and stood up. "You know, these taste a lot like how alfalfa smells."

"Benni," Elvia protested. "The professor's still talking."

"Two minutes," I said. "He won't even know I'm gone." I jerked my thumb at the professor, who, with an ecstatic expression and outstretched arms, imitated condor flight. A couple of bemused-looking elderly ladies at a front table leaned back slightly in their chairs as he swooped in their direction. "Believe me, Elvia, he'll never notice."

On the passenger side of Marla's blue Volkswagen van, in front of an extra-wide visor mirror, my cousin Rita practiced her smoky-eyed, pouty look. In the back seat, eyes closed, Eric bobbed his head to the Walkman sprouting from his ears.

"Where have you been?" I propped my elbows on the window ledge. "It's an open question," I added in a loud voice. Without opening his eyes, Eric threw me a two-finger kiss.

"Around," Rita said. She poked at her shoulder-length Dolly Parton hair with a bright pink fingernail.

Superficially, our looks affirm our familial connection, though I'm still not convinced of the Southern dictum declaring fifth cousins, or whatever we are, family. At slightly over five feet tall with curly, reddish-blond hair and hazel eyes, we sound the same on paper, the difference being I use one can of hairspray a year where she is personally responsible for at least a half-mile hole of ruined ozone layer.

"Garnet's going nuts," I said. "Would you give her a call so she'll quit bugging Dove who will then quit bugging me?"

"She's just here to deliver a message from Mama," she said. "And I know what it is. Come home now." She pumped a tube of mascara, and flashing the whites of her eyes, applied what had to be a fifth coat. "Thanks, but I'll pass. I'm through with the South. I'm a Westerner now."

"Well, do whatever you want. Just be careful."

"I intend to." She smiled chimpanzee-wide, and rubbed at a spot of pink lipstick on her teeth.

"Be careful?" I asked hopefully.

She laughed and snapped the visor up. "Right. Loosen up, Benni. You sound like my mother."

"Your way of loosening up is a bit risky for me," I said. The psychic mileage between age twenty-one and thirty-four beat the distance to Mars.

"You two done squabbling?" Marla said from the driver's seat. "Some people have work to get done."

"Lock the studio doors behind you," I called after them. "And get those quilts hung." Eric's head bobbed up and down, though I suspected it had nothing to do with my request.

27

By the time I walked back downstairs, Professor Murphy had finished his flight and was signing books.

"And what is your name, young lady?" He poised a chubby hand over the flyleaf of my copy.

"Dove Ramsey," I said. Now she wouldn't even be able to recycle it. Garnet owed me; it probably would have been her next birthday present.

"Lovely bird, the dove." He signed his name with a flourish. "Not a condor, but a lovely bird, nonetheless."

I spent the next hour upstairs in the bookstore attempting some half-hearted Christmas shopping. I chose a book on championship poker strategy for Dove, to make up for the condor book. The updated *Veterinary Handbook for Cattlemen* took care of Daddy. But before making a bigger dent in my list, I became engrossed in an oral-history book chronicling the lives of Midwestern farm women during the Dust Bowl years of the 1930's. Edith Bennett was saying how hard her husband took it seeing the farm blow away, how he took his pain out gettin' mad with her and how a woman always seems more able to rise above it, take more hurting and keep on going. Then she gave her recipe for Mock Apple Pie made with soda crackers. As I was mentally rolling out the crust along with her, the store's lights blinked twice and the round schoolhouse clock in the children's department chimed ten o'clock.

At the front of the store Elvia helped with the last-minute rush of customers. When I caught her eye, she raised her eyebrows in question.

"When you have time, put these on my account," I said over the crowd. I shoved the books across the counter to her.

"Thanks for coming, *gringa*," she said. "Even if you embarrassed all my senior citizens with your obscene questions."

"Just trying to add a little excitement to the dry tomes of avian academia."

She rolled her eyes and turned back to the cash register.

I hurried toward my truck, pulling up the collar of my jacket against the cold mist swirling around me. Annoyed at myself for not thinking to give the extra keys to Marla that morning, I tried not to think about the warm bed waiting for me at home.

The truck tires hissed over wet, luminous streets as I drove the two miles to the museum. Just before I turned into the parking lot, Marla's van sped past me. Rita was driving. Alone. I honked once and waved. She either didn't see me or ignored me. She must be going out to get food, I thought.

I'd discovered since working at the co-op that most craftspeople, once they finally started, didn't like to take the time to stop for meals, so munched along as they worked. Marla was no exception. I mentally congratulated Marla for putting Rita to some use.

Parking lot gravel popped and cracked like rice cereal under my Reeboks as I walked toward the museum. The front door yawned at me.

"Well, that's just great," I said out loud. So much for security. Pulling the door closed behind me and locking it, I walked past the still-unfinished quilt exhibit, across the patio and into the main studio, my feelings cascading from anger to frustration to resignation because there was nothing you could do to force people into being anything but what they are.

The area around the potter's wheel informed me Marla was still working. A pot posed half-formed on the wheel; clay, water, rags, two cans of Diet Coke and an empty bag of corn chips decorated a worktable nearby. Somewhere a radio played low—Johnny Cash was falling into a ring of fire. I hugged my jacket closer and envied him.

"Marla?" I called out. "Eric?" My voice had a tinny echo in the empty room. No one answered. I walked back toward my office. Since Eric obviously wasn't working on the exhibit, there was only one other thing he could be doing. That stupid book.

"Eric?" I called again. "Marla?"

Going down the hallway toward my office, I noticed light under the woodshop door. I pushed the door open. An acrid odor rose up, stung my nose. Across the L-shaped room, a worktable lay on its side. An open quart of marine varnish spread into a hardening pool on the concrete floor. I went over and tilted the can upright. Sticky varnish clung to my fingers. Irritated, I headed around the corner to find some rags to clean it up.

I felt my mouth open when I saw Marla, but it was like one of those terrible nightmares where you're struck dumb—I couldn't squeak a sound. She was sprawled in front of the sink, one leg twisted under her. Blood soaked her yellow tee shirt. It swam before my eyes in a kaleidoscope pattern. The brad awl sticking out of her chest quivered in the red river of what had to be arterial bleeding. I reached out to stop the vibrating wood-working instrument.

"No." My voice was a painful whisper. The awl seemed to move again. I stared at my hand. The awl wasn't shaking. I was.

CPR, I thought—I should do CPR. I searched the wool in my brain for the numbers—fifteen to two, five to one—I needed a partner—where was my partner—she looked like that doll—clean the cold lips with alcohol—stings—terrible smell—like hospitals—like death.

Stop it, I commanded myself. You can do this. You've pulled calves, you've seen blood. A circle of gray started to close around my eyes. This wasn't like cattle. This was a human being. How would I do the compressions, stop the bleeding? The awl would have to be pulled out. Acidy bile rose in my throat. I grabbed the edge of the sink counter. The cold tile shocked me back to reality. She might not be alive. Find out. I bent down, touched her neck gently. Then harder. Nothing.

I backed up. A rushing, jet-engine sound filled my ears. I ran for my office.

"Help," I croaked to the 911 operator. "Please."

"What's the problem?" she asked calmly. Her tiny alien voice sounded planets away.

"Marla's dead," I said. "The Folk Art Museum. Mission Highway." I felt my stomach roll. "Please. Somebody come."

"The police are on their way," her placid voice replied. I dropped the phone.

Get out, my brain said. Whoever did this is still here. Get to the truck. Run. I gripped the handles of my chair, head reeling. *Run.*

I stood up, swayed uneasily, fell back into the chair. Some things are more urgent than fear. Gripping my stomach, I puked into my trash can thinking absurdly as I gagged—watercress sure doesn't taste a heck of a lot different the second time around.

3

"HERE, DRINK THIS." Miguel, one of Elvia's younger brothers, and a new patrol officer with the San Celina Police Department, handed me a gray thermos cup of coffee. He'd stopped by after hearing the address of the murder on his radio.

"Thanks," I said, gripping the plastic cup with both hands.

"Watch it." He grabbed my arm, pulling me out of the way as the coroner's black van drove up next to us. His large hand enveloping my elbow was comforting. It still surprised me whenever I saw him, chesty and solid, in his blue uniform. He couldn't be the same little boy I'd once read *Goodnight Moon* to fifteen times in a row because he didn't want the light turned out.

"They won't let me go home. Why can't I go home?" I closed my eyes and shivered in spite of my sheepskin jacket. In the blackness I saw Marla's bloodstained chest again, the waterfall of so much human blood. I opened my eyes.

"Sorry, Benni." He lifted his hand and ran a square hand over his cropped black hair. "The chief said he wanted to talk to you himself."

"So where is he?"

"The detective I asked said he was down in Santa Barbara when they beeped him. You know it takes about two hours to drive up. He oughta be here soon."

"Can they do this, Miguel? Keep me like this? Don't I have rights or something?"

"They can pretty much do what they want." He gave me an apologetic look, then narrowed his dark-spaniel eyes. "It'd be better for you to cooperate. Better be careful with this new chief. He doesn't have much of a sense of humor. He may not find your smartass remarks so funny."

"I have no idea what you're talking about." I danced from one foot to the other in an attempt to get warm.

"Yeah, well, don't say I didn't warn you."

"You said he's not the real chief? What's the deal?"

"He's a temporary guy. Chief Davidson's on medical leave. Hepatitis or his liver or something. Guess this Ortiz is from L.A."

"Another transplant? They're like ants, nothing stops them. Couldn't they get a local to take the job?"

"I dunno. Maybe nobody wanted it."

"Makes you wonder why he did."

I sat down on the wide bumper of my truck. Police cars surrounded it, foiling any thoughts I might have of escape. No matter how tightly I pulled my jacket around me I couldn't stop shaking, couldn't stop thinking. Marla dead. Where was Eric? Where was Rita?

They had to know Marla was dead. At least Rita anyway. I'd seen her drive away. Where was she going? What was she thinking, driving away like that? What had she seen? My stomach lurched considering the possibilities.

"I've got to get back in the field." Miguel's deep voice jarred me back. "You going to be okay?"

"No, but there's nothing you can do about it." I watched him zip up his heavy jacket and fought the urge to beg him to stay.

"Want me to call Elvia?" he asked.

I handed back the empty cup. "No, it's too late. I'll call her tomorrow. Thanks for the coffee. You're a good kid."

He slipped a heavy arm around my shoulders and squeezed. "Hang in there. It'll be over before you know it."

After he left, I walked over to one of the detectives who'd interviewed me. He rested his forearms on a small mountain of a stomach as he chicken-scratched in a palm-sized notebook.

"Excuse me," I said.

His eyebrows were bushy canopies over mud-colored eyes.

"What can I do for you, Ms. Harper?"

"I was wondering when I can lock up and go home."

He sighed heavily. "Like I told your friend, Officer Aragon, the chief wants to view the scene and talk to you himself. None of us are going to be leaving until he gets here."

"Can't I tell him my story tomorrow?"

"Sorry." He stuck the battered notebook inside his jacket and lifted a meaty hand in apology. "Orders."

"Well, that's just great," I said. I walked back and sat down again on my bumper where, out of anxiety and a certain amount of irritation at bureaucratic pettiness, I flicked small rocks at the license plate of one of the patrol cars blocking my escape.

I gave myself ten points every time I hit the plate. Minus ten if it careened off the dented bumper. The moon inched across the sky at the same rate the chief was apparently driving up the interstate. I watched the detectives send a patrolman for coffee twice; the second time he had doughnuts. A blond uniformed officer with a crew cut offered me a cup both times. The first time, I accepted. By the time they offered the second, my stomach gurgled a definite *no*.

I was up to two hundred points when an older, sky-blue Corvette with an off-white rag top roared into the parking lot. I hoped it was the chief because I'd already decided that at four hundred points I was going home. Even if I had to walk.

A tall, fortyish, Hispanic man in round wire-rimmed glasses stepped out of the car. He ignored me as he walked past, ducked under the yellow crime scene tape and disappeared into the museum.

Frustrated, I picked up another handful of rocks and tossed one.

"That could be construed as vandalism against city property," a familiar voice said with a chuckle. "California Penal Code 594. It's a serious crime, Mrs. Harper, right up there with giving a false name to a newspaper."

"So call a cop." I turned to smile at Jack's best friend and old college buddy, Carl Freedman. I moved over and patted the bumper. "Have a seat. How'd you get through? I would have thought you'd be the last person they'd let talk to me."

"I told them I was a new investigator with the County Coroner's office." His tanned face crinkled as he flashed a cocky white grin.

"And they fell for it?" I asked, though I believed it. With his gold-blond hair, pale chambray-blue eyes and unabashed manner, he could sweet-talk the letter "g" out of the alphabet. His Hollywood smile had caused more than one woman to compare him to Robert Redford, something he played up so often, Jack used to call him the Sundance Kid.

"You've worked on your dad's paper since you could spell your name," I said. "They should all know you by now."

"I can still fool some of the rookies." He draped a wiry arm around me. "Need a friendly shoulder?"

"In exchange for what?" I leaned my head back against his arm. "Why are you here, anyway? Since when does your father let you cover the important stuff?"

"Since big brother is in Hawaii and Dad's got the flu," he said in a light voice.

"So what took you so long to get here, Jimmy Olsen? It's after two o'clock."

"Had a game of pool, a pitcher of beer and Lois Lane to finish."

"Is that what you're going to tell your dad?"

"Forget him," he said. He pulled out a pocket-sized tape recorder. "Now, tell your old buddy all the gory details."

Before I could answer, a husky, irritated voice interrupted him.

"Who are you?"

The Hispanic man I assumed to be the chief scrutinized us with cold blue-gray eyes. He wore faded Levi's, a pink polo shirt and a white windbreaker. His straight black hair was cut close and parted on the side—a lawyer's haircut. A thick, neatly trimmed black mustache hid his mouth, but by the set of his jaw, he wasn't smiling.

Carl bounced up, grinned and held out a hand. "Carl Freedman, *San Celina Tribune*. How about a personal interview for the Lifestyle Section next Sunday? How do you like living on the Central Coast, Chief Ortiz? Got any interesting hobbies?"

"Impersonating a county official can buy you a lot of trouble," the man said, ignoring Carl's hand. "Get lost."

Carl faced me, his back to the chief, and crossed his eyes. "You going to be okay?"

"Oh, sure," I said. "Now that Joe Friday has arrived."

Carl mouthed, I'll call you later.

I nodded and gave him a grateful smile. His silliness had helped me forget for a minute the reality of what had happened. As flaky as he was in other areas, Carl was good at that. I don't think I would have made it through those first few weeks after Jack's death without Carl distracting me with stories about the crazy assign-ments his dad gave him for the Lifestyle section of the newspaper.

The chief stared at me silently. Out of sheer nervous-ness, I threw a rock and hit the license plate. When he didn't comment, I threw another one. Finally, he spoke.

"Albenia Harper?" His voice was as flat and controlled as a news anchor's.

"That's me." Plink.

"I'm Chief Ortiz."

"That's you." I threw two and gave myself double points.

"I need to speak with you."

"So speak." Three hundred fifty and counting.

"Would you please stop that?" His voice carried a slight edge this time.

Plink. I knew I was pushing it, but I'd been up there almost four hours; fatigue had short-circuited the more judicious side of my nature, which wasn't one of my strongest traits even when I wasn't cold, tired, scared and had a mouth that tasted like coffee-flavored puke.

"Ms. Harper." Somehow he managed to put the threat of all his power and authority into two words.

Prudence kicked in. I dropped the rocks in the dirt, stood up and brushed off the back of my jeans. I was a smartass, but not a stupid one.

"Are you through?" he asked.

"I guess so." I looked up into eyes the same color as a winter ocean. Odd for a Hispanic. They studied me coolly from behind his gold wire-rimmed glasses.

"Then I'd like to ask you a few questions." He pulled a small leather notebook and gold Cross pen from the pocket of his windbreaker.

"I've already told two of your detectives everything I saw."

"And now," he said evenly, "you can tell me."

So I repeated my story a third time, leaving out the same small detail I had with the others. I didn't tell him about Rita. It was a stupid move, but I felt a perverse sense of family loyalty and wanted to hear her side before throwing her to the blue-uniformed wolves. I didn't believe she'd killed Marla. Frankly, the whole thing baffled me. Now, if it had been Rita killed by Marla, that might have been understandable, maybe even justifiable.

As I spoke, Chief Ortiz's face remained expressionless. Occasionally, he jotted something in his notebook. When I finished, he didn't comment but stared over my head into the dark forest of eucalyptus trees behind me. I knew what he was trying to do and I was determined not to feel intimidated.

I leaned against the truck and crossed my legs. Then my arms. After a few minutes, I uncrossed both. I chewed on a hangnail. All the coffee I'd consumed started to burn in my stomach. Trying to ignore the ache, I studied the interesting mud patterns on my shoes. I contemplated asking him for a breath mint. After five minutes of silence, I had to admit he was making me nervous, and that really annoyed me.

"You said a Mr. Eric Griffin, the museum handyman, was up here with Ms. Chenier," he finally said.

"That's right."

"And no one else."

"Right." I dropped my eyes, then realizing it probably appeared suspicious, looked back up. He raised a skeptical eyebrow and adjusted his glasses.

"How did they get here?" he asked.

"I'm not really sure." I forced myself to meet his gaze.

"Where were you this evening?"

"At Blind Harry's Bookstore downtown. Until ten or so."

"Did you see Ms. Chenier at any time this evening?"

"When she came by to pick up the keys. Eric didn't have his."

"And who was with her?"

"I told you. Eric."

"What were they driving?"

"Marla's van. I gave them my keys and they left. That's it."

His unblinking examination finally got to me and I dropped my eyes, not caring how it appeared. I studied the ground around his feet. He wore beat-up leather topsiders—no socks. Shoes say a lot about a man. His screamed L.A. yuppie. More specifically, Orange County—where everyone from birth to ninety dresses like a student from an East Coast prep school or a Beach Boys fan. I nervously smoothed back some curly strands of hair tickling my face and looked back up at him.

"This is a waste of time," I said. "I've told all this to two of your detectives. With how long it's taken to get this thing going, her killer could be in Oregon by now."

He gave me a long look, acknowledging that my comment hit home, he didn't appreciate it, and was choosing to ignore it.

"What was your relationship with Ms. Chenier?"

"We worked together."

"Were you friends?"

"I suppose. I've only worked here three months. I don't know anybody real well. Why?"

"You seem pretty flippant for someone who just found their friend stabbed to death."

He wasn't the first person in my life who had deemed it their right to decide that my response to something wasn't appropriate. I didn't feel the need to inform this jerk I was taught that people with backbone didn't fall apart in public. If you absolutely had to give in to tears, that's what showers were for.

"I'm sorry my emotional reactions don't meet your standards," I said, with as much deference as I could manage. "May I go home now?"

His dark eyebrows squeezed together in a scowl. "Let me see your hands."

"What?" I instinctively shoved them in my jacket pockets.

He tucked his notebook and pen in his windbreaker and held out a large brown hand. "Ms. Harper, your hands, please."

Reluctantly, I pulled them out. They were grimy from the rocks and crusty from dried varnish. I presented them, palms down.

He touched the gold band on my left hand. "Has someone let you call your husband?"

"Don't worry about it," I said.

With an enigmatic expression, he took my hands, turned them over and felt my fingertips with his thumbs.

I shivered even though his hands were surprisingly warm. His contact reminded me of the smooth feel of Marla's neck. I wanted to pull my hands back, race home, scrub them clean.

"I'll need a set of your fingerprints," he said, dropping my hands.

"Why?" Fear twisted my stomach. It never occurred to me I'd be a suspect.

"Just procedure. It shouldn't bother you if you have nothing to hide." He looked at me pointedly. "I'll need to talk to you again tomorrow."

"Fine." I edged past him, heading toward the museum, when he called to me.

"Ms. Harper."

I turned around. "What?" I didn't even attempt to keep the annoyance out of my voice.

"I've been in law enforcement for twenty years. I know when someone is lying. What aren't you telling me?"

I took a deep breath, trying not to let my panic show. "I have nothing else to say," I muttered, staring at the bridge of his glasses.

He gave me another long look. "I'll need a list of the co-op members and their addresses."

"I'll print one up for you tomorr—"

"Now."

"Yes, sir," I said under my breath.

After printing an address list on my word processor and giving it to the bushy-browed detective, I waited on the front porch of the museum for the last of the criminal investigation team to leave. Someone had finally brought me my purse, so I assumed it wouldn't be much longer before I was allowed to lock up. Then I really needed to think. I couldn't let the artists walk in on that mess. Someone would have to clean it up. The thought of doing it myself made me reach out and grab one of the posts supporting the porch.

I ran through my mental list of co-op members, stopping at Ray Winfry, the decoy carver. He was dependable and kind, and more importantly, had served a tour in Vietnam. Maybe this wouldn't faze him much.

41

Rita presented a whole separate problem. I needed to track her down and find out what had happened. And Eric. I didn't even want to think about him. Could he have killed Marla? I remembered the argument they'd had and realized I'd forgotten to tell anyone about it. I decided it could wait until tomorrow. I didn't think I had it in me for another round with Ortiz. I closed my eyes, pinched the bridge of my nose and told myself this would all be over soon.

The heavy Spanish door of the hacienda slammed open, causing me to jump. Two men in dark jumpsuits maneuvered the gurney over the threshold. They bumped Marla's navy-bagged body down the three steps indifferently, as if moving an old sofa. Tears started to fill my eyes and a sourness inched back up my throat.

"Ms. Harper." A deep voice came from behind me.

I ignored it, my attention held captive by the long, bulky bag. When it threatened to come out of the safety belts, one of the attendants casually shoved it back in place. I rubbed the back of my neck with an icy palm in an attempt to stop the queasy churning in my stomach. Was this how Jack was treated? I felt an irrational anger at the callousness of the attendants. Logically, I knew they had to treat their job that way or go crazy, but I wanted to scream—she's a person, not a sack of feed.

"Ms. Harper, look at me." The imperious voice wouldn't give up.

"What is it?" I whipped around to face Chief Ortiz.

He leaned against one of the rough posts, eyes mild behind owlish glasses.

"Your name," he said. "Albenia. Where did you get it?"

"My parents gave it to me." I frowned at him. Where was this line of questioning going?

A faint smile played around the corners of his mouth. "I assumed that. Where did they get it?"

I sighed in exasperation, not believing I was discussing name origins at two in the morning with some L.A. yuppie posing as the chief of police while the body of someone I'd talked to only six hours ago was being bounced around like a bale of hay.

"My mother's name was Alice. My father's name is Benjamin. What does this have to do with Marla's murder?"

"Interesting." He nodded and pulled at the end of his mustache. "Are you called Albenia?"

"No."

He raised his eyebrows and waited.

"Benni," I snapped.

"Did you know that in Latin your name means blonde?"

"What does that have to do with anything?"

Before he could answer, the sharp *clamp* of the back of the coroner's van distracted us. We watched it pull slowly out of the parking lot onto the highway. Realizing then what he'd been doing, I turned back and nodded.

"Thanks," I said reluctantly.

He shrugged and stuck his hands in the pockets of his jacket.

"No one took my fingerprints," I said.

"Come down to the station tomorrow. It's just a formality."

"You mean I'm not the chief suspect?" I said sarcastically. "I can leave town if I want?"

"I think your proclivity to tidy up, not to mention your graphically vivid physical reaction, pretty much eliminates you as a suspect."

"Oh." I considered his comment. "Then why do you need my fingerprints? Why do you have to talk with me again tomorrow? I won't know any more than I do now."

"You think not?" His aloof mask returned. "I only said you weren't *a* suspect. I never said you weren't suspect."

On that note, I changed the subject. "Who's going to tell Marla's family? I put her mother's address on the list I gave your detective." My voice faltered. That horrible knock in the middle of the night. Every woman's secret fear—for her husband, her son, her daughter. Except it didn't happen like that for me. The sheriff's deputy went to the Harper Ranch first. I was always sorry Wade was the one to tell me. It would have been easier to hate a stranger that first terrible moment.

Ortiz's mask slipped for a split second. A pained look flashed across his face, then disappeared.

"It'll be taken care of." He pulled his hands out of his pockets and walked toward the remaining emergency vehicles. "I'll see you tomorrow," he said over his shoulder.

"Right," was all I could think of to say. At that moment, I was tired of making wisecracks, tired of trying to avoid questions, tired of being more involved in this than I should have been. And I was just flat-out tired.

After locking up the studios and the museum, I walked out to my truck. Two other vehicles were left in the parking lot: a nondescript beige four-door and Ortiz's Corvette. Detective Bushy-brows whispered low to Ortiz, then climbed into the four-door.

I cranked the ignition, waiting for it to catch. The Chevy had needed something done to the engine for months but I'd put off getting it checked. Jack and Wade always worked on our trucks, so I didn't have a clue about how to find a trustworthy mechanic. With all the extra work Wade had at the ranch, I didn't want to bother him, so I'd just babied it along, irrationally hoping whatever was wrong would right itself.

I cranked it again, then hit the steering wheel in frustration, my eyes filming over. Through the blur I glanced over at Ortiz leaning against his car, his arms crossed, watching me. When he started moving toward the truck, I tried again.

"Come on," I begged. The ignition gave a loud screech. Though I couldn't see it, I'm sure he winced. There isn't a man alive who doesn't when he hears that sound. Finally, the engine caught. As I swung past, my headlights spotlighted him for a moment. He inclined his head in a single nod.

His small acts of kindness didn't fool me. They had a purpose. Obviously a man who believed in living by the rules, when he found out I'd withheld information concerning Marla's murder, there'd be no telling what he'd do.

Hopefully, I wouldn't be the one to tell him. When I found Rita, she'd be the one in the hot seat. Just what she deserved. Until then, I'd stall him with a little verbal tap-dancing. The way I figured, it was 35 degrees outside and the man wore no socks. How smart could he be?

4

I WOKE UP crusty-eyed and cranky from lack of sleep. From my front-porch lounge chair, sipping a mug of warm almond milk in an effort to soothe my caffeine-raw stomach, I watched my neighbor, Mr. Treton, grumble over his rain-pummeled impatiens. He was retired Army, a thirty-year man, and hated insubordination of any kind. He poked at the flattened flowers with his cane, silently commanding them to attention.

A sharp, salty breeze penetrated my cotton sweats, but the sky was clear. The weather was no longer my most pressing problem. That left Rita. My fruitless phone search for her had left me frustrated and edgy. Between sips of milk and calls of encouragement to Mr. Treton, I chewed my nails and worried.

I had called Ray early and he'd agreed to help me clean up the museum before the rest of the artists arrived. Out of a sense of duty, I called Constance. Her housekeeper informed me in a stiff voice that Miss Sinclair never rose until she was good and ready. For anything.

My next step seemed inevitable. I needed to go by Marla's place and see if Rita ever made it home. Since it was a given that the police would also be checking her house, I hadn't worked out my plan of action, but it was still early. Something would occur to me.

After a thorough inspection of the grayish-green plant life that had sprouted overnight on my bread, I decided to treat myself to breakfast at Liddie's Cafe downtown.

The phone rang as I was pulling on a clean pair of Wranglers and Jack's favorite navy blue flannel shirt.

"My best friend finds a body and I have to hear about it from my little brother," Elvia accused in her smooth contralto voice.

"I swear I was going to call you in two minutes."

"I can't believe it. We just talked to her last night." I heard a voice call Elvia's name. "Just a minute." She gave the voice a long, detailed explanation about credit card rules while I inspected a bloody hangnail on my left thumb.

"Sorry," she said. "It's crazy here already. Except for the profits, I hate the holidays. Are you okay? Come by the bookstore later and give me the details."

"I'm fine. I'll drop by this afternoon after my talk with the chief. I'm sure I'll be in the mood to do some real complaining by then."

"Why?"

"Hasn't Miguel told you about San Celina's new chief of police?"

"Only that he's from L.A."

"Well, that's about the nicest thing you can say about him, if you catch my drift."

"Uh-oh, I know that tone. Maybe you'd better try and keep a civil tongue in your head."

"You haven't met this guy," I said.

"Well, at least try."

"Elvia, I always *try*."

*

Liddie's Cafe, located two blocks from the civic center and police station, boasted the largest parking lot in town. Even so, the only vacant spot was in the back row, where I squeezed my truck between a white city-issue Ford and a county animal-control truck.

The red-and-brown walls, last redecorated when Eisenhower was in office, seemed to vibrate with the screechy voices of morning-anxious people craving their first cup of coffee. Open twenty-four hours, Liddie's was popular with everyone from the lowliest freshman at Cal Poly University to the mayor himself, who ate breakfast there every Thursday with whichever city council member he could dupe into picking up the check.

I craned my head above the chattering groups of threes and fours. This was maybe not one of my best ideas. A skinny Asian man in a Chevron Oil cap rose from his stool at the red Formica counter and dropped some coins next to his plate. I pushed through the crowd and headed for it. Counter seats at this time of day always went to the swift of foot.

"Benni Harper, how are you, honey?" a bass voice boomed as I walked by.

"Hey, J.D." I stopped in front of the long, six-person booth he occupied. "I can't believe you're eating alone."

"Well, I'm not anymore," he said. His voice carried a strong Texas twang and sounded as unstoppable as a cattle stampede. "Sit down here, honey, and tell me what happened last night. That son of mine never could get all his facts straight."

Jersey Dwayne Freedman, Carl's father and publisher of the *San Celina Tribune* as well as owner of half the businesses in town, had known my family for over thirty years. He moved to San Celina from Texas the same year my parents came from Arkansas, when I was only three

48

years old. With his thick white pompadour, impeccably tailored Western suit and turquoise-chunk string tie, he could be the poster boy of any Cattlemen's Association in the country, though the only cattle he'd ever branded was on his gas barbeque on Sunday afternoons. He hadn't called me "little lady" yet, but when he did, I wouldn't fall over in surprise.

"You must be feeling better." I slid into the red vinyl bench seat across from him.

"Felt worse last night than a calf with the slobbers." He gave a bullish snort. "But I imagine I'll live. Got to. Can't let that liberal marijuana-lovin' son-of-a-gun win."

J.D., as well as four other people, had recently run for a vacant city council seat. The council was currently split between the liberals (artists, academics and environ-mentalists) and conservatives (ranchers and oil people). With off-shore drilling, animal rights, the constant battle between ranchers and wine growers and the Hemp for Life people fighting for legalization of marijuana, who-ever won the election could make a big difference in San Celina politics in the next two years. The runoff was between J.D. and a professor of political theory at the university.

"What'll it be today, Benni?" Nadine, head waitress at Liddie's since before I ordered from the children's menu, appeared at our table. Without asking, she flipped my cup over and poured coffee. She set the pot down and grabbed a long yellow pencil from her pinkish-gray curls. "Tell me what happened last night. Were you scared? This is so exciting. Just like *Murder She Wrote*."

"Buttermilk pancakes and a chicken-fried steak," I answered, inwardly cringing at her tone. But then the whole thing was like a TV show to her. A piece of gossip. An article in the newspaper. She probably didn't even know Marla. "I'm fine, but I'm not sure how much I'm suppose to say. Because of the investigation and all."

"Sure, I understand," she said, sniffing. "Saving all the best parts so J.D. there can sell more papers. Don't mind me, I've just known you since before you could walk, that's all."

"Now leave the girl alone, Nadine," J.D. said.

Nadine gave him a cranky look and wrote my order on her pad.

"Don't be mad," I said. "I'm already knee-deep in cow crap with the new police chief. I don't need to make it worse by talking out of turn."

"What happened between you and the chief?" she asked, her eyes lighting up.

"Let's just say he and I didn't hit it off. I don't think I met his standard of a respectful citizen. 'Flippant' was the word he used."

"You?" she said and laughed. "I don't believe it."

I made a face at her. "He's a pain."

"Well, I don't know. He's a strange one but he's all right." She shifted her skinny hips. "Brings his work in here and spreads it all over the table in neat little piles. Stays for hours. Good tipper. Real polite but not a talker. Doesn't joke with the uniforms that eat in here. Never even seen him just shoot the breeze with anyone. Kind of odd, don't you think?"

"Hey, Nadine, why don't you quit flapping your gums and take my order?" a raisin-faced man in the next booth called.

"You just hold onto that rank old horse of yours," she said. She leaned over and smacked his head with her order pad, then turned and patted my hand. "Your order will be right up. Don't worry, hon. A good breakfast will set you right."

"So, you and our half-breed police chief had a squab-

ble." J.D. stuck a large bite of his ham-and-cheese ome-
lette in his mouth. Wrinkles like bird tracks formed at
the corners of his bright blue eyes.

"J.D.," I said. "I don't like him, but that's downright
tacky."

"Honey, he is what he is. Wasn't my first choice as a
substitute for Davidson, but the mayor wanted him 'cause
he was bi-leengual. Big whoop-dee-do." He twirled his
forefinger in the air. "In my day you learned to speak
English or tough shit."

I ignored him and concentrated on dumping enough
cream and sugar in my coffee to make it acceptable to
my irritated stomach.

"So, our Mr. Ortiz puts a burr under your saddle, does
he?" he asked.

"He's very overbearing, in a laid-back, L.A. sort of
way." I stirred my coffee absently. "If that's possible."

I stared over his shoulder at the most recent addition
to the sometimes unbelievable craft items the owner of
Liddie's continually tried to pawn off on unsuspecting
tourists. The latest entry was a resin-covered clock of
Elvis, with a slightly Navaho look to his face. His eyes
were a shade of blue that I'd never seen on a living
human being before. The number six hit him square in
his bulging white crotch.

"Well, it ain't going to be easy for him substituting
for Davidson. We'll just see how the boy handles this
murder. How are you, by the way?"

"I'll survive," I said. "I'm a tough old broad."

"Well, you should be. You was raised by one. How is
Dove doing these days?"

"Ornery as ever. I haven't told her about last night yet.
And I hope"—I looked him directly in the eye—"that no
one tells her for a few days. She hates me living alone,
and this'll just give her a pile of mesquite for the fire."

"I'll keep quiet, but I can't guarantee anyone else in this town. You tell her 'hey' for me." He pushed his empty plate aside and looked at me seriously. "Now, enough of that. Tell me what happened."

"Carl called me as soon as I got in last night, or rather early this morning. He took down all the facts. Trust him for a change."

He shook his head doubtfully and sipped his coffee. "Took me two hours after the murder was reported to get word to him. He's got people at every bar in town trained. My messages don't always get through. And when they do, he doesn't always remember them."

"Here you go." Nadine plunked a large dinner plate of pancakes and chicken-fried steak down in front of me. I covered the steak with white gravy, sprinkled it with pepper, dotted it with Tabasco sauce.

"Stomach of iron," J.D. said to me.

"Sustenance for battle. Now, tell me what you know about this Ortiz character. I have another meeting with him today and you know what they say, know your enemy."

"Honey, I do believe we hired him on as one of the white hats." His bristly gray eyebrows rose in amusement.

"Maybe." I poured syrup on my pancakes. "Anyway, what's the scoop on him?"

"Well now, he seems a smart enough fella for a—"

I shot him a warning look.

"Cop," he finished, grinning.

"Why would a man his age want a temporary job in a town like ours?"

"Old friend of Davidson's for one thing, and I also heard through the grapevine that he wanted a quiet place to work on something he's writing."

"Oh no, I hope he's not another cop writing his first

mystery novel. That's all the world needs, one more bad mystery novel." I snickered and stuck a large forkful of pancakes in my mouth.

J.D. shrugged. "Who knows? Doesn't look like he's going to be having too many quiet days ahead of him with this murder. Maybe he'll put us in his book. Are you sure Carl got everything right?"

"Don't worry. The story will be on the front page this afternoon. Give him a break, J.D."

"Easy for you to say." He crumpled his napkin and tossed it on his plate. "Wish that boy liked to work as much as he loves to party."

"You're coming to the pre-showing at the museum Friday night, aren't you?" Changing the subject always seemed like the best way to handle J.D. and Carl's relationship.

"You betcha. Lots a votes there." He grabbed his tan Stetson off the metal hat rack attached to the end of the booth and slid out. "Besides, I'm afraid of old Connie Sinclair. She'd come after me with a bullwhip if I don't support her little causes."

I laughed with him and licked my fork. Only J.D. could get away with calling Constance by such a common nickname.

When I pulled my truck into the museum parking lot, it appeared less ominous in the bright morning light. Even the eucalyptus grove that appeared so dense and frightening last night seemed innocuous beneath the cloudless blue sky. I pulled up next to Ray, the duck carver's, white Ford pickup, climbed out and inhaled the coughdrop-scented air. I mentally crossed my fingers. If the weather held until after this weekend, we'd be home free.

Ray was in the woodshop wrapping a twist-tie around a large green trash bag. He wore boot-cut Wranglers, blue

Nikes and a red-checked shirt that almost matched his brick-colored mustache.

"Watch it," he said. He pointed at the bleachy-smelling liquid covering the jagged dark stain on the concrete floor.

"How did you get in?" I stared at the bag in his hand, trying to avoid looking at the spot where Marla died. Maybe we could cover it with a rubber mat or something.

"I went by Constance's and got her key."

"Thanks."

He gave a stiff nod and tossed the bag over in a corner with two others.

"Did you have to tell her? I tried to call but the housekeeper wouldn't wake her." I nibbled on my nails. "She's not going to be happy about this."

"She already knew. I don't know who told her and I didn't ask." A crooked-tooth grin peeked out from under his thick mustache. "She was on the phone to the police chief when I walked in. He was getting an earful, that's for sure. I guess she has her own ideas about how he should go about solving this."

"Good for her." I smiled at the thought of Chief Ortiz being lectured by Constance Sinclair. I'd buy a front row center seat to that.

"She said she'd be down here to talk to the artists later this morning. Calm us all down was how she put it."

"And who's going to calm you all down after she talks to you?"

He readjusted the orange and blue Unocal hat on his head. The grin peeked out again. "Guess that's your job." He started mopping up the disinfectant on the floor.

"Lucky me." I perched on one of the stools and picked up a wooden train someone was sanding. "Can I ask you something?"

"Sure."

"How long have you been a member of the co-op?"

"Three years. I was one of the first to be accepted." He stuck the industrial-sized mop into the metal wringer and squeezed.

"Then you know everyone pretty well." I spun a wheel on the train.

"Well enough." He continued mopping but looked up, his face guarded.

"Did you know Marla very well?"

"To speak to. She and I didn't have cause to have much contact. She's only been a member for about ten, eleven months."

"What did you think of her?"

"What's your point, Benni?" he asked in a careful voice. He agitated the mop in the bucket of soapy water.

"I guess I want to know if you think anyone in the co-op could have been involved in her murder."

"I reckon she irritated a few people. She was pretty mouthy. But I don't think anyone would kill her."

"What about boyfriends?" An obsessive boyfriend would wrap this whole thing up in a neat package.

He shrugged. "I told you, I didn't know her that well. I guess she had some."

"Anyone here?" It suddenly dawned on me how little I knew about the personal lives of the people who belonged to the co-op.

He stopped mopping and regarded me impassively.

"I don't know why she was killed, Benni," he said. "Why don't we leave it up to the police to find out?"

"Oh, sure." I set the train down and slipped off the stool. "I was just curious. Really, thanks for coming up here and doing all this."

I retreated to my office, annoyed at my clumsiness in questioning Ray. The FBI certainly wasn't going to ask me to join any time soon. I plugged in my electric pencil sharpener and grabbed a handful of pencils. I sharpened every pencil in my desk down to lethal nubs, trying to decide what I should do about Rita. I answered the phone on the first ring simply because it was something to do.

"This is Chief Ortiz," his brusque voice said. No wonder he had no friends. "Will most of the artists be coming into the studios today?"

"Well, good morning to you too, Chief Ortiz," I replied.

"Right, sorry," he said, not sounding sorry. "Well?"

"Yes, most likely."

"I'm sending over two detectives. Cleary and Ryan. See to it that they have a private place to question people." I heard fumbling, a few muttered Spanish words; then he was back. "I can see you at two o'clock. Come a few minutes early and get your prints done. I'll leave word at the front desk."

"I . . ." I started to say I was too busy. My intention was that Rita would be the person talking to him, not me. I just hadn't figured how I was going to work that out.

"What?" His voice practically barked.

"I'll see you then," I said lamely.

"Good," he said and hung up.

Sticking my tongue out at the buzzing receiver made me feel juvenile, but a whole lot better.

Less than an hour later, the detectives showed up. Detective Ryan, the bushy-browed one from last night, and Detective Cleary, a somber-faced black man with skin the color of aged oak. With exaggerated politeness they commandeered my office and methodically called in each artist and questioned them. I wandered through the studios and tried to eavesdrop. Finally, I just came out and asked one of the quilters, a gossipy, myopic woman named Meg, what they were asking.

"They wanted to know where we were at the time she was killed. How well we knew her. Did we know of anyone angry at her. Things like that." She held up a lap quilt she was working on, a copy of Georgia O'Keeffe's painting 'Corn.' "What do you think?"

"It's beautiful," I said. "That's all they asked?"

"That's all. Why, what did they ask you?" She leaned forward, crumpling the quilt in her lap, her face awash with curiosity.

"Same thing." I avoided her avid gaze, deciding I'd better limit my questions until I found Rita. "I have to go out for a while. I have some errands to run, then I'll be at Blind Harry's. If anyone needs me, I should be back by three or four."

I glanced at the unfinished quilt exhibit as I walked through the main hall. I wondered if Eric would ever show up. If he didn't, it looked like my Thanksgiving would be spent hanging quilts, something I wasn't really upset about—at least it would keep me busy. I tried briefly to imagine Eric stabbing Marla. It just didn't seem probable. For one thing, she was five inches taller than him. And he seemed too shallow to work up the kind of passion it took to kill someone. But then again, I'd only known Eric three months. What did I really know about him?

Detective Ryan called to me as I was about to walk out the front door. "Can I use this?" He pointed at the phone behind the tiny gift shop counter.

"Sure," I said. "Take as long as you like."

Take all day, I thought. I didn't know how many detectives Ortiz had working on the case, but I was hoping it was just Cleary and Ryan. This had to be the best time to cruise by Marla's place and see if there was any sign of Rita. If the police were there, I'd keep driving. No one would ever know.

57

Easy, Dove would say, as shooting a turkey.

Of course, I should have remembered what Daddy always added to that statement in his calm, ironic voice.

"Or your own foot."

5

MARLA RENTED HER paint-peeling, 1930's bungalow from Floyd, her boss at Trigger's. It squatted in a neighborhood where fifty-year-old houses shared street lights with muffler repair shops and aluminum recycling centers. Half-covered by a huge orange bougainvillea bush that clashed with the faded red clapboard walls, it appeared deserted when I swung into the driveway. After banging on the torn screen door and pressing the rusty doorbell until my forefinger throbbed, I came to the brilliant conclusion that no one was home. There was no indication the police had been there, but then what did I expect, a twenty-foot banner?

Though Trigger's was the last place I felt like going, I knew I'd have to talk to Floyd. There was only a slim chance he knew where Rita was, but it was a possibility I couldn't overlook.

Trigger's Saloon was two blocks away, and though it was only eleven o'clock, the parking lot was already half-full. I pulled up between a chopped Harley with "Midnight Confessions" painted in script on the purple gas tank and a school-bus-yellow crew cab pickup.

I sat in my truck and stared at the bar. A flat-roofed cinder-block building the size of a small bowling alley, it sported the usual Silver Bullet, Budweiser and Dos Equis signs in the darkened windows, as well as two large white satellite dishes on the roof. It played live country-western music six nights a week, was the bar of choice for oil-field workers and cowboys, concrete and otherwise, and served the best beef dip sandwiches in the county. It was also the last place my husband was seen alive.

The air in the bar felt thick and cold and rippled with the scent of wet, smoldery beef, the vinegar of men's sweat. I scanned the room uneasily, studying the high-backed booths lining the walls, the three crowded pool tables, the long bar presided over by a depressed-looking elkhead with battered cowboy hats stuck in its antlers. A smoky haze hovered over the room like a misty tarp. From the juke box, Alan Jackson moaned about the haunted, haunted eyes he saw one midnight in Montgomery.

I almost ran out.

But something—responsibility, loyalty, *stupidity*—compelled me to walk up to the bar where Floyd swabbed the counter with a stained white towel. His fiftyish face held a tired look. A sparse, graying beard attempted to cover a cherry-red skin rash.

"Floyd?"

"That's my name," he said. He traded the tired look for a suspicious one.

I stared at him for a moment. The questions on the tip of my tongue had nothing to do with Rita. What I really wanted to ask was—Do you remember Jack? Did you serve him that last beer? Did you talk to him last? The one thing I'd never been able to let go, was the feeling that if Jack *had* to die before me, the last voice he heard should have been mine.

Floyd's cross voice brought me back. "Is there something you want, lady?"

"My cousin Rita." I forced myself to focus on him. "She works here. Have you seen her lately?"

"Sure."

"When?"

"Two nights ago?" He phrased it like a question. His scraggly eyebrows intersected in a frown.

"Sunday night?" I prompted.

"Yeah, I guess so." He pulled out a can of Copenhagen and stuck some behind his bottom lip. "She's supposed to work tonight."

"I need to get in touch with her," I said. "It's extremely important. Can you tell her to call Benni when she comes in?"

"If she comes in. She ain't all that dependable."

"You heard about Marla, didn't you?"

"Yeah." He nodded and folded his towel in half, in quarters, then stuck it under the counter. "Tough break for me. She was a good bartender. Never cheated me once. Least, far as I could tell. She'll be hard to replace."

I looked at him in amazement. Tough break for him? What about Marla? Nice guy. One of his employees is murdered and all he can think about is her replacement.

"Well, Rita was with her that night and I think she might have gotten scared and taken off. Do you have any idea where she might go?"

"Ain't she living with Marla? You check the house?"

"Yes, no one answered." When he didn't offer anything more, I decided to take a chance. The worst he could do was say no. "Maybe there's something in the house that will tell me where she's gone. Have the police been here asking for a key yet?"

His expression became irritated. "No. You think they will?"

"Probably. I'd like to see the house before them. Do you have a key?"

"I don't want any trouble," he said with a scowl.

"Just give me five minutes. Please. I want to see if her clothes and stuff are gone. Her grandmother is worried. Please." I gave him my best pleading look. Being short and somewhat adolescent-looking can have its advantages. It's harder to pull off the helpless female act if you're over five-six or carry a briefcase. I hated using it, but your resources are your resources. It doesn't always work, but this time it did.

He eyed me sourly and reached under the counter. Pulling out a huge set of keys, he twisted one off. "Make it fast."

"Thanks." I smiled widely, feeling a bit proud of myself for finally accomplishing something concrete in my search for Rita, even if I did set women's lib back a game point or two.

My feeling of triumph lasted until I entered the house. I purposely stayed away from anything of Marla's, knowing the police would be looking through her things soon, if they hadn't already. Rita's room was empty except for an old bed, a couple of pasteboard boxes and a lone fly two-stepping across the window screen. I sat down hard on the saggy mattress. My options were few. Nonexistent, actually. I locked the back door and drove back to Trigger's, rehearsing what I would tell Ortiz. None of it sounded plausible. I'd withheld important information on a homicide investigation. There was no dancing around that.

By the number of pickups and motorcycles crowding the parking lot, Trigger's lunch rush had begun. When I walked back up to the bar, Floyd was filling a pitcher from the tap with one hand and picking up a wad of bills with the other.

"Find anything?" He set three mugs and the full pitcher on a large tray. A gray-pig-tailed man in a blue "Built Ford Tough" tee shirt winked at me as he picked them up.

"She's gone." I tossed the keys on the bar. "Thanks. If she happens to come in, tell her to—"

He interrupted me. "You got a visitor."

"What?"

"Cop." He spit into a white mug and gave me an annoyed look. "Had to tell him where you were. Told you I didn't want no trouble."

"Thanks for nothing." I turned and searched the noisy room for Ryan's stomach or Cleary's calm, dark face. How did they find me? No one could possibly have known where I'd been going.

"Okay, I give up," I said. "Where are they?"

"He." Floyd jerked his head toward a corner booth where a dark-haired man wearing a conservative gray suit, a crisp white shirt and a furious expression, stood up and crooked his finger at me.

The epithet I muttered caused the skinny cowboy standing next to me to burst out laughing. I was, obviously, going to be given the privilege of explaining myself earlier than I'd anticipated.

Walking slowly toward the man in the gray suit, I decided on the casual approach.

"Chief Ortiz," I said. "I hardly recognized you in your grownup clothes."

His facial impersonation of a mannequin impressed me, though I decided not to share that particular thought. He pointed to the seat across from him.

"Sit down."

So much for the casual approach. I slid across the slick brown vinyl, avoiding eye contact. After he sat down, we played more of the silence game. While he worked at intimidating me, I occupied myself with studying his hands which were tapping a soft cadence on his thick white coffee mug. They were huge, strong-looking, with short, neat nails, and though clean, stained black in rough crevices no soap can reach. A mechanic's hands. I looked up at him in surprise.

The expression on his face was unreadable. I refused to give in and look down, hoping my face didn't show the dog-caught-in-the-garbage-can look I suspected it held.

Finally, he spoke.

"Just what do you think you're doing?"

An excellent question. One I'd asked myself several times in the last twelve hours. I looked him straight in his peculiar gray-blue eyes and told him the truth.

"I have absolutely no idea."

For a moment he appeared stunned. Not the answer he expected. Not the answer I expected. His mouth made a sharp downward curve.

"You can tell me about it now," he said. "Or we can go down to the station. Your choice."

My day had been full of choices, none of which had been appealing in the least. He wouldn't believe I intended telling him everything at our afternoon meeting, so there seemed no point in mentioning it.

"You know, you might find people more cooperative if you were a little friendlier," I pointed out, trying to stall for time.

He started to slide out of the booth. "Okay, Ms. Harper, let's go."

"No, wait. I'd rather talk here."

"Then talk."

I drummed my fingers on the wood table and studied his maroon paisley tie. "Look, I'm going to be straight with you."

"Now, there's a novel concept." He sat back and crossed his arms.

I gave him one last irritated look before telling him everything I'd seen in the last twenty-four hours including Eric's argument with Marla and how all Rita's possessions were gone. I emphasized how she couldn't possibly have anything to do with the murder.

"And how do you know that?" he asked.

"I just do. She didn't have any reason to." I paused and took a deep breath. "She's my cousin, Chief Ortiz."

"Your family has some sort of genetic immunity to capital offenses?"

"That's not what I mean. I know her. She's a lot of things, but she's not a killer. I'm not saying she didn't see anything. She probably did, and that's why she's hiding. She could be in danger. We have to find her." My voice faltered slightly. Remembering what happened to Marla, a cold knot of fear twisted my stomach.

He adjusted his glasses impatiently. "*We* aren't going to do anything. I'm going to say this once, Ms. Harper, so listen up. Stay out of this investigation. I'll find your cousin. I'll find Ms. Chenier's murderer. And I'll do it without your help. Got it?"

"Excuse me, but where does it state that looking for your family is against the law?"

"Ms. Harper," he said, his voice deceptively soft. "The only law you need to worry about is the one about interfering in a police investigation. We have plenty of room in our holding cells downtown."

"I'll keep that in mind." I held his gaze and waited. "Is that all?"

"Don't forget to go by the station and give your prints." He glared at me. "We especially need them now that you've tampered with a possible crime scene."

"No problem." I slid out of the booth and stood up. "Now can I go?"

"Yes." He waved me away with his large hand, his mind already on something else.

I walked slowly toward the exit, fighting the urge to break and run. I heaved a sigh of relief as I hit the crisp afternoon air, then groaned as I caught sight of my lopsided truck.

I jerked the cab door open, grabbed the tire jack from behind the seat and was on my knees attempting to work it under the rear axle when gravel crunched behind me.

"Looks like you have a flat," Ortiz said.

I didn't turn around. "I can certainly see why you were hired as chief of police."

Inserting the handle in the jack, I pushed as hard as I could. Not a budge. The truck was heavier than I thought. To be honest, I'd watched Jack change tires on the Chevy more times than I could remember in the fifteen years we'd owned it, and I'm sure at one time I must have changed one myself. I just didn't recall it being this difficult.

"Need any help?"

"No." I felt a flush start up my neck.

"Truck's pretty heavy."

I whipped around, thinking about what else I could do with a jack handle. He wore that self-satisfied look men get when they know they can do something you can't.

"Look, Ortiz, I castrated my first bull when I was ten years old. I doubt that changing a tire is beyond my limited female abilities."

He looked down at me with an amused expression. "Suit yourself, Ms. Harper. Had I known, I would not have presumed to offer help to a person of such prodigious capabilities."

He walked past me, hands in his pockets, whistling

softly under his breath. It took all the social proprieties I'd ever been taught not to stick my foot out and trip him. Halfway across the parking lot, he stopped and turned around.

"The starter," he called.

"What?" I snapped.

"Why your truck was having trouble turning over. It sounds like the starter. You probably need a new one."

That was just great. One minute he's threatening to arrest me, the next he's giving me engine advice.

"Anything else, Mr. Goodwrench?"

"I don't know." His blue eyes lit up. "I guess I'd have to pop the hood and find out."

Without warning, behind my eyes, a match flared. The familiar words sparked a memory of Jack in grease-stained jeans, tanned back dripping, bent over the open hood of a truck. . . .

"Are you all right?"

I started at the suddenly close, throaty sound of Ortiz's voice. My head felt thick and woolly, as if I'd run a fever for days. Somewhere a door slammed open. Wood against wood. A tumble of gusty voices filled the parking lot. Instinctively, my ears searched them. I closed my eyes and thought I felt the ground tremble.

"Ms. Harper? Is something the matter?"

I looked with dazed surprise at the hand gently gripping my upper arm and felt my cheeks grow warm.

"I'm fine." I ducked my head and stepped back. For a split second, his hand hung in empty air. "I'm sure you must have better things to do than harass honest citizens." I gave a small, embarrassed laugh.

"Yes." He gazed at me thoughtfully. "I certainly do."

Before stepping into the beige, unmarked police car, he turned and called in the confident voice of someone accustomed to being obeyed.

67

"Don't forget that starter."

I lifted a noncommittal hand in reply.

After he drove out of sight, I turned back to the deflated tire and gave it an aggravated kick. Then I picked up the jack handle and tried again. And again. Twenty minutes and a bruised thumb later, I stood up, brushed off my muddy knees and dug through my purse for the last birthday present my ever practical and mothering friend, Elvia, gave me.

The Auto Club was there in ten minutes.

6

"SO, HOW DID this Chief Ortiz find out you were checking out Rita's place?" Elvia asked. We sat in her unofficial office, a round oak table in the corner of the coffeehouse. Stacks of purchase orders in dinner-mint pastels made a patchwork of the tabletop.

"Floyd told him." I sipped my hot chocolate and gave her a who-cares look.

"Why is he spending so much time questioning you?" She pulled a shiny pencil, the color of her buttercup-yellow silk suit, from behind her ear and pointed it at me. "As chief of police, it seems to me he would relegate that task to someone less important."

"I don't know." I shrugged. "I didn't think to ask."

"Just like an only child. You never question special treatment. After all, it's only your right." She examined the tip of the pencil and frowned. Elvia's major in college had been psychology and the bookstore gave her the resources to pore through every new self-help book that hit the stands. Her latest fascination was birth order.

"I love it when you categorize me. Makes me feel so special."

"From how you've described him, he sounds like an oldest to me. Does he have any siblings?"

"Honestly, Elvia, between the threats of arrest and engine advice, it didn't come up." I drained my mug, stood up and pulled on my jacket. "I have to go. Those quilts won't hang themselves, and I have a feeling I won't be seeing much of Eric over the next few days."

"Do you think he had anything to do with Marla's murder?"

"It's hard to imagine, if only because killing someone would actually take some physical effort. Maybe he's just running scared. Who knows what kind of illegal activities he's trying to hide from the police."

"What are you going to do about Rita?"

"Keep looking for her."

"Even after what the chief said?" She frowned and tapped the end of the pencil against her cheek. Elvia was a rule-follower, as was I—most of the time anyway, unless there was a valid reason not to.

"What am I suppose to do? I don't want to tell Aunt Garnet that her precious granddaughter is missing and is possibly connected with a homicide. That scares me a lot more than Ortiz's threats. When I find Rita, this whole thing will be straightened out. She'll give her statement and that'll be that."

The folds between Elvia's eyes deepened.

I reached over and rubbed them with my forefinger. "You're going to get wrinkles."

She pushed my hand away. "Rita's been nothing but trouble since she got here. You don't need that in your life right now." She stood up and for a moment looked me straight in the eye. Slipping on her tiny black Italian pumps, she rose three inches. At the bottom of the stairway, she laid a pink-nailed hand on my arm. "Are you going home for Thanksgiving?"

"No, and it'll give Dove something to complain about until Christmas." I held up my hand before she could ask the next question. "And I feel funny going to the Harpers'. They always have a bunch of family come in from Texas and it just doesn't feel right."

"You shouldn't be alone on Thanksgiving."

"Spoken like a true oldest," I said, teasing. "Always telling people what they should do. Really, I'd rather not be around a lot of people."

Her delicate, coppery face was sober. "I mean it. You shouldn't be alone. Come over to our house. Mamá's been asking about you."

"I don't know." Being around Elvia's six brothers and their families seemed as overwhelming as the family Thanksgivings I was trying to avoid.

"Fine," she said. "Then I'm coming over to your house. We'll make chile rellanos and chocolate no-bakes just like we did in junior high. I'll iron your hair. Straight hair is back in style, you know."

"Okay, okay." I held up my hands in mock surrender. "Anything but that. Last time you ironed my hair—what was it, 1973?—you almost gave me a cheek tattoo."

"We were crazy, weren't we?" she said. "Dinner's at one."

On the way back to the museum, I stopped by the police station and signed my statement. A tiny, bleached-blond female officer expertly rolled my fingers across the fingerprint pad as she chattered about her ten-year-old son's scout badges. As she gabbed and rolled, I couldn't help but feel vaguely criminal. Techno-cynic that I was, I worried my fingerprints would show up in a computer somewhere with the information that they were found at some liquor store crime scene in Modesto.

I drove back to the museum and spent the rest of the day making quilt frames and attaching Velcro to the backs. I called Eric's house and left a terse message on his answering machine. "You are dead meat, buddy. I'm holding Dack and Cassandra hostage. You know who this is." Then, just for spite, I stuck the computer disk containing his novel in my purse. He'd have to find me now.

At eight o'clock, after the last of the artists had left, I locked up. As I was walking out to my truck, a small blue Toyota sedan pulled up and a husky young man in a denim shirt and navy tie printed with white peace symbols hopped out, a gold Blind Harry's gift bag in one hand and a maroon garment bag in the other. I recognized him as one of Elvia's clerks. His freckled face flushed a soft pink when he handed me the bags.

"She told me to hum the theme song from *Mission Impossible* when I gave you this," he said. "I didn't want to tell her I didn't know it. Do you think she was kidding?" His face wrinkled in distress.

"No, but don't worry about it. Just tell her I got hysterical with laughter." He hurried back to his truck, a perplexed look on his broad face.

I opened the gold bag and pulled out a small paperback book. *How to Become a Successful Private Detective—Earn While You Learn*. A pink Post-it note stuck to the front commanded in Elvia's large, loopy handwriting: "Check out page 67, and the dress is an early Christmas present. If you wear anything besides this on Friday night, I'll personally burn all your jeans. E. P.S. Wear your black heels and your hair in *something* besides that braid."

I zipped open the garment bag to find an almost weightless Kelly-green silk dress with a lower neckline and shorter skirt than I probably would have chosen. But, knowing Elvia, it was the latest fashion and cost a bundle. I had to admit I was grateful; I hadn't even thought about what I was going to wear to the auction

Friday night. I looked from the book to the dress and wondered which mission she considered more impossible.

I closed the bag, sat down on the bumper of my truck and flipped to the page Elvia indicated. Missing Persons Investigation. I smiled as I scanned the chapter. She meant it as a joke, but she might have helped me more than she realized. I tucked the book into my purse, grabbed my dress and went home.

I was getting ready to search the refrigerator for some sort of edible plant or animal life, when the phone rang. I glanced at the clock. It was eight-thirty, about the time Dove settled down with the newspaper. Gossips' heads were going to roll. Dove hated hearing anything last.

"Your daddy's worried," Dove said in a crabby voice. She always ascribed any sentimental feelings she had to someone else. "I ought to whip your butt for not calling me. I hope you're packing an iron."

"Watching the Humphrey Bogart Film Festival again, are we?" I said. "I found the body but I don't think I'm in any danger."

"You shouldn't be alone. Can't count on that trampy cousin of yours to be around. I could send Garnet out. She took a karate class once. Back in '71, I think. When all that women's lib stuff was going on."

"Good try, Dove." I laughed at the thought of Aunt Garnet in her J.C. Penney spectator pumps, legs spread in a karate stance, protecting me from an assailant. "But, no go. I'll be fine."

"You coming tomorrow?"

"No, but tell everyone 'Hi' for me."

I waited in silence for her lecture. But, as she is apt to do, she feinted, and brought up an even touchier subject.

"You find Rita?"

"Yes," I said, hesitantly. "I gave her the message."

"And she ignored it as usual." Dove groaned loudly. "Another night of Garnet's whining. She's driving me crazy as popcorn on a hot skillet."

"Well, good luck," I said.

"You sure you're going to be okay there alone?" Dove asked. "I think Garnet made it to a belt in that karate class." Dove's voice was hopeful. I guess raising six kids and one grandkid taught you to never say die. "Red or green or some color. She was pretty good, I hear. Especially with the yell."

"No, Dove."

"Rats," she spit out and hung up.

I regarded the buzzing phone with humor and tried to remember a time when Dove actually said the word "Good-bye" to me.

I kicked off my boots and settled down on the sofa with the book Elvia sent me. I read the Missing Persons chapter three times. The information seemed obvious— "Learn a person's habits and the types of people they associate with. Find those people and you'll find your missing person." It sounded so easy. But the only person I knew Rita hung around with on a regular basis was dead. I tossed the book on the floor in disgust and wondered if I should try Floyd one more time. Maybe he'd be more open without the chief of police sitting in his bar.

I lay on the sofa trying to decide whether I should go to Trigger's or see if any food had mysteriously appeared in my refrigerator, when the phone rang. A nervous, whispery voice took care of those problems and handed me a whole new one.

"Benni?" said Rita. "Thank goodness you're home. I need some money. Fast."

7

TO SAY I lost control would be an understatement.

"Where have you been? Do you realize what kind of trouble you're in? Do you realize what kind of trouble *I'm* in? I need to know what happened. Why did you drive away? Are you okay? What do you mean, you need money?"

"Benni," she said, when I finally inhaled. "Calm down. No need to pitch a fit." Her sleepy Arkansas drawl made me want to yank her through the phone, pouty lips first.

"Easy for you to say," I snapped.

"Well?" she asked.

"Well, what?"

"Can you get me some money?"

"You're not getting anything until you tell me what happened last night."

"Just a minute." I heard her put a hand over the receiver and mumble something.

"Who's with you?"

"Skeeter."

"Who?"

"You met him. Tall, blond mustache, good-looking in a scroungy sorta way." I heard a grunt, then a giggle.

"Oh, Mr. Belt Buckle," I said. "Is that who you've been staying with?"

"Look," she said. "Can I count on you or not?"

"Rita, I have to know what happened. You do know Marla is dead, don't you?"

A moment of silence, then a hesitant, "Yes."

"You need to talk to the police, Rita. I know you didn't have anything to do with it, but they don't."

"No police." It came out a little too quickly for my comfort.

"Rita, do you have any idea what kind of trouble you're in?"

"Look, if you'll bring me some money, I'll tell you what I know and you can tell the police. Otherwise, I'm gone."

I contemplated her offer. If I said no, I'd be no better off than when I'd started, and perhaps, a little worse. In person, I might find out something or maybe even convince her that talking to the police would be the smartest thing to do. A little voice whispered in the back of my mind—you'd better call Ortiz—but, after a small twinge of guilt, I ignored it.

"I don't have much money to give you and I'm not giving you that until you tell me what happened."

"Okay, okay," she said, with a dramatic groan.

"Where does this Skeeter live?"

"Just a minute."

I strained to understand another muffled discussion.

"He says it's probably better you don't know. We'll meet you in an hour at Port San Patricio. You know, out by Eola Beach?"

"Yes," I said, impatiently. "I grew up here, remember? Where exactly will you be?"

"Well, don't get your dander up."

"Just tell me where, Rita."

"You know the big building at the end of the pier? Where they clean all the fish?"

"Where the Blue Seal Inn is."

"Meet me there. In the bar. Skeeter says the restaurant is closed but the bar's still open. I'll be in a booth in the back. And, Benni . . ." She hesitated for a moment.

"What else?" I cradled the phone on my shoulder while reaching for my boots.

"Thanks," she said softly. For the first time, her voice sounded serious and a little frightened.

"It's going to be all right," I said with faked confidence.

"Oh, I know that." Her voice suddenly took on the relaxed tone of someone who'd just handed their problems to someone else.

The clock above my fireplace struck nine o'clock. With good luck, I'd be home to catch the eleven o'clock news; with outstanding luck, I'd have Rita with me.

I drove by the automated teller machine at my bank and drew out a hundred dollars, hoping I wouldn't need it. I intended on Rita coming home with me, though I suspected the chance of that happening was, as Dove would say, about as probable as a three-legged mule winning a kicking contest. I didn't even want to contemplate what Ortiz would do if she didn't return with me.

As I drove down the interstate toward Eola Beach and Port San Patricio, a strong wind came up. It slapped the sides of my truck like a giant palm trying to push me off the road. The heavy cloud cover made the air feel dense, thick; like breathing through a feather pillow. After fifteen miles, I turned off the interstate onto the narrow, winding highway that led to Eola Beach. As the ocean loomed closer, its sharp brine permeated the cab of the truck. I licked my lips and tasted salt.

A half mile before Eola Beach, I passed the Oakhills Mineral Springs Resort. The parking lot was almost full with an eclectic mixture of pickup trucks, BMW's and Japanese imports. With their private outdoor hot tubs, it was one of the county's more popular dating spots. Jack and I celebrated our twelfth anniversary in Number Five with a bottle of California champagne, a Don Williams tape and a pizza that was cold by the time we ate it. Seeing it depressed me and I wondered, as I had more than once in the last few months, whether staying in San Celina was such a good idea. The problem was, I had no idea where else to go.

The main street of Eola Beach was dark and quiet. Like many of the tiny beach communities on the Central Coast, Eola Beach subsisted on the money made in the three-to-four-month summer season. I crept past boarded-up frozen banana stands, bikini boutiques with empty window displays, and the only establishment with any life to it, a small, nameless neighborhood bar.

Port San Patricio, a half-mile further north, shared its small peninsula with a Unocal pumping station, the offices of the U.S. Army Corps of Engineers, Boating and Waterways Department and, if my nose was accurate, most of the pelicans and sea gulls on the Central Coast.

A damp, cold wind whistled in my ears when I stepped down from the truck. The air smelled tart and brackish, like old pickle juice. Only two other vehicles sat in the small lot at the end of the pier; an old Ford Bronco I assumed was Skeeter's, and a small Toyota pickup with a faded bumper sticker—"Commercial Fishermen Feed the World." I met no one on the long walk to the end of the pier. The low whumping of the Unocal station intermingled with the faint sounds of seals barking, a sort of bipartisan symphony.

The Blue Seal Inn sat inside a huge, barnlike building at the end of the pier. When I pulled open the heavy, port-holed door of the inn, a whoosh of warm air hit me. Behind the bar, a dark-eyed man with long hair the color of a palomino's mane pointed at me with a hand-held soda dispenser.

"You Benni?" he asked.

I nodded. He pointed toward the back as if he were aiming a pistol.

"She's over there," he said.

I edged past a pool table being used by an old man in a captain's hat toward a row of black vinyl booths.

Rita sat alone in the large corner booth, a tall pale drink in front of her. Her teased blond mane careened slightly to the left and her usually flawless makeup appeared slapdash; flakes of black mascara dusted her cheeks and one copper-and-pink shadowed eye didn't quite match its twin.

"Am I glad to see you," she said.

I slid into the bench opposite her and gave her a severe look, feeling for all the world like her mother.

"Did you bring the money?" She stirred her drink with a skinny red straw.

"Where's this Skeeter guy?" I asked.

"Around. He thought it would be better if we talked alone." She took a quick sip, then nervously stirred again.

"He's probably right about that. Tell me what happened, Rita. From the beginning. Then we'll talk about money."

She sighed and gave me an impatient look. "Marla . . ." Her voice wavered. She stopped, swallowed, then began again. "Marla, Eric and I got there about eight o'clock. He and I hung around listening to the radio while she worked, but then we got hungry, so Eric and I decided to go get some stuff to eat."

"When was that?"

"I don't know." She stuck the straw in her mouth and chewed on it. "Eight forty-five? Maybe. Yeah, that sounds right."

I gestured for her to go on.

"Well, we drove over to that liquor store about a mile away. You know, by the dairy. We got chips, a couple of cans of pop, some beef jerky. Then we came back to the museum and just sorta hung out. Me and Eric talked. Marla was working. Then she and Eric went into the museum to talk. They got into a little spat. Then he came out and told me Marla wanted us to go get some beer."

"What was the fight about?"

She stuck her mangled straw back into her drink and shrugged. "I don't know. I didn't really listen to them. Marla was pissed, though. Something he was supposed to do that he didn't."

"Sounds like Eric, all right." I wondered what he would be doing for Marla. "What time did you leave to get the beer?"

"Nine-thirty, maybe?" She twisted her face in concentration. "It didn't take long and when we got back, she was . . ." She choked back a small sob.

"Why did you leave, Rita? Why didn't you call the police? Or the paramedics? She might have still been alive."

Remembering how much blood there'd been, I seriously doubted it, but I was angry at Rita's callous departure. I couldn't imagine doing that to anyone.

"Eric told me to," she said with a small whine. I resisted the urge to slap her. "He said she was already dead and there was nothing we could do about it. He said if we hung around, they'd just try and pin it on one of us. He's had experience with the police. He knows." She looked at me defiantly. "He said it'd all die down after a while."

"Wait a minute," I said. "When I saw you driving away, you were alone. What happened to Eric?"

"He was in the van. He just ducked down when we saw you coming."

"You are such a dope." I hit the table with my fist. "Did it ever occur to you that people knew you were with her that evening? Do you know what that looks like to the police? I had to tell them the only person I actually saw leaving the scene was you. I just can't believe this. I have absolutely no idea how to help you."

"That's why I need some money to get out of town. Skeeter has some friends in . . ."

I held my hand up. "Don't tell me where. I don't want to know. That way I don't have to lie."

"They'll find who did it and they won't even need me. Please, Benni, I'm scared."

"You should be," I said. But I was, too. Just how was Eric involved in this? Could he have killed Marla? I hadn't seen him since last night and I was willing to bet the police hadn't caught up with him either. Would the police give her twenty-four-hour protection until they caught whoever killed Marla? I doubted it.

"Was Eric with you the whole time at the liquor store?" I asked.

"Mostly."

"What's that supposed to mean?"

"He had to get gas so he left for a while."

"How long?"

"I don't know," she said in exasperation. "I wasn't keeping track. Fifteen, twenty minutes maybe. What does it matter?"

I looked at her with disbelief. It really hadn't occurred to her that Eric could have murdered Marla.

"Think about it, Rita."

She looked at me with glazed, sullen eyes. A flicker of understanding caused them to widen. "You mean . . ."

"I think you'd better come back and tell the police what you just told me. Then we'll figure out how to hide you so Eric can't find you."

"I don't know," she said hesitantly.

"No way, sugar," a nasally voice said behind me. Mr. Belt Buckle—Skeeter—slid into the booth next to Rita. "Ain't no way you're going back there with that nut out there." He looked at me with damp, squinty eyes, a knight in denim armor. "When they catch this guy, then she can come back."

"They need her as a witness," I said.

"Not until they catch him," he replied and drained the rest of her drink. "Till then, I'll look out for her."

I rubbed my temples, advance therapy for a headache I knew was coming. "And what am I suppose to tell the police? Not to mention Aunt Garnet."

"You're a sharp gal. You'll think of something," Skeeter drawled. "We'll keep in touch." He slid out of the booth, pulling a stunned-looking Rita with him.

"Well, leave the message at the county jail," I said, "because that's where I'll probably be staying."

Skeeter laughed and adjusted his stained white Stetson.

"Benni," Rita said in a small voice. "The money?"

I cocked my head at Skeeter expectantly.

"Sorry," he said, grinning. "I'm brave, but I'm broke."

I pulled out my purse and held out the money. "I can't believe I'm doing this."

"Thanks." She stuffed it into her small white purse.

They were halfway across the bar when I remembered something.

"Wait," I said. "You never finished the story. What happened after you and Eric drove away from the museum? Where did you go?"

"I dropped him off downtown, in front of the court-house, and I did what he told me with the van."

"And what was that?"

"I drove it down the coast to Santa Maria and left it in a grocery store parking lot with the keys inside. Then I called Skeeter to come pick me up. We went to my place, got my stuff and split."

"All right," I said wearily. "At least let me know you're okay."

I sat at the bar for a long time after they left, debating with myself about whether I'd done the right thing. Not that it mattered now. I had no choice but to go to the police. I touched my fingers to my now pounding temples. Not tonight. And I certainly wasn't going to ruin my holiday tomorrow. I was already in so deep, what difference could one day make? Especially since I had no idea where Rita was going. I picked up my purse and started to walk toward the door.

"Hey," the bartender called. "The drink."

"I didn't have anything," I said.

"Your friend said you'd pay for hers. That'll be three bucks."

"She's no friend." I threw the money down on the counter. "She's a relative."

He shrugged and stuck the money in the cash register.

Okay, Aunt Garnet, I thought grimly, pulling the Chevy onto the now moonbright highway. Your grand-daughter dragged me into this, so you'd better have some sewing money put aside. You just may need it to bail me out of jail.

8

I SPENT PART of Thanksgiving at Elvia's parents' house, holding babies and listening to her brothers debate with noisy passion the merits and liabilities of the Rams' new defensive coach. Señora Aragon fussed around me like a small brown poodle, filling my plate before everyone else's with her special wine-basted turkey and cilantro dressing. The brothers sent up a chauvinistic whine of protest. She scolded them in Spanish until, with sheepish faces, they quit complaining. I knew my situation was being discussed, but as long as I didn't have to do anything but sit there, I didn't care. Elvia was right, as she often is in my case. It was just what I needed, a family, but not my own.

When I got up to leave for the museum to finish hanging the quilts, another protest went up. This time from Elvia and her mother.

"No, no," Señora Aragon said, shaking her small finger at me. "Too much danger."

"Those quilts have to get hung," I argued.

A compromise was reached, and Miguel, his Walkman and his pistol went along for protection. When I saw how deserted the neighborhood around the museum was, I was glad for Miguel's presence. He stretched out on the floor in the lobby and listened to a football game while I finished Eric's work. Eric's tools were still spread out in the main hall, so at least I didn't have to venture back into the studios. Even with Miguel there, I didn't know if I could handle that.

I quickly became engrossed in the physical work of hanging the quilts. The co-op's quilters had already basted strips of Velcro to the backs of the quilts so it was just a matter of hanging the frames and attaching the quilts to them.

I silently called off the names as I hung them: Jacob's Ladder, Young Man's Fancy, Texas Tears, Wild Goose Chase. I traced the tiny stitches with my finger, and wondered about the women who had sewn them. The histories I'd gathered revealed small pieces of their lives, answering my general questions about when they made the quilt and why. Some just gave short, terse replies. Others gave stories that were heartbreaking. I picked up one of the framed histories, the one for the stunning Jacob's Ladder quilt. Muriel Phillips was the quilter. Born 1909. Quilt made in 1943. "I made the quilt when my three sons were called to war," she'd written. "The real war. The Big One. They was all over the world—Alaska, the South Pacific, Italy. I pieced this quilt, a little bit every night, listening to the radio, using scraps from their old shirts. They surely loved blue, my boys did. That's why there's so much blue in the quilt. My youngest, Tommy Lee, the one who was sent to Italy—he never came back. I gave this quilt to his wife, Nona, and when she was dying of cancer in 1954, she gave it back to me. My husband and I slept under it for 38 years until he died last year of his heart." I hung the history next to the quilt, peering closely at the picture of Muriel Phillips. The perky smile under her crown of white curls disguised all the sadness in her life.

I saved Grandmother Harper's Double Wedding Ring quilt for last. I studied the intricate stitches and wondered who of Jack's ancestors made love under this quilt, who was conceived, who died. The interlocking circles were made up of tiny scraps of material in the odd shades and patterns of blues, pinks, flowers and plaids popular seventy-five or eighty years ago. The ivory muslin background was faded yellow in spots; in the center of one ring a pale brown drop of blood stained the lightness.

When I was nineteen and newly married, Mom Harper started telling me I was to have this quilt. The Lone Star, honoring their Texas heritage, was to go to Wade's wife, and I, as Jack's wife, would receive the Wedding Ring quilt to pass down to future Harpers. As time went by and Jack and I never had children, Mom Harper stopped mentioning it. Now that I was no longer her daughter-in-law, I took it for granted Sandra would inherit them both. I told myself it didn't matter, that it really had nothing to do with what I had with Jack. Not really.

After it was hung, I sat cross-legged in front of it and enjoyed the serenity of the whole pattern, wondering which of Wade and Sandra's children would inherit it, picturing it going on down through the Harper family, further and further away from me.

Maybe we should have had those tests. We just kept putting it off, thinking—a baby will come in its own good time. Maybe it was fear—which of us would it be? We'd owned cows who'd taken a while to conceive. Wade always allowed them the standard two tries, then wanted to sell them, but Jack would take a shine to three or four every year and convince his brother to give them another chance. He'd sneak them treats of alfalfa cakes and croon to them in a low, gentle voice as he fed them, a voice I knew as well as my own sigh.

When it wasn't the cows but me that needed his special attentions, Jack made the most wonderful hot chocolate—the kind made from scratch with real cocoa. He'd pour a thick white mugful, top it with whipped cream and bring it to me on a pink glass plate with roses etched on the bottom that once belonged to his grandmother. He'd drink his straight from the pan, feet propped up on the coffee table, a warm hand caressing the nape of my neck.

"Isn't this the life?" he'd always say.

I left the plate at the ranch when I moved out.

The next morning, I arrived at the museum early but didn't beat the yellow and white truck of the Coastal Goodtimes Party Rental people. I handed the placement chart I'd drawn to the two workers, a skinny Hispanic man not much bigger than me, and a sullen red-headed boy with a rooster comb Mohawk. With a small feeling of trepidation, I left them to the job of readying the studios for the pre-showing.

After calling Marla's mother for the time and place of Marla's funeral, I typed an announcement and tacked it to the co-op's bulletin board. With that done, I puttered around, typing more quilt histories, writing a thank-you note to the local VFW for a hundred-dollar donation, picked off and inspected every brown leaf I could find on the fig tree in the corner of my office. Finally I had to face the inevitable.

Red is a power color, I tried to convince my reflection in the co-op's bathroom mirror. I slid my palm over the front of the scarlet linen shirt I wore. I'd run out of clean flannel shirts and was forced to wear one of my own. I'd spent fifteen minutes that morning sitting in front of the dirty clothes hamper trying to decide just how tacky it would be to dig one out. The Aunt Garnet gene in me won. I rolled up the sleeves and made a face at myself. There wasn't a color in the spectrum that was going to make me feel confident about telling the police about Rita.

On the drive to the police station, I mentally rehearsed my story, realizing after a few minutes the one good thing about the truth was, it didn't take much rehearsal. As I neared the station, the square knot in my stomach blossomed into a full-fledged macrame wall hanging.

The municipal parking lot was packed. I was forced into circling three times before even a metered spot was free. San Celina had recently decided to pad the city coffers by installing meters on most of the downtown spaces. It was a favorite coffee break complaint among the old-time residents. Something else to blame on the influx of Southern Californians buying up all the land, bringing their big-city ways to the Central Coast. Plinking in every bit of change in my purse, I won seventy-five minutes. Enough time to tell my story. Unless they arrested me. Then, a parking ticket would be the least of my worries. In the chief's parking spot, his Corvette sat arrogantly topless under an ominous cloudy sky.

The new police station was one of the few buildings downtown that didn't adhere to the Mission theme. It was a flat-roofed stucco building painted in subtle tans with brown wood trim. Neatly cropped ivy laced the walls, and a sluggish, beige-and-blue-tiled fountain gurgled at the entrance. It looked more like an office for a group of successful orthodontists than a police station. There must have been some kind of crime wave taking place in San Celina because it took ten minutes to work my way through the line in the lobby to the desk officer, a redheaded kid with a small cowlick. He looked as if he'd graduated from San Celina High School all of three minutes ago. A large revolver was strapped around his skinny waist.

"Can I help you, ma'am?" He smiled, displaying those kind of braces that are suppose to be invisible but aren't. Braces and a loaded revolver. Now there's a scary thought.

"I'd like to see Detective Ryan or Cleary."

"Just a minute."

I studied the various notices on the wheat-colored walls of the lobby. Their bowling team placed second in the city championship last year. The FBI's Ten Most Wanted looked as hollow-cheeked and menacing as ever. I'd moved on to memorizing the faces of missing children when a smooth, tenor voice called my name.

"Ms. Harper? Is there something I can do for you?"

I turned to face the dark, curious face of Detective Cleary. The bulge from his gun was apparent under his snug tweed jacket. Someone in his life was a good cook, or he hadn't bought any new jackets for a while.

"I have some information about Marla's murder," I said.

"What is it?" He crossed his arms and cocked his head, throwing me off a bit. Blurting the whole story out in the lobby was not what I'd expected.

"I found Rita," I said. "My cousin. Do you know about her?" The eager look on his face answered my question.

"Where is she?" he said. "Is she with you? Get her in here."

"Well, she's not exactly with me."

His dark brown eyes blinked rapidly as he rubbed his jaw. "Just a minute. I think I'd better call the chief." That was exactly what I'd hoped to avoid. I swallowed hard and considered bolting. No use. He knew where I worked and probably where I lived.

Cleary reached over the counter and punched a number on the desk officer's phone. After a few short sentences in a voice so low I couldn't make out the words, he jerked his head at me.

"He wants to talk to you himself."

No kidding. I followed him through a maze of beige desks down a long hall, past a women's restroom I contemplated ducking into, to a closed oak door with a brass nameplate—"Aaron Davidson—Chief of Police." He knuckle-rapped sharply twice and swung it open. "Here she is, Chief." The small, sympathetic smile he flashed in my direction as he closed the door behind me didn't ease my mind or the tangled rope in my stomach.

Ortiz sat in a tall black executive chair, his blue eyes alert, his olive-skinned face expressionless. He gestured to a matching office chair in front of his desk. Tilting his chair back, he tented his fingers and regarded me. I avoided his gaze with a quick glance at my surroundings. Oak was the only word to describe the office. Everything matched, down to the brass-and-oak desk accessories. They say you can tell a lot about a person by their work surroundings. But this office was a loaner, so any stories it had to tell wouldn't be his. The top of the desk in front of him was bare. I wondered if he kept a file cabinet at Liddie's. I decided not to ask.

"Where's your cousin?" he finally asked, his voice smooth as the burnished wood desk in front of him.

I told him my story and waited for the meltdown.

"Did he touch anything after they found the body? Did your cousin? Did they remove anything from the premises? Did he call anybody?" His voice became louder with each sentence.

"I don't know." I tried to make out the signature on the painting behind him. It was a surrealistic desert scene with cacti shaped like green bullets. It looked like Crap. The artist's name, not the painting.

"Why did he go for gas? Where? Had his hands been recently washed? Were there stains on his clothes?" Two deep lines formed on either side of his black mustache.

"I don't know." A strong urge to chew on the tip of my braid, a childhood habit, came over me as I readjusted myself in the stiff chair.

"Why did he duck down when he saw you drive by? What did he and your cousin talk about after they discovered the body? Which way did he start walking when your cousin dropped him off?"

"I don't know. I . . . didn't think to ask."

He slammed a hand down on his desk; the unexpectedness of it caused me to jump. He rose, tore off his glasses and pointed them at me.

"Exactly. You didn't think to ask those things because you're not a cop, which is why *I* should have been the one talking to her, not you." He shoved his glasses back on, walked over to the window, and stood there muttering to himself in an incomprehensible mixture of Spanish and English.

I froze, wondering what I should do. Bolting out the door was my first choice, clearly not a viable one. Too many guns between me and my truck. Still, doing nothing had never been my style.

"She never would have called *you*," I said. "And I tried to get her to come in and talk to the police but she refused. I couldn't force her. You have more information than if I hadn't seen her at all."

He turned and looked at me, the flinty lines of his face grim. "You could have taken me with you."

Good point. But it didn't take into consideration family loyalty.

"She didn't have anything to do with Marla's murder. She was just an innocent bystander. I think you should find Eric. Were his fingerprints on the murder weapon?"

He was silent so long, I thought he wasn't going to answer.

"That is none of your business," he said, walking back to his chair and sitting down. I watched with apprehension as a small muscle twitch in his jaw.

"Anything else you care to add, Ms. Harper?"

"No." I scooted forward in my chair. "That about covers it. Now can I go?" Even I cringed at the adolescent ring of petulance in my voice. Except that's how it felt. Like being sent to the principal's office. Of course, detention here took on a whole different meaning.

He leaned back in his chair and crossed his legs, ankle to knee. Pulling at his thick mustache, he studied me with solemn eyes. I stared back. Boldly. I think.

"Ms. Harper," he said quietly. "What am I going to do with you?"

I had a few suggestions but I suspected my vote didn't count for much. Dove's voice came through loud and clear in my mind—Kiddo, sometimes your best bet is to keep your trap shut.

He stood up, walked over to the door and held it open. I jumped up, and squeezed past him.

"Just one minute." He grabbed my shoulder as I started to walk away. "I have something I want to show you."

He held my upper arm in a firm grip and steered me down the long hallway outside his office to a large white door marked "Authorized Personnel Only." It opened to a stairway leading down two flights. Another white door. No writing on it. He slipped a small blue plastic card in a slot at the side of the door. A loud click. He pulled the thick door open, and with the flat of his hand, he gave my back a gentle but very definite shove.

"Where are we?" I asked. It was obvious once I looked around. The cold, bland air, the beige walls, the fingerprinting equipment, the Breathalyzer, the DMV-like photo setup and a long hall of open metal doors revealing small rooms with single attached bunks. Detention in its highest life form.

"I wanted you to see where you'll be staying if you pull one more stupid stunt like last night."

"Very funny." I crossed my arms. "Isn't psychological intimidation a form of police harassment?"

"We can only hold prisoners six to eight hours." He studied the blue card in his hand with exaggerated interest. "We have no facilities for food or clothing, although I do have the authority to make an exception. We could send out for food." He leaned against the door and stuck his hands in his pockets. "Tell me, do you prefer Taco Bell or Burger King?"

"You're not scaring me." I glanced around, noticed a phone in the narrow white room where they took mugshots. I was tempted to go over and use it.

And what, I said to myself, call the police? I felt a hysterical laugh gurgle at the back of my throat. I turned my head in an effort to hide my smile.

"I'm glad you find this so amusing," Ortiz said mildly. "You know, this isn't college high jinks. It's a bit more serious than locking a goat in the science lab."

I looked at him, incredulous. "How do you know about that?"

"I know a lot about you, Ms. Harper."

"Why me? I'm not the criminal here."

"All information ends up somewhere. You must know that. As for why?" He slipped the blue card in the slot and pushed the door open. "I think that's obvious. You're involved in this up to your"—his eyes did a quick scan—"fairly attractive neck, so it behooves me to know about you."

I pushed past him and headed up the stairs. "Believe me, I didn't choose to find Marla's body or be related to Rita. I've been dragged into this from the beginning, and as of now, I'm out of it."

"I'm glad to hear that." He opened the last door and we were back in the hallway leading to his office. "Then I can count on you to call me the next time you talk to your cousin?"

I contemplated whether I should lie or not.

"Ms. Harper?"

"She probably won't call," I said. "She's very flaky."

"Ms. Harper." His voice held a warning.

"Okay, *okay*," I said. "You've had your fun. Can I go now?"

"Certainly. You're not under arrest. You're free to leave whenever you like." He smiled widely, with incredibly white, slightly crooked teeth. "Have a nice day."

Same to you, bud. I walked back to my truck lambasting myself on my knee-jerk obedience to authority figures. The bright pink parking ticket fluttering under my windshield made me kick the driver's door with my boot, adding one more dent to its pebbled complexion.

"Great," I said, ripping it off. I leaned against the truck and read it. The instructions on how to pay were incomprehensible. I turned it over to see if a secret decoder ring was attached. I'd had one or two tickets since this whole program started, but I couldn't remember how I'd handled them. A car swung into the empty parking space next to me.

"Having car problems?" Ortiz asked.

I shook the ticket at him. "This is all your fault. Don't I get some kind of validation? I was talking to you the whole time. Isn't that considered city business or something?"

He gestured for me to hand it to him, scanning it as he unbuttoned the top button of his shirt and loosened his tie. After a few minutes, I began to wonder if he couldn't figure it out either.

"Well?" I demanded. "Are you going to do something about it?"

"Certainly."

"Good." My anger at him dissipated a millimeter.

"If you write out a check for twenty-five dollars, I'll be happy to stick it in the mail for you."

I grabbed the ticket back. "Thanks a lot."

"Maybe you should pay the other two while you're at it," he said amicably.

That's why I couldn't remember what to do with them. "Don't worry about it," I snapped.

"I'd hate to put out a warrant for your arrest."

"I bet you would." I crumpled the ticket and tossed it over my shoulder into the bed of my truck.

"You look like a Whopper, small fries, diet Coke kind of person to me." He removed his wire-rims and slipped on aviator sunglasses. "But I could be wrong. I guess I'll have to do a little more research." He flashed a smug smile and left me with a lungful of exhaust.

I stood there, trying to think of a snappy comeback, when a remark I'd made to J.D. about knowing your enemy sparked an idea. I reached for the crumpled ticket, flattened it out and stuck it back under my windshield. Hopefully, Ortiz and I would never have the opportunity to talk again. But if we did, I was going to be prepared.

San Celina's city government offices were a short block from the police station. The three-story Mission-style building, with its rough, gray-white walls and red tile roof, housed Public Works, the City Clerk, the Mayor and all his entourage and the Personnel office. There's one good thing about growing up in a fairly small town: you end up with friends in a lot of convenient places.

The long, gray terrazzo-tiled hallway gave me time to think about how to phrase my request. I pushed open the bumpy glass door labeled "Assistant Personnel Director."

"Hey, Angie, I've come to collect on an old debt."

Her milky-pale face lit up with surprise. A huge pair of tortoise-shell glasses slipped down her thin nose. With her middle finger, she shoved them back up with a quick, darting motion.

"Why, you little shrimp." She gave a high, feminine laugh that didn't match her intellectual looks. "Where have you been hiding? Do I owe you money? My mom's just hatched a whole bunch of Rhode Island Reds. Would a couple of chickens cover it?"

Angie and I were 4-H partners through two calves, one goat, one lamb and numerous fowl during our pubescent years. We'd spent countless sticky, humid afternoons at the Mid-State Fair perched on our animal pens, boot heels hooked in the rungs, dropping peanuts in our icy Cokes and grading two-legged beef as it swaggered by.

"I'm collecting for the time that I told your mother you were spending the night at my house when in fact you went down to Eola Beach with—What was his name?"

She laughed again, gestured for me to take a seat and used her eyeglasses as a headband for her long, sand-colored hair. "Ricky Dean Abbott." She rested her pointy chin on her hand. "Shoot, I haven't thought of him in years. Last I heard, he moved to Oklahoma and was raising turkeys."

"Appropriate occupation if I remember him correctly."

"I don't know where my mind was. He kissed like a vacuum cleaner set on thick plush."

"I don't think your mind was what you were thinking with."

She shook her head, pushed the folder in front of her aside, and folded her hands. "Wasted the best two months of my life on him. Okay, I owe you. We don't have any openings, not that I see you as the civil servant type. What can I do for you?"

When I explained what I wanted, she grinned. "Feels like high school again," she said. "I could get in real trouble for this and I don't mean picking up trash in the schoolyard."

"You won't get in trouble, I promise."

She twisted her face in a wry expression and stood up. "Seems to me I've heard those words before."

Five minutes later she came back with a thin blue file.

"This is grade A prime cut here," she said with a chuckle. "He's single, got a steady job and certainly isn't hard on the eyes. As the girls in Maintenance say—give him a blood test and call the preacher."

"Single?" I said. "I didn't even think about that."

"Divorced, actually. You've been out of circulation a long time, honey. That's the *first* thing you look for."

"Anyway, I don't care about that. This is a defensive action."

"Sure." She winked and stuck the folder in her top drawer. "Look, I can't actually let you read this, that would be unethical, but I am going to lunch, so feel free to use my office as long as you like. Just don't get caught, okay?"

"Me? You were the one who almost blew it when we found out Ricky Dean was cheating on you with Leeann Riley."

"Can I help it if night air makes me sneeze? You made me sit in the bushes with you outside his parents' house until two in the morning to catch them. To this day I blame my bladder problems on that night."

"But we didn't get caught."

"Can't call you a liar there." She pulled her glasses back down and looked at me intently. "I'm glad to see you taking an interest in something finally. He's not a bad start."

"I told you that isn't the reason."

"Right." She stood up and picked up her purse, patting my shoulder as she walked out the door. "And good ole Ricky Dean Abbott's favorite holiday is Fourth of July."

9

"YOU LOOK LIKE you're a million miles away," Meg said. She walked into my office carrying a large manila envelope. The small room was filled with the earthy scent of her patchouli perfume. It reminded me of high-school dances, Brut cologne, the press of damp hands against the small of my back.

I had been sitting for the last hour tossing pencils at my pencil cup thinking about the last few days up to and including what I'd just read about Ortiz. What a surprise he turned out to be.

"Just thinking about tonight," I said. "What's up?" Meg, our resident potluck organizer and general busybody, usually dropped by my office only when being pressed into service as an emissary.

"It's about Marla." She placed the envelope on my desk, pushed it toward me. "Or rather about her funeral."

"What about it? Does anyone need directions?"

"That's what I wanted to talk to you about." She bent over and pulled up the knee socks she wore under her gauzy Indian skirt. Something was always off kilter on

Meg: a torn pocket, curly bangs cut too short, eyeglasses taped in odd spots, but her quilts, exquisite copies of Georgia O'Keeffe paintings, were always perfect.

"No." She hesitated for a moment. "We, that is the rest of the co-op, were wondering if you were going."

"Of course. Isn't everyone else?"

She pushed the envelope closer to me. I peered inside. It was full of crumpled bills and some change. "We collected some money for flowers. Could you get them? I don't think anyone else is going to make it."

"No one?" I looked at her, perplexed.

"Oh, Benni," she said. "I know you got along with her okay, but she wasn't real well-liked by the rest of us." Her laugh was high and strained. "Except for a few. She was real well-liked by a few."

"What's that suppose to mean?"

Red-faced, she fanned thin fingers as if to cool herself. "Oh, forget I said that. That was horrible."

"Quit playing games, Meg," I said irritably. "Just tell me what you mean."

She dropped her head and studied her reddish hands. "It's just that she had a thing about other women's men, if you know what I mean."

"Marla?" I knew she was a flirt, that seemed to come with her bartending job, but she didn't seem the type to steal another woman's man. But then, since I'd known her, I hadn't had a man. That certainly opened up some possibilities of people who might want her dead.

"Anyone I know?" I asked.

"You didn't hear it from me." She leaned over my desk, giving into the temptation to spread a little gossip. "Ray," she whispered. "And Eric. And who knows who else?"

"Oh." Things were starting to get clear. In a murky sort of way. "Did anyone tell the police?"

She shrugged. "I didn't, but I can't say what anyone else said. I figure who people sleep with is their own business. I know Ray or Eric didn't kill her."

"And just how do you know that?" Great, I thought, I'm beginning to sound like Ortiz.

"I know them. They wouldn't kill anyone. Ray's a big teddy bear, you know that—and Eric, well, you know." She gave a nervous laugh. His laziness was well-known in the co-op. Of course, it doesn't take that much effort to stab someone, especially if you're angry.

"I hope you're not going to make a big deal about this." She stood up, tugged at her thin skirt as she went out the door. "Really, I think it was probably some homeless person looking for money. Or one of the guys she goes out with from Trigger's."

After hearing Meg's weak defense of Ray and Eric, I realized how naive I must have sounded to Ortiz when I defended Rita.

Ray and Eric. Each a very strong possibility. I laid my head down on my desk, my mind reeling with questions. How much of this did the police know? What should I tell them? If Ray didn't have anything to do with it and his wife found out about him and Marla, it could ruin their marriage. But what if he did do it? And what about Eric? Where was he, anyway? A sharp knock on the door interrupted my jumbled speculations.

"Got a headache?" Ray asked. His gentle concern and easy smile made him seem about as likely a killer as Mr. Rogers. Then again, I was never quite clear on exactly what it was he did in Vietnam.

"No, just tired." I smiled back, but couldn't help regarding him in a new light. I hadn't even suspected anything sexual going on between him and Marla. Of course, Jack always said I was the densest woman he'd ever seen when it came to male-female relationships. I was always the last one to figure out among our friends who was interested in whom. No feminine intuition whatsoever.

"It's four o'clock. We're all going home now. You need anything else done for tonight?"

"No, I've got a few more quilt histories to frame, then I'm leaving, too. Then I think I'm going to sink into a long, hot bubble bath."

"Just remember to come up for air," he teased.

Ten minutes later, my mind was on that hot bubble bath when I climbed the stairs to the second floor of the museum to look for some frames for the last two quilt histories. I had searched through the storage room, certain I'd ordered enough, but in an artist's co-op, frames of any size or condition always seemed to sprout little legs and walk away.

The air was warm and thick in the four spacious rooms where Constance's ancestors had once slept, made love, had babies, died. Sneezing and coughing, I scrounged through rusty old trunks and poked through boxes containing old tubes of paint, stacks of blank, yellowing canvases, and one large box full of every sort of bead, trim and feather you could imagine—an obvious donation that no one could quite figure out what to do with. The floor creaked under my weight. I wondered if the idea Constance brought up at the last co-op meeting about using these rooms as more exhibit space was feasible from a safety point of view.

After checking a six-drawer chest in one of the rooms and finding nothing but more dust and an old mouse nest, I decided to forget it. I'd just mat the histories and stick them directly on the wall with some double-sided tape. I shoved the last drawer in, struggling a few minutes when something hung it up. I pulled it out and peered into the back of the chest. Dusk and the hacienda's filmy windows made seeing anything difficult, but there was something stuck to the back of the chest. Curiosity overcame sense. I tentatively stuck my hand in and yanked at the plastic-wrapped object. When I pulled it free and inspected it, I could have kicked myself for not leaving well enough alone.

The plastic freezer bag was full of rubber-banded bills and it didn't take a genius to realize there was something fishy about this money.

I turned the bag over and over, trying to make a decision. If I called the police, which is what I knew I should do, they'd be all over the museum and the pre-showing and auction would be ruined. Our next fund-raiser wasn't until spring. So, after ten seconds of serious contemplation of the consequences, I stuck the bag back in the chest and pushed the drawer closed.

I'll tell the police, I told myself as I locked the front door. Just as soon as the auction is over.

My answering machine was flashing when I got home. As I unbuttoned my shirt, I listened to my one caller.

Dove hates answering machines, so she pretends that she is actually talking to a human, leaving time for your answer. Her messages always sound halting and semi-lucid.

"Benni, is that you?" Long pause.

"Who else would be in my house, Dove?" I don't know why I felt compelled to answer. That authority thing again.

"Don't get smart with me, young lady." One, one thousand, two, one thousand . . .

"What do you want, old woman?"

"Garnet wants to see you."

Aha. The real reason for the call. "I can't. I'm too . . ."

"And don't give me any of that you're-too-busy crap. She's your great-aunt and she deserves some respect.

And I deserve some peace and quiet. And don't you turn me off."

"Great suggestion." I hit the stop button, thankful for at least one positive thing about technology. But by the time I undressed, curiosity got the better of me and I punched it back on.

"I knew you'd be back," her voice cackled out of the machine. "You always were as nosy as a chicken. Call me. I mean it." The answering machine chirped.

"Don't hold your breath." I took a quick shower to scrub away the worst of the dirt and dust embedded in my pores, then pulling my hair up in a Pebbles ponytail, I settled down in a nice warm bath and worried about the trouble I knew was coming after the auction tonight. I didn't remember seeing any sinks in the jail, or showers, for that matter. I couldn't sleep without my nightly shower. I sank deeper into the bubbles and groaned.

After a few minutes in front of my vanity mirror decid-ing they were laugh lines and not wrinkles, I took care of the impossibly boring ritual of war paint. For once, my curly hair semi-controlled itself down my back. Though I briefly contemplated pulling it back with a rubber band, I decided the lecture from Elvia wasn't worth it. The green silk dress felt as airy as cotton candy and made a fine rustling sound against my nylons. It had been a long time since I'd worn a dress, and it felt, if a bit awkward, pretty good. I slipped on my Levi jacket to retain some level of familiarity, with the intention of ditching it before Elvia saw me. It was soft enough to make a pretty good noose.

The caterers arrived minutes after me and started unloading cases of champagne and foil-covered trays of hors d'oeuvres. Though the champagne had been donated by one of Constance's friends who owned a winery, I'd spent more on the food than I'd intended, hoping full stomachs would help open people's wallets a little wider.

Ten minutes later, Constance Sinclair exploded into the room wearing a black crepe de Chine dress and a kamikaze expression. At four feet ten with stiff white hair and the mannerisms of an overbred greyhound, she yapped orders at the fish-mouthed catering staff—move that table there, stack those glasses that way, what's this Folger's doing here, we paid good money for gourmet.

Her early arrival and autocratic manner didn't surprise me. Most of her friends would be here tonight. Nothing less than perfection would bring a smile to her pinched, persimmon lips.

"Everything seems in order," she finally decreed.

In the next forty-five minutes, most of the invited guests had arrived and were mingling with the artists. The champagne was flowing more quickly than I'd anticipated, so I considered starting the auction early before everyone was too tipsy to write a check. On the other hand, their slight inebriety could work in the co-op's favor.

"Where's the rest of the champagne?" Constance's silvery eyelids disappeared as she, with wide, slightly bulging eyes, considered our stock critically.

"In the studios," I said. "I'll have the caterers bring it out when we need it."

"Connie!" J.D.'s voice bellowed over the heads of a large, chattering group of people just arriving. "What a shindig. Can I make a campaign speech?"

If anyone could make the stiff-backed Constance Sinclair come anywhere near simpering, it was J.D. Freedman.

"Oh, J.D.," she said. Her tight pink face spread into what looked like a grimace of pain but I think was suppose to be a flirtatious smile.

He winked at me and took her elbow. I smiled at them and couldn't help but wonder. J.D. had been a widower for ten years and Constance had never married. There must be some reason why he called her Connie.

I felt a hand slip around my waist. I turned to face the lopsided grin of Carl. He drained the glass he held in his other hand.

"Quite the little soiree you have here. Never thought you had it in you, you old cowpuncher. You look incredible, by the way."

"Thanks," I said. "I hope we get a lot of donations tonight. That is the whole point to this."

"Surely you'll be able to wring a few bucks out of San Celina's richest and finest. We do love the arts here on the Central Coast."

"Who's watching the paper?" J.D. asked, looking annoyed.

"Julio knows what to do," Carl said lightly. "Trade ya." He exchanged his empty glass for my full one before I could protest.

"It's your job while your brother's gone to supervise the evening shift," J.D. said. "And I haven't seen you for two days. Where have you been?"

"I've made the supervisory decision to let Julio handle it for a few hours." He pulled at the sleeves of his tailored leather jacket and ignored the rest of his father's question.

J.D.'s face turned a dull red. "Cathy called me today."

Carl shrugged and sipped his drink. "So?"

"So she says you're three months behind in your child support. I'm paying you a good salary, son. Why don't you spend a little less time having a good time and make sure your kids have some food on the table?"

Carl's head stiffened. A blank expression fell over his face.

Constance tugged at J.D.'s thick arm. "There are some people I invited specifically to meet you." She flashed me a frown and flicked her eyes toward Carl, her message clear as distilled water. I wanted to tell her that no one could change Carl and J.D. I'd watched this ballet more times than I could count in the last twenty years and the two lead dancers had their steps down cold.

"Just a minute, Connie." J.D. pointed a finger at Carl, inches from his pink button-down-collar shirt. "I sent her the money, but I'm deducting it from your next paycheck and nothing better go wrong tonight or else."

Two spots of rosy color stained Carl's cheeks as he watched his dad lumber across the room greeting people in his oversized voice.

"Come on, Carl," I said, pulling at his sleeve. "Take a look at the food I ordered. They carved a quilt pattern on top of the cheese wheel."

"What a crock of bullshit," Carl said. He followed me to the hors d'oeuvre table and picked up another glass of champagne. "You wouldn't happen to have anything stronger hidden away somewhere, would you? This tastes like cat piss."

"Carl, you shouldn't let him get to you."

"You don't have to live with him. He doesn't tell you what to do with your life every single, solitary minute."

"Neither do you."

"With those support payments I'm having to make? I can't afford to eat at Taco Bell, much less get my own place. Now she says the kids need gymnastic lessons. I told her to buy a swing set at Sears and let them fall off that. And she's taking opera lessons. That's where my hard earned money is going, down her stringy throat."

"Eat something." I held out a plate of rumaki and shrimp puffs, trying to avoid any more discussion about his ex-wife. I'd known her in college. A tall, gorgeous redhead, she was well known even then for being a person easily impressed by money and prestige. Everyone thought she only married Carl for his money. And time seemed to prove that true. But Carl had really loved her and I knew their breakup had been hard on him.

"I'm not hungry," he said, pulling a small flask out of his jacket and taking a swig. "But I do have a question for you. I heard through the grapevine that your cousin was a witness to the Chenier murder." He picked up a glass of champagne, gave it a disgusted look, then drained it. "I can't believe you'd hold out on me like that. J.D. got all over my ass for not getting all the facts."

"She wasn't a witness," I said hastily. "She was just with Marla before it happened. She didn't see anything."

"You've talked with her?" An eager expression lit up his face.

"Get that look out of your eyes," I said. "There's no story there. She didn't see a thing. Besides, she's out of town right now."

His pale marble-blue eyes narrowed. "I've known you a long time, Benni, so quit jerking me around. You've got something up your sleeve. What did your cousin . . ."

"Benni!" A soft, high voice interrupted him. "Everything looks so great. Grandma Harper's quilt never looked better. Pretty dress."

"Thanks," I said to my sister-in-law, Sandra. "I'm glad you came. Is Mom Harper with you?" I turned to her thankfully, ignoring Carl's aggravated look.

She shook her head, her brown eyes sober. "No, she stayed home with the kids. They're all coming tomorrow to the festival. We're stopping at the mall first to see Santa Claus."

Carl grabbed my arm. "There's someone I need to see. I'll get back to you later." He strode away, his back rigid with irritation.

"Did I interrupt something?" Sandra asked. Her smooth forehead puckered with worry as she tugged at a strand of straight brown hair curled in a slight flip, a hairdo she'd worn the whole sixteen years I'd known her.

"Don't worry about it," I said. "I wasn't giving him exactly what he wanted and we know how much men like that. Speaking of pushy men, did Wade come with you?" I surveyed the room quickly.

A tremulous smile fluttered across her waxy pink lips. "No, he's . . ." Her eyes grew shiny with tears. "To tell you the truth, Benni, I don't know where he is."

"Sandra, what's wrong?" I laid a hand on her softly rounded shoulder. "Oh, he isn't drinking again, is he?" Wade's nights out with the boys had caused problems between them before. The number of times Jack and I drove to town in the chilled darkness of early morning to pick up Wade and his truck blurred in my memory into one huge sleepy trip.

"Not that bad." She shifted her eyes from my face to her square, blunt-nailed hands. Though she was a large, sometimes awkward woman, Sandra had a quiet gentleness about her that made her easy to be with, something I especially appreciated the first few days after Jack's death.

"What is it?" I asked. "You know I'll help wherever I can."

"I hate to bother you with this . . ." Her face flushed with embarrassment, or as I peered closer, possibly anger, something I rarely saw in Sandra all the years we'd lived at the ranch.

"You're family, Sandra. Let me try and help."

"I think Wade's cheating on me," she blurted out, then burst into tears.

I patted her on her shoulder as she cried quietly into her napkin. When I realized people were beginning to stare, I steered her toward a corner of the room, near an open window.

"Are you sure?" I asked.

"There's no other explanation."

"For what?"

"This." She opened up her large leather purse, pulled out a folded white Trigger's cocktail napkin and handed it to me. "I found it in his jacket a couple of months ago."

A phone number was raggedly jotted onto the crumpled napkin. My stomach lurched when I read it. "Have you tried calling it?"

"I only got up enough nerve to try about a week ago," she said, her voice trembling. "No one answered. Not that I'd have had enough courage to say anything anyway."

"Have you talked to Wade about it?"

"No. I don't know how to bring it up."

"Maybe there's an explanation. Maybe it's not what you think." I was trying to convince myself as much as her, because what was going through my mind right then was unthinkable.

"Could you talk to him? He's always listened to you."

This is not your problem, I told myself, as I studied the napkin and its incriminating numbers. Let Sandra fight her own battles.

"Okay," I said. "I'll see what I can do. Let me keep this for now."

"Thank you," she said with a sigh. "You can have it. I don't ever want to see it again."

"I'll talk to him tomorrow at the festival. I'm sure there's a logical explanation for this. Maybe it's just a feed salesman or something."

She gave a small laugh. "Thanks, Benni. I knew you'd know what to do. Gosh, I miss you out at the ranch."

"Go enjoy the exhibit." I squeezed her arm. "I'll see you tomorrow."

As I watched her move toward the food table, I mentally kicked myself for what I'd so blithely offered to do. I stared at the napkin, my heart sinking, knowing good and well why no one was answering the phone. The only question was, just exactly what Wade was doing with Marla's phone number in his jacket pocket.

10

I STOOD AT the window with my back to the crowd and searched for answers in the dark parking lot. It never ceased to amaze me how I managed to tangle myself up in other people's problems. There were times when I wished I could move away to a place where no one knew me, where no one would walk up to me with those magic words—"Do you think you could . . . ?"

"Ms. Harper," a low, masculine voice said about a foot from my ear. "I hardly recognized you in your grownup clothes."

"Think up your own lines, Ortiz." I turned around and confronted his smiling face. Inspecting his perfectly tailored navy suit, I wondered where a gun could be concealed. Did police chiefs even carry guns or was that something they left to the peons in uniform?

"Something going on out there I should know about?" He leaned over and peered out the window.

"What are you doing here?" I asked.

"Just supporting the local arts."

"Right." I looked back out the window.

He leaned against the adobe wall, watching me with his suspicious cop look. "What's got you bugged?"

"What makes you think anything is bugging me?"

"You have the face of a monkey, Ms. Harper."

"Excuse me?"

He laughed, white teeth brilliant against his dark face. "What I mean is, you show your emotions on your face. I hope you never bet your life savings on a bad poker hand."

"I happen to be very good at poker," I said stiffly. No need to mention Dove always swore I could have been a pro if I could play with a paper bag over my head. "Do you have any new leads on Marla's murder?"

"Nothing I'm going to tell you," he said, still smiling.

"Well, I guess that pretty much wraps up our cocktail chatter. Hope you brought your checkbook. Have a nice evening." I started to move away, when he grabbed my elbow.

"Who was the lady you were talking to?"

"I've talked to lots of ladies tonight."

"You know who I mean. The lady who was so upset. The lady who gave you that napkin you were studying with such interest."

"She was my sister-in-law, and what we were talking about was personal so therefore none of your business." I pulled my elbow out of his grasp.

"Anything I suspect has to do with this murder is my business." It took two seconds for his smile to turn into a frown. He reached for the napkin; I twisted around and held it behind me.

"Believe me, this had nothing to do with Marla's murder."

"I'm a cop. I don't believe anybody."

"What television show did you steal that line from?"

He tried for the napkin again, and without thinking, I stuck it in a place I didn't think even he'd attempt to follow.

He glanced quickly at my chest; a dull red flush turned his dark skin a cinnamon color.

"That wouldn't stop me if we were alone," he snapped.

"How fortunate for me we aren't," I said coolly and folded my arms across my chest. His scowl deepened.

"You're being childish," he said.

"I know." I also knew making him angry was not in my long-term interest, but until I confronted Wade, I wasn't about to show that napkin to Ortiz. "Look, this honestly doesn't have anything to do with Marla's murder but I do have something to show you."

"What?" He narrowed his eyes skeptically.

"It's probably nothing, but I'll let you decide. I'll show it to you after the auction."

"Now."

"No. This time you're just going to have to do things on *my* time schedule."

I held up my hand when he started to speak. "Save your breath. I'm not saying one more thing until after the auction."

He whipped around and walked away, his lips so narrowed in anger they almost disappeared behind his mustache.

"Relax," I called after him, glad he'd have a few hours to cool off before I showed him the bag of money. "Have some champagne."

"What's his problem?" Elvia walked up, looking like a Vogue cover in a black and white linen dress that somehow didn't have a wrinkle on it. She scanned me critically, then gave a satisfied smile. "I knew that dress would be perfect on you."

"Thanks," I said. "I'll give you the name of my personal shopper. Her specialty is impossible missions."

She laughed and fingered a strand of smooth black hair, pulled to one side with a mother-of-pearl hairclip in the shape of a sea horse. "What did you do to make our new police chief angry this time? You really must quit provoking the public servants. Especially the ones that can make life miserable for one of my brothers."

"It's not me. He gets some perverse pleasure out of baiting me."

"Hmm," she said and took a sip of champagne. "So, what gives?"

Glancing down at the small beaded purse hung over her shoulder, I reached down the front of my dress and pulled out the napkin. "Could you keep this for me until tomorrow?"

"Sure." She took the napkin and slipped it into her purse. "May I inquire as to why you have a cocktail napkin stuffed in your bra? You haven't needed help in that area since you were fourteen."

"Very funny. Can I fill you in tomorrow? I don't even know the whole story yet."

"What have you got yourself into this time, *mi amiga?*" She tapped long, icy nails on her plastic champagne glass. "And the real question is, will it earn you another private tour of our city's penal accommodations?"

I gave her a rueful look. "You heard about that."

"It was quite the talk of the station, according to Miguel."

"That's so embarrassing."

"More embarrassing to actually have to stay there."

"True, but that's not going to happen. I hope."

"Those last two words worry me."

"They worry me more. Just keep your checkbook handy, okay?"

She shook her head slowly and gave a low chuckle. "You've had more excitement in the last four days than you've had in fifteen years."

"This kind of excitement I can do without. Now, help me start herding these people toward the studios so we can commence with the real purpose of this party."

The bidding at the auction was vigorous and competitive, spurred by a generous holiday spirit or perhaps spirits of the liquid persuasion. One especially keen bidding war was waged by Carl and his father for a Texas Star quilt. At four hundred dollars, a good-natured J.D. gave in to his younger son, and Carl carried it triumphantly away.

"Thanks for the show," I teased Carl as people made their way out to their cars. "You and J.D. bid like it was a prize bull on the block."

He smiled and patted the quilt he had slung over his shoulder like a serape. "I love beating out the old man. Even for a blanket. Of course, I'm going to have to borrow the money from him to pay for it."

"Why does he put up with you? And, if you realized how much work went into it, you wouldn't be so blasé. That's probably the most expensive blanket you'll ever sleep under." I poked him on his free shoulder. "Or is it a present for some special lady?"

"Sure is." He pulled it off his shoulder. "Here."

"Oh, no," I said. "I'm not wrapping it for you. I haven't even finished my own wrapping yet."

"I don't want you to wrap it, Benni," he said, his face serious. "I want you to have it."

"Me?"

"Just take it." He turned a soft pink under his tan.

"I can't. It cost you four hundred dollars. There must be someone you want to give it to."

116

"There is. Now take it or else Ashley sleeps with it."
Ashley was his Airedale terrier.

"You wouldn't."

"Jack was my best friend. I know this Christmas is going to be hard for you. Think of it as sort of a present from him too." He shoved it at me and looked down at the ground.

"Thank you," I said softly. "You're a good friend, Carl Freedman."

"Yeah, well, sorry I barked at you earlier."

I hugged the quilt to my cheek and looked intently into his glassy eyes. "It's all right. Are you okay to drive? I lost one guy already. I don't want to lose another."

"I'm fine," he said. "You worry too much. Come by the paper and I'll take you to lunch."

"I will, real soon."

After he left, I set the quilt down on the counter and turned to go through the museum to the studios to lock up.

"What was it you had to show me?" Ortiz stepped suddenly from around the corner, causing me to jump at the sound of his voice.

"Someone should put a bell around your neck," I said, my stomach instantly tightening with anxiety. I glanced around at the caterers still cleaning up. They and Ortiz were the only people left. Safety in numbers, I told myself. He couldn't pistol-whip me with witnesses around.

"It's up here," I said, sighing. As we started up the stairs, the man in charge of the catering staff asked me a question about the equipment.

"The first room on the right," I told Ortiz. "Look in the last drawer in the old oak dresser. I'll be there in a minute."

I was in the middle of haggling with the catering supervisor about two damaged chairs when Ortiz came barreling down the stairs, a look on his face vicious enough to fell a herd of elephants.

"Are you out of your mind?" he said in a voice as close to a snarl as I'd ever heard.

"What?" I looked up, surprised at his overreaction.

"I've had it with you," he said. "I'll find something to charge you with if I have to sit up all night with the D.A. myself."

He pushed past me into the lobby, punched some numbers into the phone and started snapping orders in a low voice. Slamming down the receiver, he turned to me and said in a barely controlled voice:

"Explain."

"What are you so upset about? I found it when I was looking for some picture frames this afternoon. I'm sorry I didn't tell you sooner, but I knew you'd ruin the auction and we'd worked so hard on it."

"You knew about it this whole time?" His mouth literally dropped open. "You're nuts. You're unbelievable."

"What's the big deal, Ortiz? It could have been there for months. We don't know for certain it has to do with Marla's murder."

"What are you talking about?"

"The money. What are you talking about?"

His fingers dug into my upper arm like giant crab pincers as he practically dragged me up the wooden stairs. He opened the door to the room where I'd found the money and shoved me in.

Lying in the middle of the small room, his head in a pool of what looked like dark red ink, lay Eric.

"I . . . I . . . ." Pushing my way past Ortiz, I stumbled down the stairs with him in close pursuit.

"Well?" he asked.

I collapsed in the chair behind the counter in the lobby. "I feel sick."

"You can get sick later. I want an explanation."

"You can't really believe I knew about this." I felt tears prick at the corners of my eyes.

"What am I suppose to believe? You sent me up there."

"To find a plastic baggie of money. I didn't know he was up there." The edges around my eyes started to go black; I bent over and tried to keep from fainting.

"Look at me," he said, pulling me back up. "What money?"

"You're a creep, you know that?" I pulled my shoulder out of his grasp. "I feel awful."

"Not as awful as your friend upstairs. What money?"

"I found a plastic baggie full of money. I think it was a gallon size, although it could have been a quart. I didn't really measure it. It looked . . ." I heard myself start to babble but couldn't stop.

"That's it?" he said.

"Yes, that's it. What did you think? That I walked around all night knowing that Eric was lying up there? What kind of person do you think I am?" Anger started to overcome shock. My stomach stopped rolling but my head started to hurt.

"That is a question that has kept me up nights. What time did you find the money?"

"About five o'clock or maybe a little before. I didn't exactly look at the clock." I pressed on my left temple. It was pounding so bad I would have sold my hair for three aspirin.

He ran a hand over his face in frustration. He was standing there, glaring in my general direction, when four uniformed officers burst into the lobby.

He pointed a finger at me. "Stay put." Then he turned and started giving orders in a sharp voice.

I grabbed the quilt Carl gave me off the counter, cradled it in my lap and rested my head on it. Inhaling deeply, I willed myself not to throw up. I closed my eyes, saw Eric's head in the dark puddle, and opened them again. In a half hour, the museum was a clone of four days before with technicians and uniforms everywhere. Ortiz seemed to have forgotten about me as he supervised the crime scene. My luck ran out when he walked back over.

"Go home," he said in a voice cold enough to freeze ice cream. "I don't have time for you tonight. We'll talk tomorrow."

"I can't," I protested. "I have to lock up."

"Give me your keys. I'll lock up."

"And how will I get in tomorrow?" I don't know why I was fighting him, leaving was exactly what I wanted to do. Just being contrary is what Dove would say. What I would say was I was sick and tired of being ordered around by this guy.

"Look," he said, his voice going into the dry-ice stage. "I want you out of my sight. I'm so angry at you right now, I don't know what I'll do. I suggest you stop arguing with me while I'm still rational."

"Fine. But do you plan on showing up at six tomorrow morning to set up for the festival?"

"I'll drop the keys off in your mailbox when we're done."

"You don't know where I live."

He looked at me with disdain.

"Right," I mumbled. I took the keys to the museum off my key ring and threw them on the counter.

I picked up my quilt and walked out, acutely aware of his frigid stare and the embarrassed looks of the officers working on the scene.

Grabbing the Levi jacket lying across the front seat of the truck, I slipped it on, not gaining much comfort from the cold, damp cotton. The image of Eric's body flashed through my mind, and the implication of it was so overwhelming, I didn't know what to do. When I reached my rented house and pulled into the driveway, a sudden feeling of alienation and fear struck me and I wanted to be someplace familiar, someplace from the past. It was too late to drive out to the ranch, so I threw the truck in reverse and drove downtown to a place guaranteed to be both familiar and open.

11

A STRAWBERRY MALT on a cold November morning is not physically soothing no matter what personal history is attached to it.

Liddie's Cafe was almost empty since most students had left for the holiday and the two A.M. bar rush was still an hour away. My waitress, a young brunette with a bottle-brush hairdo and long pumpkin-colored nails, didn't blink twice when I ordered two large strawberry malts. Working this shift, she'd probably seen stranger.

Pulling my Levi jacket close around me, I stretched my legs lengthwise across the red vinyl bench seat and rested the back of my head against the icy window. I closed my eyes and wondered if anyone would care if I stayed there forever. My waitress checked back once. Twice. Then left me alone. I drifted in and out of that lazy dreaminess overly warm rooms and indistinct conversations bring on. The voices swelled around me, becoming louder, more animated as the bars closed and people continued their partying over breakfast.

"I thought I told you to go home." Keys clattered across the table.

I took my time opening my eyes. Ortiz stood at the end of the booth, hands in his pockets, tie pulled loose and crooked, deep shadows under squinting blue eyes that seemed naked and vulnerable without his glasses. The dark stubble sprouting along his jaw line gave his face a faintly criminal cast.

"Contrary to what you'd prefer," I said, "this city is not under martial law and I am old enough to be out after curfew." I grabbed the museum's keys and stuck them in my pocket.

"It's dangerous for a woman to be out alone this time of night."

"This isn't L.A., and even if it was, where I go and when really isn't any business of yours."

"Robbery, assault and rape exist even here and, unfortunately, that is my business," he said, his jaw setting stubbornly.

"Get lost," I replied.

"Look, I realize I overreacted. I'm sorry. But what did you expect? I go up and there's this body—"

"Which I keep telling you I knew nothing about, and sorry doesn't begin to cover it. You've acted like some kind of Nazi general from the beginning of this whole thing."

"And you've interfered from the beginning. Withholding information, witnesses, evidence—"

"Look, in the last four days you have lectured me four times. I don't want or need another one. I am sick of—"

"Good." He slid into the seat across from me. "So am I."

"Hit the road, Sergeant Friday. This isn't a television show. I don't have to talk to you."

My spike-haired waitress walked up, a pleased smile curving her pale tangerine lips.

"So your guy finally made it," she said. "You all done there?" She gestured at my empty glass.

"Take both of them." I shoved the untouched strawberry malt toward her. "And no, my guy didn't make it. He died nine months ago." I looked at Ortiz. "But then you already know that. You know everything, right?"

Her eyes darted to Ortiz, who shook his head slightly, then back at me. She pursed her lips, picked up the glasses.

"Anything for you, sir?"

"Coffee." He settled in, stretching his arm across the back of the seat, loosening his tie more. "Look, I said I was sorry. What more can I do? And my name is Gabriel. Gabe."

I leaned my head back against the window and closed my eyes, hoping if I ignored him, he'd go away. Minutes passed. The swish-swish of the waitress's nylons, the clink of cup against saucer, the acidic scent of strong coffee told me he wasn't leaving. Inhaling the steam of his coffee, I imagined how it might warm the lump behind my breastbone, a lump as hard and cold as a hailstone.

"I am sorry," he said, softer this time. "About tonight. About your husband. I didn't know until a little while ago how he died. Officer Aragon told me. It must be tough."

The image of Eric's body, lack of sleep, the unexpected kindness in his voice, or maybe a combination of all three, caused moist heat to burn in the back of my eyes. Tears formed in the corners but I held back, my throat aching with the effort. I had to do something—scream, curse, throw his coffee mug across the room, run out. But they all seemed to take so much effort. So I kept my eyes closed and talked.

"Jack loved strawberry malts. One time, when we were sixteen, he drank four in a row. His father had grounded him for cutting algebra, so we hitchhiked into town and sat here until two in the morning until Wade found us and took us home."

I opened my eyes and stared straight ahead at the shiny Elvis clock behind the cash register; the minute hand circled his thick body, just as he'd sometimes swung his arm at the end of a song.

"The night he died, I was at my dad's ranch, making strawberry preserves. I think about that a lot. Jack's dead and all those jars of strawberry preserves are still there in my grandmother's pantry waiting to be eaten."

I turned and looked at Ortiz. Under the gold cast of the coffee shop lights, his dark face was still, impenetrable. I had grown up with that look—Elvia's brothers, her father, the smooth-cheeked Spanish boys in high school in tightly pressed chinos. It could mean as little as a sore tooth or as much as a knife in your belly. His blue Anglo eyes never left my face.

"There were so many strawberries," I said. "Two bushels. They were starting to go bad and my grandmother hates waste, so I hulled every last one of them. My hands looked like they were dipped in red ink." I stared down at my fingers, seeing the red again.

"Do you ever wonder why things happen the way they do? I never asked Dove who gave her those strawberries but I've tried to imagine what would have happened if they'd never been planted, or someone forgot to water them, or a disease killed them before they could bear fruit or that person just, on the spur of the moment, gave the strawberries to someone else. I would have been home. He wouldn't have gone to town."

"You don't know that," Ortiz said. He traced his finger around the rim of his cup. If it had been crystal, a fine note might have rung.

"Yes, I do." I swung my legs around and faced him.

125

"It didn't have anything to do with you. It was his choice. A reckless choice, as Frost might say, but still, his choice."

I clenched my fist, wanting to hit something, some-one. "Every drink he had that night involved me. When he stepped into that jeep, I stepped in, too."

"It's not that simple," he said.

"You're wrong. It's just that simple. When he left me, he took everything I had." I stared at my clenched fist, then looked up. "Tell me, do you have children?"

He looked back with surprise. "Yes. A son."

"Then you couldn't know."

"Know what?"

"That it's different. When you're married and don't have children, everything you have is wrapped up in one person. When they aren't there anymore, it's like . . ." I stopped. What was it like? What could I say? That it was harder and harder each day to remember Jack? That at some point the unthinkable happens, when you least expect it; you realize you've stopped loving the person and started loving the memory, the memory only *you* have, and you're afraid if you forget or you die, it would be like the two of you never existed.

"What?" he asked after a few minutes.

I looked at him and thought, I can't bear this.

"I knew him before he could shave," I said.

He was wise enough to realize there was nothing he could say.

The noisy background chatter slowly leaked away like the air in a helium balloon as group after group of cus-tomers paid for their breakfasts and left. I suddenly felt that if I could get to my bed, I could sleep for days. I laid my head on the table, cradling it in my arms, not caring how it looked.

I felt or thought I felt, through the thick cotton of my

jacket, a pressure on my arm. I looked up. His hands were wrapped around his mug. His eyes seemed full of pain. Or maybe it was just fatigue.

"You're tired," he said. "You need to go home."

Suddenly, talking about Jack to Ortiz, telling a stranger things I'd never told anyone, sickened me. It made me feel disloyal and angry—at Ortiz, at myself.

"Do you think the same person killed Marla and Eric?" I said abruptly.

"I don't want to talk about that right now," he replied in a weary voice. "Especially with you."

"Did you find the money?"

He raked his fingers impatiently through neat black hair. "There wasn't any money."

"There was," I insisted. "It was a big plastic bag full of money."

"Are you sure?"

"Of course, I'm sure. What kind of question is that?"

"Look, if your cousin calls, you can tell her she doesn't have to worry about Eric Griffin anymore."

"Was she in any danger?"

"Apparently not from him. But someone else?" He shrugged, drained the last of his coffee, studying the bottom of his cup as if the answer would appear in the dregs.

"So all we have to do is find out what Eric and Marla had in common."

Annoyance flashed across his face. "I will. You won't. I've had about all I can take of you being involved in this. I haven't had a decent night's sleep in four days. I don't want to have to worry about you on top of everything else." He slapped the cup down in the saucer. The sharp clink caused me to wince. "Come on, I'll walk you out."

"Who asked you to worry about me? And I'm perfectly

capable of walking myself out."

"I'm doing it for me, not you. How would it look if a citizen was mugged while the chief of police sipped coffee a hundred feet away?"

"You're absolutely right. It would look terrible. Are you going to stay and walk everyone out?" I gestured around the restaurant at the other customers. "You could be here all night."

"For once, could you just not argue with me?"

I started to protest, but the exhausted look on his face stopped me. Though it irritated me, a surge of pity welled up. It couldn't be easy having to deal with the stress of two murders in a place where you have no family or friends.

"Oh, all right," I said, reaching for the check. He snatched it up first and slid out of the booth.

"I'll get it." His face dared me to protest.

I picked up my purse, too tired to argue. We didn't speak as we walked out to the parking lot. Freezing night air turned our breath to floating white powder. The sky was clear, moonless, black. The old mercury vapor street lights illuminated everything with a blue, spooky cast that caused an involuntary shudder to run up my spine.

"Cold?" Ortiz asked.

I pulled my denim jacket closer, wishing it was my sheepskin. "Just a goose walking over my grave."

He laughed out loud, startling a nervous cat crouched underneath my truck. "My grandfather used to say that."

"Your Kansas one?"

He gave an ironic smile. "So you found me out."

"Derby, Kansas." I shook my head. "Who would have ever guessed?"

"Well, I spent my last two years of high school in California, and I have lived there over twenty years. I assimilate easily."

"A real asset in undercover work, I bet."

His laugh was a low growl that, simply because it was masculine, sounded comforting. "What have you been doing, reading my personnel file?"

I lowered my chin and smiled into my jacket. "All information ends up somewhere. You said so yourself."

"There's nothing more disconcerting than having your own words thrown back at you. Those records are suppose to be confidential. Even I have to fill out a form in triplicate to obtain one. How did you manage?"

I shoved my hands in the pockets of my jacket and kept quiet.

"You know someone in Personnel." He tilted his head to see my face better. "You probably went to school together. It shouldn't be too difficult for me to find out. Breaching confidentiality in that job is probably grounds for dismissal."

A small surge of panic for Angie flashed through me. "Look, I'm sorry. My friend shouldn't have to pay for what I did. Please don't make trouble for her."

His eyes crinkled with amusement. "Humility. Now there's a quality I've never seen in you before. I could get used to it."

"Oh, shut up." I laughed and made a fist, punching him lightly on the chest the way I did Jack when he teased me.

He grabbed it, covered it with his large hand, and shook it gently, his eyes cloudy and serious.

"Albenia Harper, you are driving me nuts. Why do you think that is?"

"Gabriel Ortiz." I pulled my fist away and poked him in the chest with my finger. "You're the one writing a master's thesis on Kierkegaard. Why is anything the way it is?"

A small groan rumbled in the back of his throat.

Before I realized what was happening, he slipped his hand behind my head, his fingers tangling in my hair, and pulled me to him. His embrace was powerful and his kiss intense, searching; it tasted of coffee and peppermint and salt.

I don't know what made me kiss back—desire, anxiety, loneliness. But as our kiss deepened, somewhere in the twisting caverns of my mind, Jack's brown eyes lurked, dark and tender, and the memory caused me to stiffen and pull back. Ortiz's arms tightened for a split second, then let go.

"I can't," I said, feeling dazed and nervous and irrationally guilty, as if I were cheating. My rapid breath blew a small white cloud that floated up and mingled with his.

"I'm sorry," he said, something close to a look of desperation on his face. "That was . . . I don't know why . . ." His voice trailed off. Then he frowned. "Go home." He turned and walked toward his car, his back rigid, the gravel crunching like tiny bird bones under his feet.

I stared at him open-mouthed. He was acting as if I'd done something wrong. I was as embarrassed as he was, but you didn't see *me* snapping anyone's head off.

"Don't make such a big deal about it, Ortiz," I called after him, my voice quivering more than I would have liked. "It certainly isn't to me."

He stopped, turned slowly around and looked at me, the hard, shadowy planes of his face blank.

"Let's just blame it on the moon." I pointed up at the black, empty sky, wondering why in the world I was trying to make this easier for him. I guess being married as long as I had, it just came out without thinking. Old habits die harder than loco weed.

His face relaxed slightly. "You'd better go home," he said softly and turned away.

I climbed into my truck and sat there for a minute, hugging myself; his kiss had affected me more than I wanted to admit. I leaned my head on the steering wheel, inhaled deeply and tried to sort out my feelings.

The physical memory of his warm lips, the scratch of his raspy mustache, the comfort of his strong arms, lingered on my skin. I felt aroused, embarrassed, ashamed. Jack had been dead only nine months. What kind of person would even be thinking what I'm thinking? Especially about someone they'd only known four days?

A person who's alive and kicking is what Dove would say.

After three tries and some creative language, the truck's engine turned over. I flipped my headlights on. Seconds later, Ortiz's came on. That small protective act made me smile. It was exactly what Jack would have done.

He followed me to the corner, but when I turned right, he kept going straight. I sighed in relief. The way I was feeling and after what happened between us, my place at three A.M. would have been a mistake. A big mistake. And by the fifth or sixth time of telling myself that, I almost believed it.

12

"YOU LOOK LIKE . . ." Meg started.

"Don't say it." I lowered the brim of my blue Dodgers baseball cap in an attempt to conceal a face that needed about six more hours sleep.

"I was just going to say you look like death warmed over." She twisted a strand of toffee hair and giggled nervously. "But that's a bad choice of words, I guess. Isn't it awful about Eric? I hope this isn't some kind of serial killer who has it in for artists."

"Is everything all set to go in the quilt booth?" I didn't want to discuss Eric's death with anyone else this morning. I was awakened at six A.M. first by Elvia wanting to know if I was all right, then Carl, wanting to know if I had any information the police weren't releasing, and finally Dove, giving me a second chance at the bodyguard services of one elderly aunt.

"We're ready to roll," Meg said, glancing at her watch. "One hour to blastoff. There are people arriving already. One old lady wanted to have her picture taken in the place where the two murders happened. Gross, huh?" She wrinkled her pale, freckled nose.

"No one is allowed upstairs or to point out the place in the woodshop where Marla was killed," I said. "Pass that around. I'll bring them before the co-op board and have their studio privileges revoked if I catch anyone showing those places to the public. Let's try and leave Marla and Eric with a little dignity."

"I'll tell everyone," Meg said evenly, not dispirited by my prickly tone. "There's coffee in the pottery booth," she added diplomatically.

"Thanks," I answered, a bit chagrined by my attitude. I didn't want to tell her I'd had four cups already and that lack of caffeine wasn't my problem. I looked up at the cloudy sky, hoping the weather forecast was accurate— low clouds burning off to a sunny day. The sooner I could cover the bags under my eyes with sunglasses, the better.

By ten o'clock, cars were parked half a mile down the highway and the craft booths in the museum parking lot were snaked with lines of people. It appeared the murders actually improved attendance, at the festival rather than harmed it.

The VFW and a couple of Boy Scout troops had fired up their steel barrel barbeques early and were slowly cooking ribs and chicken over oakwood in the Santa Maria style barbeque no event in the county was ever without. My stomach growled when the scents of the spicy beef and chicken hit my nose, making the chocolate doughnut I'd had at seven o'clock seem like a mirage.

I was standing next to a booth selling anodized earrings in the shapes of endangered animals when I felt a dry, rough hand slip under my braid and squeeze my neck.

"Hey, squirt. Heard you found another body." I turned around and smiled up into the gray eyes and sun-webbed face of my father.

I slipped my arm around his solid waist. The smell

of his clean cotton shirt and English Leather aftershave was familiar and comforting. "Daddy! Am I glad to see you." I leaned my head against his shoulder. "It was our handyman, Eric. I think it's connected with the other murder, but I don't know how." I shivered. "Kind of spooks me a little, but I'm mostly okay. Where's Dove and Aunt Garnet?"

"Garnet woke up with a cold in her ear this morning, so they aren't coming. I was sent to cheer you on."

"Dove didn't tell me that when she called this morning," I said. "Well, cheer away. I can certainly use it."

"Don't think Garnet was up when Dove called. You know, I don't feel real comfortable with you working where there's been two murders."

"Really, there's nothing for you to worry about," I said. "They have nothing to do with me except that I was unfortunate enough to discover them. I'm getting a rather gruesome reputation around San Celina these days."

"You be careful, you hear?" He reached over and pulled the brim of my cap down. "You still keep Jack's .45 in your bedroom?"

"Sure do," I said, pushing my hat back up.

"Don't forget to . . ."

"I know. Aim for the oysters."

He chuckled at our old joke. "Guess so long as I'm here, I'll drop by the feed supply and see if my order's in. Got anything you want to send back to the sisters?"

"No, but tell Dove I'll call in a couple of days. And tell Aunt Garnet I'm sorry she's feeling bad and couldn't make it."

"Right." He pulled at his long white sideburns and gave me a slow hound-dog grin.

"Well, I am sorry she's feeling bad," I said, returning his grin.

I had started walking back to the museum to see how the exhibit was faring when I ran into Sandra. Her face was pallid, and the shadows staining the delicate flesh under her eyes made me guess that she'd slept as little as me last night.

"I've been looking for you for an hour." Her breath came in hard little puffs. She shifted sixteen-month-old Casey to her other hip. "Wade's here. You said you'd talk to him."

"Right," I said, wishing I hadn't made that impulsive promise. Getting involved in someone else's marriage problems was just asking for a boot in the butt. "Where is he?"

"Over by the food booths and he's in a real bad mood. He didn't get in until after three last night and he was mean as a badger when I asked him where he'd been."

"Don't get your hopes up," I said. "If he won't talk to you, I'm sure he won't to me either."

"You were always good with him," she insisted. "Almost as good as Jack was. I don't have anyone else to ask."

Taking Jack's place in the Harper family constellation was discomforting and yet, oddly appealing. At least it made me feel as if I still belonged someplace.

"I'll catch up with you later and let you know what happened." I reached over and gave a quick raspberry kiss to Casey's downy cheek, causing him to giggle. "I can't believe I'm missing all of Casey's growing up."

"You should come out more," she said.

"I will." But we both knew I wouldn't.

Wade stood around the smoking barbeques with a group of men dressed in such a similar manner they could have been a convention of ex-Marlboro Men. Jack would have fit right in. I wondered if I would ever get over the expectation he would just appear one day from behind an oak tree and tell me it was all a big joke.

"Hey, Wade," I said. I picked up a soft dinner roll and took a bite.

"That'll be a quarter," he said good-naturedly, and pushed down the brim of my hat. One of the most irritating things about being short is a great many people seem to feel since the top of your head is visible, it is public domain. My head has been ruffled, patted, and tweaked more than most cocker spaniels.

"Can I talk to you for a minute?" I readjusted my cap and tossed the roll at him.

"Talk away." He dodged it and moved the toothpick hanging from his mouth from one side to the other.

I glanced around at the men lolling around the smoking barbeque.

"Alone," I said in a low voice.

"Sounds serious, Wade," a thin man with an Adam's apple as sharp as an arrowhead said as he flipped a rack of ribs with long silver tongs. The dripping juices sizzled when they hit the hot fire. "What have you been up to?"

"Nothin' good, that's for sure," Wade replied. He followed me to a grove of eucalyptus trees a short distance away. With the hope he was kidding, I looked at him grimly.

"Why the long face, blondie?" He pushed his gray cowboy hat back and leaned against the peeling trunk of a eucalyptus tree.

"Wade, I'm just going to be blunt, okay?"

"Why change now?" he asked, smiling.

"Sandra's upset."

The smile froze underneath his stiff brown mustache. "She's always upset this time of the month. It's just female stuff. She'll be okay in a couple of days." He

136

rolled his toothpick again and gave a lazy smirk.

He couldn't have made me madder if he'd held me down and pierced my ears with a ten-penny nail. So I decided to just spit it out.

"She thinks you're cheating on her, and as far as I can see, she has pretty good reason to."

"Don't know what you're talking about."

"A certain cocktail napkin with the phone number of a certain woman who is now dead. Ring any bells?"

A surprised look fractured his smile. "How'd she get ahold of that?"

"Doesn't matter. What about it?"

He rubbed the back of his neck and frowned. "It's not what you think."

"And just what am I thinking?"

"Stay out of this. It's between Sandra and me."

"So talk to her about it."

"I will. When I'm ready."

"Not good enough. Besides, I'd like to know myself just how you were involved with Marla."

Driving his fist into the eucalyptus trunk, he turned and pointed a work-cracked finger at me. "You need to mind your own business."

"You need to talk to your wife," I snapped back.

"I said when I'm ready." He started to walk away, then turned back and scowled at me. "Just butt out, Benni. You're not part of this family anymore. What happens between us isn't any of your concern."

It was a good thing I didn't have a shotgun in my hand right then, because I would have loved to pepper the "W" on the back of his jeans with a load of birdshot. I was livid, but a part of me was embarrassed, too—his remark hit too close to home. He was right; they weren't my family anymore. But after all those years, it was hard to disconnect.

"Looks like you might make enough today to buy a few more pounds of clay."

I turned to face a genial-faced Ortiz. He was casually dressed in faded black jeans, a pale blue sweatshirt with "L.A. Marathon" printed on it, and his beat-up topsiders. The washing machine had obviously lost his socks again.

"I hate to think the murders helped attendance, but I think they did." I peeled a piece of bark off the tree and avoided meeting his eyes. Okay, I thought, this is how we're going to play it—light and easy—as if nothing happened.

"Probably has. Believe me, people are basically morbid. How are you doing?" He stretched his arm up and pulled off a leaf I would have had to jump to reach.

"Fine." I looked up at him suspiciously. Why was he always turning up at the oddest moments? Was he tailing me? Did police chiefs do that sort of thing? And how much of my fight with Wade did he hear?

"It's hard not having a place where you fit," he said softly. He held the leaf he'd picked under his nose. "One of the things I hate the most up here is the smell of eucalyptus. Reminds me of the Vicks my mom used to rub on my chest when I had a cold. Did your mom ever do that?"

Well, he heard the last part anyway. I wondered if he'd heard the part about Marla.

"Do you make it a habit of eavesdropping on private conversations?" I asked.

"Whenever I can."

It was such an honest answer, I didn't know what to say.

"We know about your brother-in-law's affair with Ms. Chenier," he said, tossing the leaf on the ground. "He wasn't the only one."

"He wasn't?" I looked at the ground and wondered if they knew about Ray, if there were others I didn't know about.

"That's all I'm going to say." He kicked at the pile of crackly, aromatic leaves we stood in. "I assume that whole napkin business has to do with your brother-in-law's affair. You really should give it to me."

"I don't know what you're talking about." I peeled off another strip of bark.

He sighed and ran his fingers through his hair. "Well, I can't fault you for loyalty. Technically, I could haul you in right now. You're just as much a suspect as your brother-in-law."

"Me? Are you crazy?"

"Does 'You are dead meat, buddy. I'm holding Dack and Cassandra hostage. You know who this is' sound familiar?"

My message on Eric's answering machine. I felt my face turn red.

"Who's Dack and Cassandra?" His tone was off-hand but the question wasn't.

"It was just a joke," I said, laughing uneasily. "You don't really believe I killed him."

He let me squirm for a minute before answering. "You're not my first choice. But I can't say the same for your brother-in-law."

"Wade would never kill anyone."

"Everyone has the potential for murder."

"Is that the cop or the philosopher talking?" I asked.

"Depends."

"On what?"

"What kind of day I'm having."

"So who wins today?"

"It's still early. I'll have to wait and see."

"Well, Friday," I said. "As always, it's been just the

greatest fun talking with you, but I need to get back to the festival. Make yourself useful. Buy something."

"I want that napkin," he said. "And I want you, the man says like a broken record, to stay out of this investigation." He reached over and pushed down the brim of my cap, a slight smile on his face. "And I told you, the name is Gabe."

"Whatever." I irritably pushed my cap back up. Everyone thinks they invented the wheel. "Why don't you find someone else to bug, Ortiz?"

"Whether I bug you or not is entirely up to you. I'll stop when you get out of this investigation. It's that simple." He gave me a serene look, then walked away.

I'd begun climbing the steps to the museum when Carl called to me. He ran up the steps and fell in beside me.

"I saw you talking to Ortiz. Anything new on the Eric Griffin murder?"

"I don't know one bit more than what I told you at six o'clock this morning and, for your information, I was being given a lecture, not a progress report. You, of all people, should know that."

"Sorry," he said, holding up his hands. "Just trying to do my job."

"I know," I said. "I'm sorry I'm so grumpy. I just haven't gotten much sleep these last few days. And Ortiz just has a way of getting under my skin. Really, I've told you everything I know."

"Good enough." He put his arm around me. "Don't worry about the chief. He'll quit harassing you once these murders are solved or shelved."

"He'd better," I said, telling myself that wasn't regret I was feeling, just relief.

"I'm still waiting for you to come down to the paper for lunch," he said. "You need some fun in your life. Maybe we should make it dinner and a movie."

"Carl Freedman," I said, laughing. "If I didn't know better, I'd swear you were asking me for a date."

He smiled crookedly, his blue eyes serious. "Is that so hard to imagine?"

I looked at him in surprise. I didn't want to say it had never crossed my mind. He was Jack's best friend. One of my oldest and dearest friends. I'd never even considered him in that context. Since his divorce four years ago, Carl had entertained me and Jack more times than I could remember with hilarious reenactments of some of his unbelievable dates. I couldn't imagine being one of them.

"What's wrong, you need some new joke material?" I asked, not entirely sure if he was kidding or not.

"Benni," he said in a pained tone. "You know it would be different with you. You're not just some bimbo. Give me a break. Just think about it and call me."

"I will," I said to his back as he turned and ran back down the steps.

Sitting at my desk, I thought about the complicated path my life had taken. A week ago, I was coming home to a lonely chicken pot pie and chocolate no-bake cookies and now I was involved up to my ears in two homicides and my brother-in-law's affair with one of the victims, was contemplating dating my dead husband's best friend and having uncomfortably erotic feelings for a blue-eyed Hispanic man from Kansas, of all places, whom I couldn't be around for ten seconds without starting a fight. So I did what most women do when faced with a life too complex to sort out. I decided to clean out my purse.

I discovered at the bottom of my saddlebag-style purse, one of the parking tickets I'd forgotten to pay. It was only five months old. That cheered me. I thought it had been much longer than that since I cleaned out my purse.

Also down at the bottom, next to a paperback book I was looking for a few months ago, lay a small red-labeled computer disc. Eric's book. I swallowed hard. We'd never know what happened to Dack and Cassandra now. I knew I should give it to the police. It was possibly evidence, but the thought of a bunch of cops sitting around laughing at Eric's writing made me feel sad and a bit protective. I wasn't sure what family he had, but this really belonged to them. Out of curiosity, I flipped on my word processor and slipped it in.

Dack's carnal capabilities were impressive, though I doubted the technical accuracy of six times in less than an hour. Eric had obviously overestimated what women who read romance novels were expecting. His writing was overdone and superficial, but there was something humorously appealing about his abuse of almost every basic writing rule I'd learned in the one creative writing class I'd taken in college.

Write what you know. The words of my professor flooded back to me. There was an elaborate subplot threaded through the eight finished chapters, concerning a blackmail scheme Dack and Cassandra had going. No hint about who they were blackmailing. Just someone with a very nasty secret.

Write what you know. Eric seemed to know a lot about blackmail. Too much. Or maybe, it suddenly became apparent to me as I stared at the words on the screen, just enough to get himself killed.

13

IT STARTED RAINING again Monday morning, but I lay in bed and enjoyed the sounds of the whooshing river running through the gutters.

The festival turned out to be a bigger monetary success than we'd hoped, with the co-op's cut being over a thousand dollars and most of the artists getting enough orders to keep them busy for a few more months. Though the studios were open, the museum was closed for the day, so I intended on catching up on some of the sleep I'd lost in the last few days. However, something niggled at the back of my semiconscious mind and kept me from drifting back to sleep.

Then it dawned on me. Today was Marla's funeral. I groaned out loud and hit my pillow. My dramatic response was wasted on an empty room. The clock-radio on my oak nightstand read nine o'clock in cheery red numbers. The funeral was at eleven and I still had to get to the florist, so I dragged myself out of bed and headed for the coffee maker.

An hour later, I was dressed in what was my most respectful funeral garb—a narrow navy blue wool skirt, white linen blouse and navy cardigan. An idea slowly took shape as I dressed. Maybe I would be able to talk to Marla's mother alone and find out something. Wade's relationship with Marla pricked at me, though I knew better than anyone that he certainly didn't have the resources to pay her blackmail.

After a quick trip to the florist, I pulled up in front of the mortuary wondering why they always looked like miniature versions of Tara. Though it couldn't have been more than fifty degrees outside, the temperature dropped ten degrees in the spacious pink foyer, pink being the operative word. It was like being trapped inside a bottle of Pepto-bismol.

The lobby's fuzzy brocade wallpaper mirrored the upholstery on the slightly darker pink French provincial love seats. The freshly vacuumed rose carpet was marred only by the tracks of Marla's friends and family.

A black-suited man with surprisingly robust skin seemed to appear out of nowhere and took my raincoat and the wet, bulky spray of yellow roses. Handing me a cream-colored program, he directed me toward the double doors of the small chapel.

A dozen or so people were scattered throughout the chapel. No one looked familiar to me. I chose a seat two pews behind a tall woman with skin as weathered as an old piece of harness, whose resemblance to Marla was unnerving. Two women flanked her, protective arms encircling her narrow shoulders. They were of such similar size, age and puckered complexion, they had to be her sisters.

The service was brief and, thankfully, the coffin closed. The minister ended with an announcement that a luncheon was being served at Mrs. Chenier's house and all in attendance were invited. He ended the service with a tape of what he claimed was Marla's favorite song—

"The Impossible Dream." Marla's mother broke into sobs during the song and was patted and cooed at by her sisters while the rest of us picked at our hands or studied our printed programs. I wondered if anyone was thinking what I was: that Marla, in a manner of speaking, wouldn't have been caught dead with that song being sung at her funeral. "Let's Give Them Something to Talk About" by Bonnie Raitt would have been more her style.

There was no opportunity to question Mrs. Chenier at the funeral, so I decided to go to the house. Maybe it would happen more naturally there. I walked up to Mrs. Chenier, extended my sympathies on behalf of the co-op and picked up a photocopied map with directions to her house. When I walked out into the cotton-candy foyer, I ran into Detective Cleary.

"I thought the police only attended the victim's funerals in the movies," I said.

"No, ma'am." His coffee-colored face was impassive as he tucked a brown notebook inside his jacket.

"So, does anyone look like a killer here?" I flashed him an encouraging smile.

"I don't know, ma'am. I'm just following orders."

"And doing a fine job of it." I knew full well I wouldn't get an opinion or a single piece of information out of him. Ortiz had probably threatened to demote him to parking patrol if he as much as breathed in my direction.

"Yes, ma'am." He folded his hands in front of him like a preacher.

"Well, it was nice talking with you again, Detective Cleary. You can tell your boss you successfully squeezed past me without letting slip so much as a smidgen of information."

"Have a good day, ma'am." He smiled and gave me a

wink before he walked out into the rain.

After a short, damp service at the cemetery, I drove to Mrs. Chenier's lemon-colored stucco house. It was located in a small middle-class neighborhood north of the university. The forgotten tricycles and Big Wheels scattered across wet sidewalks and the neatly trimmed front yards gave testimony that the thirty-year-old houses were going through their second, or third, generation of enthusiastic young homeowners.

More people were at the luncheon than at the funeral, probably because of the neighbors stopping by with a casserole or pie, then staying to sample the buffet and whisper about the way Marla died. The clove-spiked ham, green bean casseroles and Jell-O molds so reminded me of Jack's funeral, I almost gave up my plan to question Mrs. Chenier. But the thought of Wade being involved with Marla's death made me stay.

I hung around longer than was socially acceptable, trying to manuever time alone with Mrs. Chenier. Finally, her sisters retired to the kitchen to clean up, everyone else had left, and Mrs. Chenier and I were alone in the musty, Early American living room, looking through calico-print photo albums showing Marla from birth to as late as three weeks ago.

"She was such a talented girl, my Marla," she said. "She only worked at that bar until her ship came in. That's what she always told me. Ma, she'd say, I'm going to buy you a mink coat when my ship comes in. That's what she always said." Mrs. Chenier's tanned, shriveled face twisted inward and a single tear ran down a deep crease in her cheek.

"She was very talented," I said. "I'll bring the rest of her pots by later this week. Unless you want us to sell them. Her pottery was starting to develop a real following."

"Go ahead and sell them." She pulled a tissue out of the sleeve of her brown, lacy-necked dress and dabbed at her eyes. "Heaven knows I need the money. Marla helped me, you know. That's why she had to work at that place instead of just doing her art. Her father was a drunk. Dropped dead and left me nothing but this house. And the taxes were three years behind when he passed on." For a moment, anger flashed in her eyes.

"I'll get the best price I can for them," I assured her. "We'll feature them in our museum gift shop." If what Ortiz said about people was true, we could probably double the price and they'd sell like crazy.

"She was a worker, my Marla. She always had something going. Did I tell you what she said? She said, Ma, when my ship comes in I'm going to buy you a mink coat. A white mink coat. That's what she said." Her milk-chocolate eyes filled with tears.

This was not going as I intended. As I turned the pages of the album, scanning the pictures of Marla in all ages and moods, I tried to think of a way to get more information without being cruel.

"Have the police come up with any leads?" I asked.

"Hmph," she spit out, her eyes angry again. "They haven't done nothing. Plenty of questions. That's about it."

"Have they said why they think she was killed?" I kept flipping through the photo album, trying to sound casually curious.

"Crime of passion, they called it. They wanted to know who were her boyfriends. Was there anyone special she was seeing." The angry look again.

"Was there?" I studied a picture of Marla at ten in one of those "sitting on a pony" pictures taken in grocery-store parking lots, her face scrunched into a scowl. She looked like she wanted to flip the photographer the bird. I smiled—that's the Marla I remembered.

"My Marla had her share of boyfriends." Mrs. Chenier sniffled and tucked the tissue back in her sleeve.

"But no one special."

"She dated around, but like I told the police, she wasn't about to settle down. She had a big project going that kept her busy most the time. She said that she'd be set by Christmas." She touched her cheek tentatively. "Said our ship was only a few miles from shore."

My hand froze as I reached for another page of the album. I tried to keep my voice even and bland.

"What was she working on?"

Mrs. Chenier pushed at her stiff tan curls. "She was always working on something. But she said this time she wasn't selling out for peanuts. That we'd been on the bottom long enough."

"Did it have anything to do with her pottery?"

"I'm sure it must have. What else could it be?" She looked at me oddly. I decided to change tactics.

"Who were Marla's friends, Mrs. Chenier?"

"The police asked me that. I told them the people at that artists' place. That girl she lived with. She talked about you some. She liked you real well. But Marla always liked being by herself. Even as a little girl. She didn't need people much."

I lowered my head in embarrassment. I never thought much about my friendship with Marla, if indeed there was one. Apparently, it had been a friendship to her, and I felt bad that she had so few people who would really miss her.

"Mrs. Chenier—" I decided I might as well just plunge in with the truth. "I liked Marla too, and the reason I'm asking so many questions is that I wonder whether the police are doing a thorough job of looking for her killer. I'm just trying to see if there's anything I can do to help catch the person who did this to her."

"Oh." She touched a ringless hand to her flat chest. "Well, I don't know what I could tell you that I didn't tell the police. I just assumed it was a crazy person who broke in and killed her. She shouldn't have been up at that place alone so late at night."

"Someone was supposed to be with her," I said, somewhat defensively. "But right now, the important thing is to catch the person who took your daughter from you."

She nodded, reclaimed the tissue out of her sleeve and dabbed at her thin nose. "I'll try and help, but I've told the police everything they asked."

"That's just it," I said eagerly. "Maybe there's something you know that they didn't think to ask." I closed the album and set it on the wagon-wheel-style coffee table. "You know, when I moved to town, the place I rented wasn't big enough for all my stuff. I stored a lot of it at my dad's house. I bet you have a lot of Marla's things here."

"I do," she said. "I've kept her room just how it was. She sometimes spent the night here with me. We'd make hot fudge sundaes just like when she was a little girl." She shredded the tissue in her hands.

"Did you show the police her room?"

"I surely didn't," she said. "That's Marla's private things. They didn't have nothing to do with her, her . . ." She swallowed convulsively.

"I'm so sorry," I said, laying a hand on her arm and feeling a bit disgusted with myself for putting her through this. Her arm felt cold and papery through the thin rayon material. "Maybe I should come back later."

"No, I'd like you to see her room. It would make me feel better. Maybe there is something there that could help you." She stood up and started walking down the short hall.

Marla's bedroom reminded me of my own—twenty

years ago—though her taste in rock stars had been a bit wilder than mine. As I would have predicted, posters of the Rolling Stones, Janis Joplin and Jim Morrison papered the walls. A variety of faded stuffed animals and a well-hugged Raggedy Ann doll nestled on the pillow of her lavender gingham bedspread. Though I was sure Mrs. Chenier would never recognize it, the air smelled faintly sweet of marijuana.

"I don't know how it will help, but go ahead and look around," Mrs. Chenier said. She reached over and stroked the dark stiff hair of a three-foot-high doll standing in the corner next to a tall chest of drawers. "Thank you for being concerned. It didn't seem as if anyone else cared that my Marla died. I'll be in the kitchen."

That made me feel, as Dove would say, knee-high to an ant. It's not that I didn't care about Marla's death, but our friendship wasn't my compelling reason for looking deeper into her murder. I sighed and looked around the room, not really knowing where to start. The only experience I'd ever had in investigative work was seventeen years ago on my high-school newspaper when Elvia and I tried to discover just exactly what ingredients were in the Rainbow Harvest Casserole the lunchroom served on Fridays.

Her desk seemed the obvious place to start. That's what they did on television cop shows. Her mother really did believe in keeping everything. I found book reports dating back to 1967 and an old diary of her first year in high school. I didn't even bother reading it, figuring whatever Marla was involved in was more recent. Standing back and surveying the room, I tried to think where she would hide something that she didn't want anyone, including her mother, to find. The furniture was shiny clean and the pillows on the bed plumped, so it had to be someplace that did not receive regular ministrations from Mrs. Chenier's can of spray wax.

After the usual hiding places like drawers and under the bed, I tried the "clever" places I'd hid things as a teenager: the center of the bed between the box springs and mattress, inside the shanks of boots, behind picture frames. After ten minutes of fruitless searching, I pulled out her desk chair and sat down. Why was it always so easy on television?

I scanned the room again, marveling at the time warp I was in. The Troll doll collection, arranged according to size on the dresser, was priceless in terms of memories rather than money. I stood up and grabbed the two stiff hands of her walker doll and attempted to make it perform in the way the TV commercials promised thirty years ago. Its stiff-legged gait was just as unwieldy and unnatural now as it was then. I remembered the Christmas I got one like it and how disappointed I'd been when the doll didn't perform as I'd anticipated. I smiled thinking about that Christmas, how my Uncle Arnie, fourteen then, and only six years older than me, teased me by kidnapping my doll, pulling her head off and putting gravel inside the hollow body so that she rattled like a castanet whenever I picked her up.

I twisted the head and wondered if Marla ever discovered how easy it was to pop off. The hollow space inside a doll that size could hide a lot of things. I glanced down the hallway to make sure Mrs. Chenier wasn't coming. I was sure she wouldn't take kindly to me decapitating Marla's doll. I popped the head off and peered down into the depths. Well, I knew where her marijuana stash was now. But that told me nothing about blackmail.

I scanned the bookshelves. She had the typical assortment of childhood and adolescent books, mostly mysteries. Her Nancy Drew collection looked as if it didn't miss one numbered book. I pulled one out and flipped through it. I had been more of a *National Velvet* and *Black Beauty* sort of girl, but I had a lot of friends who were addicted to Carolyn Keene. I put it back and pulled out another. I flipped through it and was surprised by a hundred-dollar bill stuck in the pages. I turned the book over and three more fell out. I kept going through the books and finally quit counting at one thousand. I quickly flipped through the others; almost every book contained some bills. Marla obviously didn't believe in banks. In one book, there was no money, only a white legal-sized envelope. It was sealed, but at this point, I figured, in for a penny. I tore it open and surveyed the contents.

It contained two money-order receipts for five hundred dollars each, made out to a Suzanne Hart, and a small newspaper article. The heading of the article caused me to stop breathing for a second.

LOCAL MAN KILLED IN AUTO ACCIDENT.

When I heard the clump of heels echoing down the oakwood hallway, without thinking, I shoved the receipts and article back into the envelope and stuck it in the band of my skirt behind my sweater.

"Did you find anything?" Mrs. Chenier asked.

"Everything's so neat. Did you ever see anything when you were cleaning that looked suspicious?" Answering a question with a question seemed like the best way to avoid actually lying.

Her features squeezed together in a helpless look as she shook her head silently.

"I've bothered you long enough," I said, wanting suddenly to just get out of this sad place. The envelope tucked in my skirtband felt as large as a backpack; the significance of its contents made me queasy. "I'll keep asking around and if I find out anything, I'll let you know."

"Thank you for trying." She walked with me to the living room where I retrieved my purse. Her sisters, embroidered tea towels in hand, watched us from the kitchen doorway. It was probably my imagination, but I felt like they could see through my sweater to the envelope stuck there like an illegal pistol.

"I'm so sorry." I touched her arm, not really certain just exactly what I meant.

"Thank you," she said and closed the door behind me.

I resisted pulling the envelope out when I climbed into the Chevy. When I was safely out of her neighborhood, I pulled into a McDonald's, ordered a coffee and picked a quiet corner to wrestle with the contents.

I studied it a long time, uncertain of exactly what I'd discovered. I still couldn't believe I took it. Any scruples I'd developed in the last thirty-four years seemed to have disappeared in the last few days. If the money I found in the upstairs of the museum was blackmail money belonging to Eric and the money Marla had was too, then these money order receipts to this Suzanne Hart led me to believe she was profiting as well. And that she, hopefully, was still alive.

That left the newspaper article. What could Jack's accident have to do with any of this? He was alone when his jeep turned over out on a desolate stretch of old Highway One. It was the reason no one found him for hours, probably the reason he died, a fact that still tore at my heart. The coroner said he most likely never regained conciousness, but no one could guarantee that. I still lay awake at nights and wondered about his last moments, whether he was in pain, if he thought of me. For the millionth time, I wished Wade had reached Trigger's before Jack left.

I stuck the papers in my purse and as I drove back to

town, tried to decide what my next move should be. Or rather, what it would be. I knew I should head straight for the police station and show them what I found, but I also knew that Ortiz would bite through a metal bit if he knew how I got it. And the thought of Jack's death being a part of this whole mess was something I needed to ruminate on. Finding this Suzanne Hart looked like the next logical step.

Sitting in the driveway at home, I inspected the contents of the envelope one more time. This was incriminating stuff and I didn't want anyone finding it until I knew what it was all about. Remembering how easily I found it in Marla's house didn't make concealing it inside my house feasible. I looked around the cab of the truck. Not a lot of hiding places there. In the corner, the glove compartment smiled at me. I pulled it open and surveyed the fifteen years of accumulated papers and junk. Taking the contents out of the white envelope, I stuck them inside a faded blue folder containing the outdated warranty information on the Chevy. Hide in plain sight. I mentally patted myself on the back for my cleverness.

So now all I had to do was find Suzanne Hart. I set my mind on the mechanics of it, not wanting to think about what she might have to tell me about Marla, Wade, Jack. A part of me wished I could stop, but I felt somehow as if I were in a spiral going around and around, caught in its twirling center. The question was whether I was spiraling up or down. And that seemed to be an answer that would only come when the spinning stopped.

14

AS WITH A lot of things in my house, I'd stuck my phone directory in such a safe place, I couldn't remember where it was. After being informed by the directory assistance operator that three numbers were the limit, the library was my next stop.

San Celina's new public library, perched on a bluff overlooking San Celina Central Park, was a two-story, gray concrete building that must have been designed by an architect specializing in federal prisons. The latest county phone book showed twenty-five Harts, any of which could have someone named Suzanne living there. I photocopied the page, begged change from the librarian at the reception desk, settled into one of the glass-and-wood phone booths and started dialing.

An hour and six dollars later, I'd reached twenty-three wrong numbers, two numbers no longer in service and one No-Suzanne-here-but-my-name-is-Leon-and-I-can-take-you-to-heaven-baby.

As I folded the photocopied page and stuck it in my purse, I couldn't help but wonder if Ortiz or any of his men were even remotely close to what I'd discovered.

This, of course, would be like cracking pistachio nuts to them—they'd just run the name through the Department of Motor Vehicles and get all the Suzanne Harts who'd ever lived in San Celina County and their current addresses. Unfortunately, I didn't know anyone who worked for the DMV. But, I reasoned, driving toward the city administration buildings, one government agency was as good as another and it was a well-known fact all bureaucrats knew each other.

"I told the receptionist I didn't want to see you," Angie moaned as I plopped down in the black vinyl office chair next to her desk. A red plastic makeup mirror and a small array of Avon cosmetics decorated her gray desk blotter.

"She knew you were kidding." I laid a candy bar in front of her. "There was a time you'd do anything for a Snickers."

She checked her thin gold watch. "Those days are long gone. It's four twenty-five and I'm out of here in five minutes. Whatever it is you want, I won't do it. You promised I wouldn't get in trouble for showing you Ortiz's file."

"Shoot, did that idiot report you?"

"Oh no, he's more devious than that. He's toying with me, like a cougar with a half-dead squirrel." She looked at me miserably through her large tortoise-shell glasses and started scooping up her makeup.

"What's he done?" I felt irritation bubble up inside me. Then again, he never actually promised he wasn't going to report her.

"Nothing concrete. Just things. Annoying things."

"Like what?" I picked up a square acrylic paperweight with pennies floating in it. They looked like small copper fish frozen mid-glide.

"Well, for one thing, he greeted me by name this morning."

"And?" I inspected the paperweight more closely. How did they do things like this? It made a loud clumping sound as I turned it from side to side on her desk. It looked the same no matter what side you laid it on.

"He brought me a doughnut." She clicked her makeup mirror closed.

I continued turning the paperweight and waited. She grabbed it from my hands and set it on the other side of the desk. I folded my hands and looked at her with amusement.

"Let me get this straight," I said. "He greeted you by name and he brought you a doughnut?"

"Yes." She pulled open her middle drawer and threw the mirror in.

"What kind of doughnut?"

"You know, he has this irritating look, like you're a sow he's sizing up for Easter dinner, and it was chocolate. With sprinkles." She glared at me.

"Oh, well, sprinkles. That clears it up for me. Sounds like you have a strong case for police harassment. Want the name of my lawyer?"

"It's a really smirky look," she said crossly.

I cocked an eyebrow at her and grinned.

"That's the look," she said, smiling reluctantly. "You two ought to start a vaudeville act."

"Yeah, right. The cop and the cowgirl."

"Sounds like a bad Clint Eastwood movie," Angie agreed, laughing. "Okay, I give up. What is it you want?" She zipped her paisley makeup bag closed.

"Do you have access to DMV records?"

"Sure, we do DMV checks when we hire people for the city."

"Could you run one for me?"

"Does this have anything to do with those murders at the museum?" She looked at me suspiciously.

I avoided her scrutiny and concentrated on the framed Disney poster behind her showing Mickey's physical changes over the last fifty years. It reminded me of the school pictures of me that Daddy displayed in chronological order on the wall of his bedroom. Mickey seemed fatter in his later years. Part of the good life, I suppose. I guess no one stays the same forever; not even Mickey Mouse.

"No way," she said firmly.

"Why not?" I whined in the way you can only with an old girlfriend.

"That is an ongoing investigation with the police department. You're treading on thin ice, my friend. Your police chief brought me a doughnut today. I don't want tomorrow's present to be handcuffs."

"All right, Ms. Chicken," I said, sighing. "It was just a thought. I really don't want you to get in any trouble. I'll find another way to track this person down."

She peered at me anxiously through her large glasses. "Are you sure you're not in over your head? Why not just let the police handle it?"

I didn't elaborate about how involved I'd become in the investigation or why. The less she knew, the better, especially since Ortiz was wise to our connection.

"Don't worry. I know what I'm doing. Most of the time anyway. I think."

She stood up, smoothed down her taupe wool skirt and pulled her purse out of a lower desk drawer. "That's what I've always liked about you. You're self-assured in such an uncertain sort of way. I'd ask you if you were free for dinner but, believe it or not, I have a date. Come by sometime when you don't want anything but food, okay?"

"Sure." I laughed and stood up. "Do you want me to tell Ortiz to quit bugging you?"

"I don't think you need to bother," she said wryly. "He probably knows exactly where you are right now, so it accomplished his purpose."

Angie's mention of dinner made me realize the small plate of food I'd nibbled on at Mrs. Chenier's house had been hours ago. Since Jack's death, meals were something that presented a daily irritation. For fifteen years I'd cooked a big dinner every night for him, whatever ranch hands were around and whichever of Wade and Sandra's children happened to like what I was serving. Jack always teased the kids on the days we had stuffed pork chops, his favorite, by blocking the door, saying there was only enough for him. They'd crawl all over him, wrestling him to the ground, giggling like little monkeys when he tickled them.

Now, with no one to cook for, I usually made do with pot pies or fast food. Sitting at a stoplight downtown, trying to decide which brand of grease I was in the mood for, I remembered Carl's half-joking invitation. Taking a chance, I headed for the *Tribune* five blocks away. Marla's funeral left me feeling melancholy and I hoped Carl wouldn't take offense at a last-minute request for company.

The receptionist, a chubby, jagged-haired brunette with deep dimples, waved me back toward the editorial department without a pause in her animated conversation with a skinny kid in shorts so baggy the crotch swung around his knees. Not many people were at their desks this late in the afternoon, though there was a flurry of activity over at the sports desk where, thanks to satellite TV, a sporting event of some sort could always be found.

"Hey, Benni, want a piece?" A man with a face the color of a banana moonpie and nerdy black eyeglasses held up a gooey slice of pizza.

"No, thanks anyway," I said. "I'm going to see if Carl wants to get some dinner."

"Make that cheap son-of-a-gun pay," he replied.

"I intend to," I answered with a laugh.

I rapped on the glass window of Carl's office, where he was talking on the phone. His face lit up when he saw me and he gestured for me to come in. It felt good to have someone glad to see me. Though I'd never thought of Carl in that way, I wondered if maybe I needed to open my mind, stop assuming that everything or everyone always remained static. If nothing else, the last nine months should have taught me that nothing is such a sure thing that it can't change.

"Be with you in a minute," he said to me. He punched the hold button and dialed an extension.

"Dad, Mayor Holland on line three."

"What brings you here?" Carl came around the desk and enveloped me in a hug. Holding me a shade longer than usual, he chuckled when I gently squirmed out of it. Maybe I wasn't that ready yet. "You look like a stewardess for United Airlines."

"I'm hungry," I said. "And I think the proper term these days is flight attendant."

He grabbed his leather jacket from the oak coat rack in the corner and slipped it on. "I'd love to have dinner with you, except I have an interview in ten minutes. Want to come? We could eat afterwards."

"Okay," I said. "Who are you interviewing?"

"The professor who's running against Dad for the city council seat."

"You're kidding."

"Nope. Dad says he runs a fair paper. That his political ambitions shouldn't bias the news. So we're giving equal time to his opponent."

"Are you going to be fair?"

He grinned at me, and for a moment, I could see just how appealing he could be to women. "Why wouldn't I be? I'm voting for him."

"Does your dad know that?"

"After the article, he will. Let's go."

I linked arms with him as we walked out of the building. "Carl, you really need to let go of that adolescent rebellion someday."

"Is that your subtle way of telling me to grow up?"

"Yes."

He chucked me under the chin. "Now, what fun would that be? Do you want to ride with me or take your own car?" He patted the fender of his small green Triumph.

"I'll take my own car. Where are we going?"

He paused before answering. "Sorry," he said. "But I told the professor I'd meet him at Trigger's. He's trying to get a feel for his blue-collar constituency."

I studied the tips of my navy pumps. No matter what I did, Trigger's seemed to loom in front of me like a huge boulder in the middle of the road. Perhaps it was a sign that I needed to get past it, move on.

"That's fine," I said, looking up at Carl. "I'm kind of in the mood for one of their beef dips anyway."

"You sure?" He laid a hand on my shoulder.

"Not entirely, but I'll go anyway." I ran my hand along the fender of the Triumph. Jack rebuilt the engine for him as a thirtieth birthday present, complaining the whole time that Carl should be driving an American car.

"That's my girl."

Trigger's Monday night customers were a mellow and easygoing bunch compared to the crazed weekend crowd. Only one pool table was in action and the songs on the jukebox ran toward sad and bluesy Don Williams rather than the perky Saturday night sounds of Carlene Carter.

Carl's tweedy professor candidate was waiting for him in a back booth, so I left them to their business and went over to the pool table to watch. After nodding to the two cowboys chalking their cues, I took a seat at a table close by. The door to the men's room slammed open and Wade and another guy walked out. Wade was telling the man some joke about cattle prods and Congressmen.

"Catch you next game," he told the guys when he saw me. He grabbed his beer and sat down across from me. "Never thought I'd see you here."

"Having dinner with Carl." I traced a name carved into the shellacked dark wood of the table. Tracy. I wondered where she was right now. What she did for a living. Did she find the love of her life here? I looked up at Wade. "He's doing an interview first."

He grunted, his tanned face wary.

"Look, Wade, I'm sorry about Saturday. Let's call a truce, okay?" I touched the sleeve of his plaid shirt.

"None of it's what you think." He stared at the table-top, not reacting to my contact. "You should stay out of what doesn't concern you."

"It's not just what I think, Wade. The police know about you and Marla."

He jerked his head up. "Did you . . . ?"

"Would you give me some credit, Wade? I didn't say anything, but apparently your relationship wasn't much of a secret. Have they talked to you yet?"

"Yes, and I told them what I knew. Which is nothing. And I wasn't the only one, you know. She got around."

"I know. And the police know that too."

He regarded me with twitchy, narrowed brown eyes, a familiar prelude to an explosion. "You seem to know an awful lot these days. You and that Mexican police chief are getting pretty chummy, I hear. Didn't take long for you to get back in the saddle, did it?"

I yanked my hand back as if I'd been burned, wanting to smack his sullen face. "You're an ass, Wade Harper."

I stood up, stumbling against a chair in my haste to make it to the ladies' room before the tears escaped. Standing in the dark tan, Lysol-scented room staring at my reflection in the chipped mirror, I wondered if anyone else was thinking what Wade had said. Why didn't I just get out of this town? Go someplace where no one knew my name, my financial status, the last time I had sex.

"You okay in there?" A low, indistinct voice came through the door. It opened and Carl stuck his head in.

"You alone?" he asked, nodding toward the three stalls.

"Yes, but you can't come in here."

"Sure I can." He stepped in and leaned against the far wall next to the tampon machine. "I saw you and Wade talking and then you ran off. I got worried."

"I'm fine. He's just being a jerk." I ran some water in the rust-stained sink and splashed my face. Carl pulled a couple of paper towels from the dispenser and handed them to me.

"Thanks." I patted my face with the rough sand-colored towels.

"What were you two arguing about?" he asked curiously.

"Nothing important. I don't really want to talk about it."

"Don't let him bug you." He took the paper towels from my hand and dabbed at my cheek. "Missed a spot. You know, Wade never did know his ass from a hole in the ground." He tossed the towel in the overflowing trash can. "Forget him. Let's eat."

"Okay," I said, sticking my head tentatively out the door.

"Don't worry, he left." He pointed me toward a booth where our beef dip sandwiches sat steaming on wide white plates. I picked at mine until he finally took it and ate the rest while rattling on about some toxic waste story he'd been working on for weeks.

I only half-listened, nodding and commenting at the right intervals, a talent most women pick up somewhere in junior high and utilize far more often the rest of their lives than any algebraic formula.

"So, I tracked this guy down in Buttonwillow and he confessed that he took five thousand for looking the other way when they dumped it . . . Benni, are you listening to me?" Carl snapped his fingers in front of my face.

"What? Oh, sure, you tracked the guy to Bakersfield and then what?"

"Buttonwillow." He reached over and tugged at a strand of my hair. "What planet are you on?"

"I'm sorry," I said. "That thing with Wade just got to me, I guess. What were you saying?"

"What were you and Wade arguing about?" he asked again, peering closely at me.

"Same old thing. You know Wade," I said vaguely.

"Was it about Jack?"

I traced my finger over the condensation dripping off my glass of Coke and didn't answer.

"You know, any problems he has shouldn't bother you anymore," Carl said. "Want me to talk to him?"

"No," I said sharply. I was getting tired of people telling me what and who I should be concerned about, as if feelings and emotional connections were something you could switch on and off like a light switch.

"Sorry," Carl said, his voice hurt. "I was just trying to help." He touched my hand. "I miss Jack, too." He shook his head. "It was just so crowded here that night. I talked to him a couple of times and then he was just gone. I wish . . ." He looked at me helplessly.

"I know," I said, wishing I didn't feel the need to comfort him. I didn't want to share my misery with anyone. Then I felt guilty for my selfishness. Who else but with me could Carl mourn?

"Do you think it'll ever get easier?"

"I don't know, honey," he said, draining his beer. "I honestly don't know."

"What was that you were saying about tracking someone?" I asked, changing the subject. Talking about Jack in Trigger's was just too much to deal with right then. "Do you have the resources to do that at the paper?"

"Not actually at the paper. I just have a lot of contacts."

"If all you have is a name, and you've tried the phone books, what would be your next step?" I opened the bag of chips that had come with my sandwich, dumped them in my plate, and looked for the brown, crusty ones.

"DMV."

"What if you don't have access to that?"

"I do, though." He poured more beer into his mug from the pitcher sitting next to him.

"But what if you didn't? What would you do then?"

"What's this all about, Benni?" He looked at me oddly. "I can run a DMV for you if you want. Who are you looking for?"

"No one," I said, wiping my salty fingers on my napkin. "This is just hypothetical."

"I thought you found your cousin." He sipped at his beer, the corner of his lip twitching as he studied me.

"I did. Well, actually she called me. I was just wondering how people track other people. I was listening to your story. It made me curious."

"What are you up to?"

"Nothing." Even as I said it, I realized it came out too quickly.

"Does this have anything to do with those murders? Am I going to have to inject you with sodium pentothal to get you to confide in me?"

Before I could answer, the thundering voice of J.D. interrupted us. "What are you two youngsters up to?" He slid in the booth next to me and crooked his finger at the cocktail waitress.

"Just eating dinner, Pop," Carl said, his face turning blank. "See the story on the chemical dumping?" he asked in a placid voice, his eyes blinking rapidly.

"Sure did. Had to cut out about twenty percent of it," J.D. said. "You got to learn to compress, son. You ramble on like an old woman."

"What'll it be, boys?" The waitress, a big-breasted redhead who must have subscribed to the same hairdo magazine as my cousin Rita, smiled at us with long, yellowish teeth.

"Bud light," J.D. said.

"Jack Daniel's, double," Carl said. I looked at him with concern and shook my head.

"Carl," J.D. said. "Where were you yesterday? Didn't you get any of my messages?"

Carl drained the rest of his beer. "I was working on the chemical dumping story. Why, what's up?"

"Son, don't you remember what yesterday was?"

Carl's brows moved together in concentration.

"It was Jenny's birthday." J.D. shook his head and sipped at the beer the waitress set in front of him. "Can't say much about a man who'd forget his own daughter's birthday."

"Well, shit," Carl said. He picked up his shot glass and swallowed the double bourbon in one gulp.

"Yeah, you are," J.D. said. "But I covered your butt, as usual. I had the toy store at the mall send over a Barbie Dreamhouse and say it was from you. Now, you'd better get over and see her today."

"Thanks," Carl said hastily, his face a soft pink. "I just got so caught up in this dumping article. Everything I put in there needs to be there. I think if you read it again . . ."

"Now, Carl," J.D. said. "I been doing this a lot longer than you and I'm telling you it's . . ."

"Benni's got a secret, Dad," Carl interrupted. "Has to do with the Chenier and Griffin murders."

"That right?" J.D. smiled down at me, a wiry gray eyebrow cocked in question. "What kind of secret you got, little girl?"

"Carl's just chasing rabbits," I said, glaring across at him. "I don't have any secrets. I was just asking a hypothetical question and your son jumps to all sorts of conclusions."

"What's the question?" J.D. asked, his face alert as a bird dog's. "Don't listen to that boy. I'm sure I've got a better answer."

"It's nothing," I said, pushing at him with my hip to get out. "Thanks for dinner, Carl. Thanks for everything. How about we do it again in about ten years?" I hitched my purse over my shoulder and headed for the door.

It was dark when I walked out into Trigger's parking lot. I was fumbling through my purse looking for my keys when a hand clamped down on my shoulder, startling me.

"Hey!" I twisted around, holding out my keys, ready to stab.

"I'm sorry," Carl said. "I'm such a dipshit sometimes, I even disgust myself." He gave his best crooked, forgive-me smile.

I pulled out of his grasp. "Don't get me involved in your juvenile squabbles with your dad. You were pissed because he was criticizing your story, so you diverted his attention to me. That's real mature, Carl."

"I know." He wiped his palm on the side of his khaki pants. "I know what a donkey I can be. I'm sorry I dragged you into it. Don't be mad."

I leaned against the truck and rubbed my eyes with my fingers. "Carl, why don't you try and work things out with J.D.? He's not as bad as you make him out to be. Besides, there may come a time when you'll want to and can't."

"That personal experience talking?" he said softly.

"Maybe," I said, though I'd been thinking about Wade and the last words he'd probably had with Jack. My memory wasn't that dramatic. The best I could recall, my last words to Jack before going to my dad's had been— "If you go to town today, pick up some Repel-X for the horses." We kissed good-bye in that quick, mindless way you do when you're going to see each other the next day.

"I'll think about it," Carl said, opening the truck door. "Just don't be mad."

"All right." I threw my purse on the seat and turned to face him. "Just talk to him, okay? Try and work things out."

"For you, honey, anything." He gave me a quick kiss on the cheek.

When I walked through the door of the museum, the antique clock in the lobby chimed seven o'clock. The museum itself was dark and quiet, but Meg's orange Toyota, Ray's white Ford pickup and half a dozen other vehicles in the parking lot told me artists were working. December was their busiest time of year. Many of them were scheduled for various festivals until Christmas Eve.

I walked back into the studios, where three women were chattering around a multicolored calico Log Cabin quilt.

"You're here awfully late," one of them said. "How was the funeral?"

"Just picking up some work to take home," I said. "It was sad. Not very many people came." I emphasized the last sentence.

The quilters ducked their heads in embarrassment and went back to work. I walked back toward my office where I closed the door and sat down, feeling incredibly exhausted. I'd only worked for three months and already I needed a vacation from this place. I wondered if I was ever going to go camping or ride a horse again.

I had one last idea left about finding out Suzanne Hart's identity. If that didn't pan out, I had no choice but to tell Ortiz what I knew. I picked up the phone and dialed Mrs. Chenier. Her soft, tissue-paper voice sounded like it was talking from the moon.

"No," she said. "I don't recall anyone Marla knew with that name. But I didn't know all her friends."

"Did she keep an address book there?" I could have kicked myself for not thinking to ask that before now.

"Oh, yes," Mrs. Chenier said and my heart started beating faster. "But the police asked me for that right off."

"Oh." My heart flopped back to normal. "I don't suppose you remember if there was a Suzanne Hart in it."

"No, I'm sorry. Is this Hart person important?"

"Probably not," I said. "But don't mention the name to anyone yet. I'm still looking into it."

"Whatever you say. Thank you so much for your help."

Every time I talked to Mrs. Chenier, I felt guiltier. I made a note to myself to get those pots of Marla's out and priced so they would sell. I was sure Mrs. Chenier could use the money as soon as possible. If they didn't sell, I'd dip into my savings and buy them myself. I couldn't help but remember the money in the Nancy Drew books. An anonymous postcard to Mrs. Chenier telling her to look in the books—What harm could that do? Maybe it *was* illegally gained, but if anyone deserved it, it was Mrs. Chenier.

I laid my head down on my desk and wished that I'd never become involved in this, never found any bodies, never met Ortiz, never had this job. Never became a widow. Wishes, wishes. If wishes were horses . . .

I forced myself up. When I started thinking in clichés, even ones involving horses, I needed to get to bed. A strong knock sounded on my door.

"It's open," I called.

Ray walked in, his face grim. I briefly wondered how long he'd been standing outside my door, how much of my conversation with Mrs. Chenier he'd heard.

"What's up, Ray?" I asked in a light voice.

"Constance wants her keys back." Since cleaning up after Marla's murder, Ray had unofficially taken over the task of opening up the museum for the artists. The two other sets of keys were on Marla's and Eric's bodies when they were found and were locked up as evidence.

"I'll make copies of these spare keys tomorrow," I said.

"Okay." He started to walk away, then turned back and regarded me with angry brown eyes. "The police came to talk with me again today."

"Oh?"

"They wanted to know about my relationship with Marla."

I stared at my desk blotter and didn't say anything.

"I wasn't the only one."

"Apparently not."

"Why did you tell the police about me?"

"I didn't," I said. "Why does everyone assume *I'm* the one turning all you guys in? Meg told me about you and Marla, and if Meg knows, you know everyone does. I haven't told the police anything about you."

His face grew stubborn. I knew the look. He needed someone to blame, someone other than himself.

"If my wife finds out about Marla, she'll take my son and split." His voice broke slightly. I felt a flash of sympathy; I knew what Ray's son meant to him. Still, that wasn't my problem. I had enough of my own.

"I'm sorry, Ray, but I guess that's one of the consequences of that sort of thing. I don't know what you want from me."

"No one is taking my son from me," he said, his voice harsh. He stabbed the Xacto knife he was holding into my wood desk. "No one."

I stared at the knife and held my breath. The look on my face must have shocked him back to his senses.

"I'm sorry," he said in a soft voice. He picked up the knife and stuck it in his tool belt. "It's just that you seem awfully involved in this. You and that police chief have gotten real friendly, I hear."

"The next person who brings up the relationship I *do not have* with Chief Ortiz is going to have to sign a complaint against me for assault."

He looked at me steadily. "All I'm saying is you should stay out of things that don't concern you." He turned and walked out the door.

As I stuck the keys in the ignition of the truck, I thought about all the things I should have answered. Of course, all I'd done was sit there and gape.

"No backtalk from you this time, bud," I commanded the Chevy, "or I'm selling you for scrap."

And for a change, someone believed me.

15

THERE WAS ONE message on my answering machine when I arrived home.

"Benni, call me." Sandra's weepy voice sputtered like an old engine. "Wade came home real mad, then left again. He said he saw you at Trigger's. What happened?"

I didn't call her back. I didn't know what to tell her. I had no idea where Wade fit into this whole mess, but I knew one thing—I'd just as soon eat a saddle blanket as talk to or about him again.

A saddle blanket would have probably tasted better than anything in my refrigerator. I would have killed right then for the beef dip I didn't eat at Trigger's. While changing into jeans and boots, I decided what I needed was a real homemade meal—steak, baked potato, corn on the cob, apple pie with vanilla ice cream. And a movie. A funny one. Williams Bros. Market out by the university had everything I needed, except the movie. The video store had slim pickings, so I grabbed *Police Academy*, remembering it being a silly, slapstick comedy that made police look like mindless idiots. For some reason, that sounded appealing.

I balanced the paper sack of groceries on one hip and had inserted the key in the front door with the other, when a whoosh and then a plink sounded above my head.

The porch light shattered.

Tiny shards of glass sprayed across my face. I dropped the paper sack and frantically brushed at my eyes. The scent of Italian dressing surrounded me. I glanced out at the street. A light-colored pickup was idling there. In the dark I could just make out the outline of the rifle. Like a stupid animal, I stood frozen, staring.

Another plink chipped the stucco above me.

I shoved the front door open, hit the floor.

Sounds like a .22, I thought, amazed at my calm as I crawled across the floor toward my bedroom. No match for a .45. If I could get to it. My bedroom seemed a hundred miles away.

A front windowpane cracked.

I scrambled for the bedroom, knees banging against the hard oak floor. Nightstand, my mind commanded. Get to the nightstand.

I fumbled for Jack's pistol. Slip in the clip. Safety off. Pull the slide back. Aim. Jack's words, Daddy's words, coming back to me. I sat back against the nightstand, rested the heaviness of the gun on my bended knees and aimed at the open bedroom door.

Somewhere, tires squealed.

Mouth dry, breath coming in sharp gasps, I sat in the dark, frozen. Police. Call the police.

The 911 operator had already received a report. A patrol car was being dispatched. I told her I had a gun. She told me to stay on the line.

"They're coming up the walk now, ma'am," the dispatcher's steady voice said after minutes of inane conversation she had probably been taught kept a scared caller from hysteria. It hadn't worked.

"I have a gun," I said. "Tell them I have a gun."

"They're in the house," she reported.

"Tell them I have a gun," I repeated.

"Police," a loud voice yelled from the living room.

"I have a gun!" I yelled back.

"Put it down," the voice commanded.

"Not until I see your uniforms!" I shrieked.

"Benni?" The faintly familiar voice broke through the loud adrenaline buzz in my ears. A dark head poked around the corner of the doorway. A bright light blinded me. I aimed the pistol at the light.

"Benni?" he asked again. I knew that voice. A sob gurgled up from my throat.

"Miguel?"

"Put the gun down, Benni. It's Miguel," he said in a soothing voice.

Another sob escaped, but I couldn't put the gun down. A primordial voice in my subconscious whispered—it's a trick—don't surrender your weapon.

"Benni, I can't put my gun down until you do." His voice sounded apologetic. "Put it down on the floor next to you. Do it now."

The deep, reassuring tone of his voice finally penetrated my brain. With trembling hands, I laid the gun on the floor next to me.

"Push it away from you," he said softly. I shoved it across the slick floor. He turned off his flashlight, flipped on the bedroom light and picked it up, his pistol already back in its holster. Shaking his head, he removed the clip, pulled the slide back and emptied the chamber.

"Geeze Louise!" he said, sounding like the Miguel I knew again. "You scared the shit outta me."

He passed the gun to the officer behind him and held

out his hand. I grabbed it, pulled myself up, then burst into tears.

"Ah, don't cry," he said, putting a heavy arm around me. As I leaned against his comfortable bulk and tried to get control of myself, he carefully led me to the tweed sofa in the living room. His partner, a tall, freckled guy in horn-rimmed glasses, was inspecting the bullet hole in the wall across from the window.

"Looks like a .22," he said to Miguel. He turned to me. "Who's pissed at you, lady?"

I stared at them a moment, wondering where I should start, when we were distracted by the arrival of two more police cars. After getting my description of the truck, I was left alone as they put out a report to the other patrol cars and assessed the damage made by the three bullets. Finally, Miguel came over, pulled out a notebook, and started asking me questions. I repeated my story of the light-colored pickup.

"That could be thousands of people in this county," he said. He started to ask who I suspected, when the front door flew open and Ortiz burst into the room. His navy L.A.P.D. sweatshirt had the crumpled look of something slept in or grabbed off the floor; the fierce expression on his face caused all of us to stop talking mid-sentence.

"What happened?" he demanded. For a moment, we all just stared at him, then three officers started talking at once. He held up his hand and scanned the room, glaring indiscriminately. His eyes paused at me, then moved on to the hole in my living room wall.

"Someone get the slug?" he asked, walking over to the wall.

"Whose smart idea was it to call him?" I whispered to Miguel.

"Probably the dispatcher," Miguel said out of the side

of his mouth. "Orders. Anything that involved you, we were suppose to call him pronto."

"You've got to be kidding," I blurted out. Ortiz turned and gave me a threatening look.

After taking my statement, Miguel helped me nail up the plywood my neighbor, Mr. Treton, had graciously cut to fit my broken window and pick up the groceries splattered across the porch.

"Man, I loved this movie," he said, picking up the video dripping with Italian dressing. I turned down his offer to take me to Elvia's with the assertion that I wasn't going to let a yahoo with a peashooter run me from my home.

After he and his partner left, I looked around and realized the only people left in the house were me and Ortiz. His expression hadn't changed since he'd arrived. Silently, he walked over to the front door and locked it, pulled down the shades on the front windows, then sat down in Jack's brown leather recliner, arms folded, eyes angry.

"What happened?" he asked.

"It's in the report. With your pull, I'm sure you can obtain a copy."

"I'm not in the mood for your bullshit."

"I told Officer Aragon everything. It's in the report."

He let out a string of Spanish words I vaguely recalled hearing spew from the mouths of Elvia's brothers when we were kids. I also remembered them getting repeated whippings from Señora Aragon for it. His outburst caused no reaction in me, seeing as I didn't actually understand what he was saying. That is, until I heard the word *estupida.*

"I am not stupid," I said. Before he could comment, the phone rang.

"Are you okay?" Dove's voice sounded faraway but

gruffly familiar. I wanted to crawl into the phone toward it.

"How in the world did you hear about it so fast? And yes, I'm fine."

"That nosy old fart who lives next door to you."

"Mr. Treton?"

"I give him a couple of jars of my clover honey and he keeps me informed."

"You're paying the neighbors to spy on me?" I asked incredulously. Ortiz's scowl turned into a confused look.

"I prefer to think of it as bartering."

"Dove, I'm thirty-four years old."

"I know how old you are. Whose sports car is that out front?"

"You don't miss a thing, do you? Are Mr. Treton's binoculars trained in on me at this moment? Are you hooked up by cellular phones? What am I doing right now?" I stuck my tongue out at the phone.

"Probably making a face," she said and cackled.

"Are you through? I want to go to bed."

"So, what about the car? Heard it's a great restoration job."

"It's the chief of police's car and he was just leaving."

"Heard he's a fine-looking man," she said. I looked over at him in his old jeans, the thick black mustache I still thought about at odd moments, and slightly perplexed blue-gray eyes.

"Pretty fine," I said.

"Let me talk to him."

"No."

"Benni . . ."

"No, Dove. He was just leaving. There's nothing you could possibly have to say to him."

"You need police protection."

"I have Jack's pistol. That's all the protection I need."

"Let me talk to him."

"No."

"I'm bringing Garnet out, then. You shouldn't be alone. I can be there in a half hour." Knowing how she drove, I didn't doubt it.

"Why, you old coot, that's blackmail."

"So call the cops. Let me talk to him."

I held the phone out to Ortiz. "My grandmother wishes to speak to you."

He looked bewildered as he took the phone.

"Whatever she wants, tell her *no*."

"I heard that," a tiny voice squawked from the receiver.

He nodded as she spoke, her voice a frantic buzz audible from where I was standing.

"Yes, ma'am," he said. "Yes, ma'am. I intend to, ma'am. I'll take care of it personally."

He handed the phone back to me, his face impassive.

"What did she say?" I asked.

He answered with a shrug.

"Dove," I said. "I'll be fine."

"I know you will, honeybun," she said in a saccharine voice.

I looked at Ortiz suspiciously.

"I'll see you soon. Have fun," she said.

"What do you mean, have . . ." but she'd already hung up.

In the meantime, Ortiz had settled back in Jack's recliner, and punched the television on to a rerun of *Saturday Night Live*. The Coneheads were going to the circus.

"Excuse me." I grabbed the controller from him and flipped the TV off. "Weren't you just leaving?"

"Can't."

"What?"

"Orders."

"What?"

"Your grandmother demanded police protection for you, and since I don't have any money in the budget for overtime, I guess I'm stuck with the job."

"Are you out of your mind?"

"Your grandmother is a very influential person in this county. Purely a career enhancement move on my part." He smiled and pushed the recliner back one notch.

"You can't spend the night here."

"She said I could."

"Well, I say you can't."

He locked his hands behind his head and crossed his legs. "She outranks you." His expression was as cocky as his position.

"Don't you own a pair of socks?" I snapped, mostly because I couldn't think of anything else to say.

"What?" He looked down at his topsiders, perplexed.

I glared, not about to admit that I was actually relieved someone was staying the night with me. The sight of his pistol lying on the end table next to him gave me as close to a feeling of security as I was going to have tonight.

"You can use the quilt on the sofa if you need it." I laid the remote control on the table next to him. "Where's my gun?"

"You won't need it while I'm here." He grabbed the controller, turned on the TV and started cruising the stations.

"It's my gun. I want it back."

"You'll get it back tomorrow," he said, his eyes never leaving the TV screen.

"I want it now."

"I said no. Now go to bed." He settled on the eleven o'clock news and pushed the recliner back as far as it would go.

"Get out of that chair."

"I told you, I'm not leaving."

"I'm not telling you to leave. I'm telling you to *get out of that chair*." His head snapped up.

"Okay, no problem," he said in the pacifying tone a person might use on a nervous horse. In seconds, he was out of the chair, sitting on the sofa. "Is here all right?"

"Fine." I went into the bedroom and slammed the door.

A few seconds later, he knocked. "Don't lock it." His voice was muffled by the thickness of the door.

I swung it open. "What did you say?"

"Don't lock this door. I might need to get in there quickly."

Another time, that remark might have made me laugh, but I was too close to the edge to find any humor in it. "Do you think he'll come back?" My voice cracked, but I was beyond caring.

"Probably not. He was either a very poor shot or he was only trying to scare you. With the caliber of gun he was using, my guess is the latter." He took off his glasses and cleaned them with the edge of his sweatshirt; his eyes drew tight with fatigue. "I'm not done talking with you. We're going to continue our conversation first thing tomorrow morning."

"I know." Right then, I didn't care. Tomorrow was a lifetime away. I was still wondering how I was going to make it through tonight.

He started to turn away, then stopped and turned back, his face apologetic. "Look, about the chair."

I held up my hand. "I'm sorry I snapped. It's just that . . ."

"I get it, Benni." His voice was strained. "I'll be out here if you need me."

Though I took a hot shower to relax, my sleep was

fitful all night. Even Ortiz's presence in the house failed to lessen the apprehension that held me tight as a wrestler's grip. More than once I woke suddenly, my throat tight, my face hot from the adrenaline coursing through my body.

I lay there and thought about the last three months, how different living in town was, how I missed the sounds and the odors of ranch life: the groaning of cattle echoing through the gullies on a clear night, the smooth feel of worn leather reins, horses whinnying to be fed at the end of the day, the tart, earthy smell animals bring to your life.

At one point, in a sort of panic, I pulled the embroidered case off Jack's pillow and rubbed my face where he once laid his head, trying to find his scent. But it had been too long; only my smell was there. I held the pillow to my face, stifling my sobs, wishing suddenly I were alone, yet glad I wasn't.

I woke for the last time at five A.M. and read the ceiling for an hour, worrying about what Ortiz was going to ask me and how much I should tell him. Now that there was a link to Jack's accident, I wanted to get to this Suzanne Hart before the police. If they talked to her first, it would get all tangled up in legalities and I'd never find out if she knew anything about the night Jack was killed.

Since sleep was obviously out of the question, I crawled out of bed, put on a pair of thick gray sweats and slunk down the hallway into the kitchen. I couldn't see Ortiz, so I assumed he was stretched out on the sofa asleep.

The kitchen was a mess as usual. I hadn't washed dishes in a week, and though I didn't honestly care about impressing Ortiz with my housekeeping abilities, I was vain enough not to want anyone to see what a closet slob I had become.

I turned the hot water on to a quiet trickle and pushed up the sleeves of my sweatshirt. I was on my second load of glasses, trying to shove the dishrag down into a thin, elegant iced tea glass given to me by Elvia, when it broke, slicing deep into the palm of my right hand. Forgetting I wasn't alone, I let out a yelp. Tears stung my eyes as I held my hand under the running water, washing the soap out of my wound.

"Cut yourself?" Ortiz whispered about three inches from my ear, causing me to jump.

"For crying out loud, why don't you cough or something before you sneak up on someone?" I grabbed a dish towel and wrapped it around my hand.

"And take away my only advantage?" he asked. "Let me see." He unwrapped the towel and pried at the slit with his thumbs.

"Stop it." I tried to pull away. "You're making it bleed more."

He continued to grip it firmly. "That's the whole idea, gets rid of any glass chips. You probably need stitches. And a tetanus shot."

"Forget it. I'll just stick some gauze on it."

"Sit down. I'll do it. Where's your first-aid supplies?"

I pointed to the cabinet above the refrigerator and sat down on a kitchen chair. After a lot of complaining about my pitiful box of supplies, he fashioned a neat though bulky bandage.

"I guess you did this so I'd have to cook breakfast," he said.

"Feel free to fix anything in the refrigerator."

He groaned when he looked at the bare shelves. "I should have guessed you're one of those modern women who can't cook. Guess we'll have to go out."

"You can go out. I'm not hungry. And I can too cook."

"Then we'll have our talk on an empty stomach." He pulled a kitchen chair out, flipped it around and straddled it.

"I'd like to get dressed first, if you don't mind."

"You're not leaving this house until we talk," he said smoothly.

I took my time dressing, partly out of choice and partly because of the awkward bandage on my right hand. I was attempting to brush the tangles out of my hair with my left hand when he knocked on the bedroom door.

"You okay in there?" he called.

I yanked the door open. "What do you want?"

"You were taking so long, I was afraid you escaped. Of course, I knew you wouldn't get far without these." He dangled my truck keys in front of my face.

"Give me those." I grabbed them and stuck them in the pocket of my jeans. "It's taking me a long time because I'm having to do everything with my left hand." I turned back to the mirror of my oak vanity and continued pulling the brush through my snarled hair.

"Here, let me." Before I could protest, he grabbed the brush out of my hand and pushed me down on the vanity stool. His long, even strokes were so relaxing that after a minute or so, I found myself growing drowsy, breathing slower, in time with the strokes.

There was a vague familiarity to his careful strokes. Not of Dove, who believed the quicker the better, or even Jack, who loved my hair but never, in the whole time we were together, brushed it. Then it occurred to me. It reminded me of my mother.

On my first day of school, though she was already bedridden from cancer, she insisted on being the one to brush and braid my hair. Years later, Dove told me that it took her a day to rest from the strain of it. All I remember was she sang "Jesus loves the little children," in a soft, breathless voice that was almost a whisper, and kissed the tip of each of my braids. For luck, she said. I tried to swallow over the lump in my throat.

"Who did you see yesterday?" Ortiz asked quietly, bringing the brush underneath my hair; his fingers brushed against the nape of my neck, causing me to shiver slightly.

"No one."

He looked at me in the mirror, a challenging look in his deep-set eyes. "You went to Marla's funeral. You talked to Detective Cleary."

"Oh, yeah, I saw Detective Cleary." I smirked at his reflection. The brush snared a knot; he tugged sharply, jerking my head back.

"Hey, watch it." I tried to squirm away. So much for sentimental memories.

"Sorry. Where did you go after the funeral?" The firm, regular strokes continued, tranquilizing me again.

"To Mrs. Chenier's house." I figured I might as well not lie, he probably already knew anyway. "You know, you look awful," I added. With his overnight stubble and wrinkled clothes, he looked more like a vagrant than the chief of police. He ignored my comment.

"Who did you see there?"

"A bunch of people I don't know."

"Then where did you go?"

"McDonald's. I had a cup of coffee. Want to see the receipt?" The brush caught another tangle; he yanked firmly.

"I think I'd better do this myself," I said, reaching for the brush.

He held it away from my grasp. "Sorry, it slipped. I'll be more careful." He grinned, then got serious again when he saw my irritated face in the mirror. "Then?"

"I went to the *Tribune*, had dinner at Trigger's with my

friend Carl, went to the museum, then I came home."

"Who did you talk to at Trigger's?" He continued brushing, the rhythm the same, the strokes gentler.

"My brother-in-law Wade, Carl, Carl's dad, J.D."

"At the museum?"

"I don't know. Some of the artists. Josie, Sally, I think. Ray."

"Did you notice anyone following you during the day?"

"No."

For a few minutes, the only sound was the whoosh of the brush moving through my hair. I closed my eyes and felt the tension in my neck and shoulders dissipate with each stroke.

"Well, Ms. Albenia Harper," he said in a low voice, "it seems to me we have a small problem here."

"And what is that?" Even with my eyes closed I sensed his scrutiny.

"You have something I want and it appears you aren't going to give it to me."

I wasn't about to open my eyes on that one.

"I don't know what you're talking about."

"Whoever is involved in this isn't messing around," he said. "What is it you're holding back from me?"

"Nothing." I started to rise, but his hand clamped down on my shoulder, pushing me back into the chair.

"I think my hair's just fine," I said.

"I'm not through yet."

"Well, I am. You know, it's a mystery to me why in the world you don't quit harassing me and spend your time actually looking for Marla and Eric's killer."

He sighed, picked up my hair and bounced it in the palm of his hand as if he were weighing it.

"That isn't a mystery," he said. "A problem, maybe, but not a mystery."

"What?"

He stared at my hair, as if there were something written there. "A problem has a solution. You have information, I want it. When you give it to me, the problem is solved."

He wrapped my hair around his hand and held it lightly; if I moved, it would tighten, like a slipknot. "Now, a mystery is an entirely different animal."

"What are you talking about?" I started to pull away, felt his hand tighten, then decided to stay put.

"A mystery has no solution. The mystery isn't who killed Marla and Eric. That's the problem. The mystery is why. All the psychiatrists in the world can't tell you that. It boils down to a question of evil, which is a mystery that will never be solved, by man anyway."

"Is there going to be a pop quiz after this, Sergeant Friday? Or perhaps I should say Professor Friday?" I asked, though I knew I was taking a chance with the grip he had on my hair.

"Sorry." He unwrapped his hand and laughed. "Been reading Marcel. French philosopher and playwright. Has a lot of interesting things to say. I have a tendency to lecture when I get excited about something."

"Gee, I never noticed that trait in you," I said.

He looked at my reflection and grinned. He set the brush down and started dividing my hair in sections.

"What are you doing?"

"You usually wear your hair in a braid, don't you? I thought I'd French braid it."

"What?"

"Don't look so shocked. You're looking at the best French braider in Derby, Kansas," he said. "At least I was at one time."

"You're putting me on."

"Nope. My mother was a working mom long before women's liberation. I have twin sisters seven years younger than me. From the time I was twelve, it was my responsibility to get them ready for school. I can iron ruffles almost as good as I braid hair."

I watched mesmerized as his hands rapidly wrapped one strand of hair around another.

"Embarrassed the heck out of my father. Insulted his Latin machismo. But whatever machismo genes I had were overcome easily by the greedy little capitalist in me. The mothers on my street would pay me fifty cents a head." His reflection smiled at my unbelieving look. "My dad made me work in his garage on the weekends. He was terrified I was going to become a hairdresser."

"He must have been relieved when you became a cop."

"He never knew. He died when I was sixteen."

"Oh, I'm sorry."

"That's why I came to California. I was giving my mom a lot of grief. You know sixteen-year-olds. She sent me to live with my dad's brother in Santa Ana. I lived with my Uncle Antonio until I went into the Marines."

"And braided your cousins' hair?" I asked, smiling.

He grinned back. "Lucky for me, Uncle Tony had four sons."

"Does your mom still live in Kansas?"

"In the same house I grew up in. She retired last year. Taught fifth grade for forty-one years."

He reached over to the vanity, found a rubber band in the clutter and wrapped it around the end of my braid. "There you go." He gave me a hand mirror and stood back, folding his arms across his chest.

It was the neatest French braid I'd ever seen.

"Ortiz," I said, laying the mirror down. "I hate to admit it, but I'm impressed. What other secrets are you hiding behind that macho cop exterior?"

187

"Now, what kind of secrets could a good ole boy from Kansas possibly have?" He winked at me and glanced at his watch. "I have to hit the road. I need to go home, shower and get to work. Lots of bad guys out there."

"I guess I owe you fifty cents," I said, walking him to the door.

"First one's on the house." He gave my braid a tug and stepped out on the front porch. He waved to Mr. Treton, who was watering his already soaked impatiens at a suspiciously early hour, then turned back to me.

"Benni, why don't you just tell me what they're after?" His voice was tight, apprehensive.

"Where did you put my gun?" I asked.

"You just don't get it, do you?" He rubbed his jaw, then reached over and touched his finger to my cheek. "I don't want the next bag they zip up to be yours."

I folded my arms across my chest and didn't answer.

"I put it back in your nightstand," he said with a sigh and stepped into his car.

Ten minutes later, I was draining the bloody water out of the sink, when the phone rang. Elvia's voice held a hint of laughter.

"I hear you had company last night," she said.

"Can't I do anything in this town without it being on the front page of the *Tribune?*"

"Come by the store. I want to hear everything."

"Calm down, it's not what you think."

"Oh," she said, disappointed. "Too bad."

For the second time that morning I didn't answer. I wasn't about to admit she might be right.

16

"SO HOW ARE you going to find out who this Suzanne Hart is?" Elvia asked.

I told her the whole story while we sat in her real office upstairs drinking cappuccinos. She looked worriedly at my bandaged hand. "Just how bad did you cut yourself?"

I sat with my right hand raised as if swearing to tell the truth. It seemed to throb less that way. "You have any aspirin?"

She dug through her desk and tossed the bottle over to me, which I missed. "Sorry," she said. "I guess I should have known to buy you plastic glasses."

"Ha." I struggled with the child-proof cap. She reached over, popped it open and gave me two tablets.

"Two more."

"Two's enough. If they don't work . . ."

"Just give them to me," I snapped.

She raised her eyebrows quizzically at my tone and handed me two more.

"Sorry," I said. "My hand hurts." She waited with a blank, patient face for me to continue.

"I don't know how I'm going to find her," I said, swallowing the aspirin one at a time between sips of cappuccino. "I just know I have to. I have a feeling she knows something about Jack's death and I want to get to her before the police."

"You really think Wade's involved?"

"I don't know," I said irritably. "Wade, Ray, the man in the moon. Apparently, Marla has been with them all. I'm going out to the Harper Ranch today to see if Sandra knows anything."

"After what's happened between you and Wade? Maybe you should take one of my brothers with you." She took a sip of her drink. Her shiny lips left a reddish-orange crescent on the side of her cup.

"I know Wade's schedule," I said. "He's usually not around the house in the late afternoon. I'll drop by then. Now, help me think of a way to find this Hart woman."

She leaned back in the rose-colored executive chair, her dark eyes amused. "I'd rather hear about what happened last night with you and Chief Ortiz. Miguel says the station house is just buzzing."

"Miguel ought to mind his own business and quit gossiping like an old biddy."

"You know, you're going to be wearing a bandage around your whole body when Ortiz finds out you have this information."

"Hey, whose side are you on?" I drained my cup. Maybe an overload of caffeine would make the aspirin work faster. "Now think. Where would you go if you were taking blackmail money?"

"You're not certain she is, though."

"No, but it looks like it. What would you do?"

"To tell you the truth, I'd get as far away from the scene of the crime, or whatever you call it, as I could."

"That's what I thought." I chewed on my thumbnail. "But where?"

"Stop that," she said automatically. I continued to chew. "Or I would stay as close as possible to the person paying me my money."

"Oh," I said, deflated. "I never thought about that."

"You sure this Suzanne wasn't someone associated with the co-op? Maybe she worked with Marla at Trigger's."

"Of course," I said, hitting the desk. "That is so obvious, I can't believe I didn't think of it. I'll go ask Floyd if she was an ex-employee."

"Do you think he'll tell you?" Elvia said dubiously. "And do you really want anyone to know you're asking about her? You don't know who's involved with this. Don't forget *why* Ortiz spent the night at your house last night."

"Okay, Watson, then you do it."

"Oh, no," she said, holding up a coral-nailed hand. "I'm not going to some country-western bar and play Charlie's Angels."

I picked up her phone and sat it in front of her. "You don't have to move out of this office. Call him. Pretend you're her sister or something."

Elvia's face looked interested but wary. "That's a possibility. But not her sister. That's information he could know." She tapped a long nail on her tiny cup, then pointed at me. "I have it. Her bank. I'll say she has some money coming to her and we don't have her new address. Give me Trigger's number."

Within three minutes we were a tiny bit closer to finding Suzanne Hart. Elvia's hunch was right. She did work at Trigger's about nine or ten months ago. Floyd sent her last paycheck to a post office box in Salinas. I grabbed the phone and dialed information in Salinas.

No listing for a Suzanne Hart.

"Well, that's that." I couldn't help but be disappointed.

"Now what?"

"Stake out the post office?" Elvia suggested.

"For a whole month? Who knows when she collects her mail?" I inspected my bandage. It was already looking a bit grungy. I picked at the graying edges of the tape. "I could go up there, I guess. If she's a cocktail waitress, chances are she's still doing that. How many bars can there be in Salinas?"

"You're going to cruise the bars looking for her?" Elvia shook her head and rolled her napkin into a ball. "That sounds appealing."

"What else can I do?"

"Dare I suggest you take this information to the police?"

"Forget it, Elvia. I told you, I'm going to find her first. Then the police can have her." I pointed my finger at her. "And you better not rat on me."

"I won't," she said. "But I don't like it."

"You never like anything I do."

"And that's never stopped you before."

"I've got to go. I want to go see Sandra while Wade isn't there. I'll probably leave tomorrow morning for Salinas. Hopefully, I won't have to spend the night there, but don't get worried if I'm not back until the next day."

"I always worry, *gringa*," she said. "Drive careful. *Be* careful."

"Yes, Mom," I said, dodging the napkin ball she threw at me.

It had been a couple of months since I'd visited the Harper Ranch. Driving under the wrought-iron arch with the "Lazy J-Flying H" brand felt familiar but discomforting, like talking to someone you haven't seen since high school. The oak trees lining the long driveway, planted by their dad, John, almost twenty years ago, dappled the truck as I drove past. A passel of young Hispanic kids played on a new swing-set in front of the ranch's original house, where Jack and I had lived. A pretty young woman I assumed was their mother sat in a lounge chair under a tree, reading a newspaper. It surprised me until I remembered Sandra telling me that they'd rented the house to their new foreman. I wondered if the foreman's wife had trouble with the pantry door sticking.

Sandra sat in a brown wicker chair on the long front porch of the new house, a six-bedroom two-story built by Jack's dad when beef prices were high. Her face lit up when she looked up from her needlework, and I felt guilty that I hadn't seen her since the craft festival. Though I never minded the isolation of the ranch, I knew it was lonely for Sandra.

"Hey, stranger," she called and gestured at the matching chair next to her. "What brings you around here?"

"Just thought I'd drop by and see how you all were doing. Brought the money Mom Harper made for the baby quilts at the festival."

"Good," Sandra said, looking back down at her counted-cross-stitch sampler. "You missed her, though. She went to town with Mrs. Larson to see a movie. First time she's been off the ranch in a month."

"What are you working on?"

She held up the sampler. It was an elaborate pattern with hearts, houses and three types of alphabets—"Keep thy heart with all diligence; for out of it are the issues of life," it said.

"I like it," I said. "Looks hard, though."

She shrugged and concentrated on the sampler, counting under her breath.

"It looks funny having all those kids playing around the old house," I said. "You painted it, I see."

"They're a nice family," Sandra said. "She's teaching me Spanish. Arturo's a big help to Wade."

"How're the herds looking so far?"

She shrugged again. The running of the ranch had never interested her like it had me. She was a town girl; she lived on the ranch for the love of her man, not the lifestyle.

"You need any help on the computer?" I asked. "Wade said you were having some trouble with the calf weights."

"Not anymore," she said sharply. Her face had an odd, strained look.

"Oh, you figured it out, then."

"No. I'm just not doing it anymore. Wade's doing the books the old way. We only use the computer for the kids' Nintendo these days."

"Wade's managing the books? How's the ranch doing?"

"Who knows? He never tells me anything. I'm just here to have babies and cook, didn't you know that?" She stabbed her needle into the fabric and gave an ironic laugh. "Keep the Harper dynasty in heirs, so to speak."

"You must have some idea about how things are going. What does Mom Harper say about Wade doing the books?"

"Benni, since Jack died, all she does is watch soap operas, call her sister in Abilene and talk about moving back there. As for the money, all I know is when I ask for it, Wade gives it to me. He was looking at new trucks last week and talking about paying cash, so we can't be doing that bad, can we?" She set the sampler down on the table next to her. "I don't know what's going on with him, but I'm telling you, if it doesn't stop soon,

I'm taking the kids and moving back to town with my mom." Her face flushed in anger.

"Where is he?"

"Out in the north pasture repairing some fencing." She gave a sarcastic snort. "Or so he says."

"Want me to try talking to him again?"

"Do what you want, but don't hold your breath waiting for him to tell you anything."

You're crazy, I told myself as I bumped across the dirt roads. Stay out of it. But it wasn't just Wade and Sandra's marriage I was concerned about. The fact that he was doing the books and he was thinking about paying cash for a new truck made me suspicious. I knew better than anyone that there was no way the ranch could afford a new truck. As with most cattle ranches these days, the Harper Ranch was land-rich and cash-poor. I wanted to know what had changed.

Wade and Arturo, a wiry, bandy-legged man in ankle-skimming Wranglers, were repairing boards on an old corral. Wade raised his head when I drove up, took off his John Deere cap, and wiped his forehead with the back of his sleeve. He said something low to Arturo, who picked up a hammer and moved to the other side of the corral.

He walked over as I stepped down from the truck. "What do you want?" he asked.

"To talk."

"I'm done talking to you."

"Wade . . ."

"I mean it, Benni. Unless you want to discuss the weather or the price of beef, you can just get back up in that truck and drive on out of here."

"I will as soon as you tell me what's going on with the ranch."

A tense look flitted across his face. "Nothing."

"Don't give me that. I just talked to Sandra. Why aren't you using the computer anymore? I can't believe you went back to the old way. It's so inefficient. After all the money we spent on getting it set up."

"That's just it," he said. "After all the money we spent, we still can't make this place earn a plugged nickel."

It was just the opening I wanted.

"Sandra says you have plenty of money coming in," I said, looking at him intently. He avoided my eyes. "Wade, you know and I know that's impossible. I did the books for ten years. Where are you getting the money to buy a new truck?"

"I was just looking at them. Doesn't cost nothing to look."

"Wade, don't screw around with me. I know you were involved with Marla and I suspect she had some kind of blackmail scheme going on. Have you stepped into her shoes? Is that where you're getting your money?"

His face twisted in confusion. "What are you talking about?"

"That napkin with Marla's number on it. The nights you're gone until two or three in the morning. Was it just an affair or were you working on this blackmail thing too?"

"I'm not blackmailing nobody. Marla and I had something going, but not for long. She knew I needed money, so she put me in touch with some guy who needed some delivery work done. Shit, then she got pissed because I wouldn't give her a cut. Some people." He spit a stream of tobacco juice.

"What are you delivering?" I asked, my stomach rolling. He couldn't possibly be that stupid.

He wiped his forehead again. "I meet this guy in Trigger's twice a week. He gives me a package. I deliver it to another guy in some bar up the coast. That's it."

"And how much are you paid to do this?"

He mumbled under his breath.

"What?"

"I said, a thousand."

"Each time?"

He nodded.

"How long have you been doing this?" Without thinking, I hit the side of the truck with my bandaged hand. A sharp stab of pain made me regret it.

"Couple of months. Look, it's not what you think."

"You're an idiot, Wade Harper. I'm not stupid and I thought you weren't, either. Those have to be drugs you're delivering. You could go to prison for years if you got caught. Why would you do such an idiotic thing?"

"We're losing the ranch, that's why," he snapped. "You were right, okay? Jack was right. We should have made all those changes. We should have done it years ago. But it's too late now. I can't make it. I can't do it. I can't do it alone." A sound something like a sob rumbled deep from within him.

"Oh, Wade," I said, reaching over to touch his arm. He shoved it away.

"I even tried to sell some of the land. To a stinkin' bunch of lawyers from L.A. They wanted to grow wine grapes. But they bought over near Atascadero. Got a better deal. I couldn't even do that right." With the toe of his worn boot, he kicked at a gopher hole.

"I'm putting the whole place up for sale. Ma's been wanting to move back to Texas and live with Uncle Bob on his place, be near her sister. Bob's manager quit on him a while back and he's getting too old to take care of it. Me and Sandra are going back with her. If no one will buy the ranch, then I'm letting the bank have it."

"You're leaving San Celina?" I asked, astonished.

"I don't know what else to do."

"Does Sandra know?"

"Not yet. I was going to talk to her about it tonight. I just decided myself yesterday, when I told the guy at Trigger's I wasn't going to be delivering any more packages. Those two murders spooked me."

"Do me a favor, okay? Tell her everything. About the drugs. About Marla. Set her mind at ease. Start fresh."

"I don't know," he said, wiping his mouth. "She's pretty pissed."

"She'll forgive you," I said. "Turn on that Harper charm. Believe me, I remember how well it works."

He looked at the ground, then back up. "I have one more thing to tell you."

"What?" I asked, alarmed at the seriousness in his voice.

"It's about the night Jack died."

Though the sun was warm on the back of my neck, I shivered. "Oh, Wade, no." By the tone of his voice I knew he was going to tell me something I didn't want to hear. Like a child, I wanted to put my hands over my ears and block out his words.

"I'm sorry, Benni," he said, his voice hoarse with emotion. "I'm real sorry."

"Just tell me what it is, Wade." I took a step forward, squeezing my hands into fists. My right hand throbbed, but it was as if the pain wasn't in my hand, but floated around it.

"I lied about that night. I did make it to Trigger's before he left. We argued again out in the parking lot. Then I left. If I'd stayed, I could have stopped him. I *should* have stayed." He looked up at the sky and swallowed convulsively.

I didn't know what to say. How could it be that no one had ever told me about this before? I guess the good ole boy network was alive and well in San Celina. I wanted to scream, cry, hit him, ram my truck into a tree.

I didn't do any of those things. It didn't really matter. It didn't change anything. Dead was still dead.

"I'm glad you told me," I said, not certain how I was going to feel about my reaction later. I only knew I didn't want to end things with Wade in anger. Jack would have hated that. For all their fights, Jack loved his brother. "Is there anything else?"

"No." He hesitated. "I don't know what else to say. He was my little brother, Benni. I should have protected him." He looked at me, eyes squinting against the sun. "I'm sorry."

"So am I," I said and climbed into the truck.

I watched Wade in the rearview mirror as I drove away. Arturo ambled over, pushed his hat back, said something to him. Wade answered, then bent over, picked up a hammer and started walking toward the corral. Through the pale brown dust kicked up by the truck, when I drove far enough away, he looked almost like Jack walking away. Then, when I got a little further, he looked just like anybody and then, all of a sudden, I couldn't see him anymore.

17

I DROVE PAST the big house without stopping to say goodbye to Sandra. I knew I'd see her again before they left. Any questions she had right now were up to Wade to answer. If he would. I thought about what he said. Should he have stopped Jack? Was that his responsibility? Are we ever really responsible for anyone else? All I knew is that if he had, Jack would be alive right now.

Driving under the arches at the end of the driveway felt different this time. Inside, I ached, as if someone had pummeled my heart. The Harper Ranch had been my home for almost as long as I'd lived with Dove and Daddy. I couldn't imagine someone else living there. I thought of all the fences I'd fixed, the vegetable garden Sandra and I spent so many hours working in, the live Christmas tree Jack and I planted in the backyard of the old house last January. The Harpers moving back to Texas made me think of the game I played as a kid—Big Step, Little Step—where the caller would sing out your name and what kind of step you were allowed to take. I felt like they all were taking one giant step forward while I was left standing behind.

It was dark by the time I got home. I didn't notice the car sitting across the street from my house until the door slammed. If it had been a sniper, I'd be dead. When I saw who it was walking toward me, I thought, I don't need this right now.

"Where have you been all day?" Ortiz asked. He must have come straight from work because he was still in a gray suit, jacket unbuttoned, tie loosened.

"Why don't you get a hobby?" I asked, climbing the steps to my porch. I fumbled with the keys, realizing for the first time that my palm was wet. I looked down at my bandage; it was soaked with blood.

"I knew you needed stitches." He took the keys from my hand and opened the door. "Get that bandage off and I'll put a clean one on." He took off his jacket and started rolling up the sleeves of his white shirt. I started to protest, then decided I was just too emotionally drained to make the effort.

"So, what did you do today?" he asked again as he held my hand over the kitchen sink and poured peroxide over it.

I yelped and tried to pull back.

"Don't be such a baby," he said, gripping tighter. "Well?"

"Why don't you take up jogging or something?"

He pushed me down on a kitchen chair and reached for the first-aid supplies over the refrigerator. It occurred to me that he was getting way too familiar with my place of residence.

"I do jog. I called the museum three times today. They said you never came in. Where were you?"

"Running errands."

He exhaled sharply as he rebandaged my hand. "We found the truck driven by the person who shot at you."

"You did? Who were they? Why were they shooting at me? How did you find them?"

"Apparently, your neighbor, Mr. Treton, has an excellent pair of binoculars."

"So I've heard."

"Anyway, he keeps them right by the window, and while he was dialing 911, he wrote down a partial license plate of the truck. That's why I was trying to get in touch with you all day."

"Oh," I said. "I just assumed you wanted to harass me as usual." His annoyed look cheered me. "So who was it?"

"Good question. The truck was reported stolen out of a grocery store parking lot about a half hour before you were shot at."

"Did you dust for fingerprints?"

"I know my job, Benni," he said wryly. "Wiped clean."

"Oh." I propped my left elbow up on the kitchen table and rested my cheek on it. "So what happens now?"

"What happens now is we go get some dinner. Unless, of course, some food has miraculously appeared in your refrigerator."

I was hungry, starving in fact. But the thought of spending an evening sitting across from Ortiz eluding his questions was not the least bit appealing. I was afraid he'd somehow worm out of me what I was doing tomorrow.

"Thanks, but I'm not hungry."

"Well, I am." He picked up the kitchen phone and started dialing.

"What do you think you're doing?"

"I think I'm ordering a pizza."

"What? You can't . . ."

He held up his palm and quickly ordered a large thick-crust mushroom and black-olive pizza and a six-pack of Cokes.

"You're incredibly arrogant," I said when he hung up the phone.

He smiled at me, unruffled. "In my line of work, that could be taken as a compliment." He gathered up the first-aid supplies and stuck them back in the cupboard. "You really need to invest in some more first-aid supplies."

"Who do you think you are? You walk in like you own the place . . ." Then something dawned on me. "Oh, no, you are *not* spending the night here again. That's final. No discussion, no argument, no way. I mean it."

He loosened his tie further and laughed. "No, not tonight. I don't think they'll try again. Besides, my reputation couldn't stand it."

"Your reputation? What about mine?"

"A woman who's found two bodies in less than two weeks? Sweetheart, your reputation is already suspect."

I stared at him for a moment, trying to decide what I should do. Part of me wanted to tell him to get lost. Another part didn't want to spend another evening with no one to talk to except the newscasters on TV.

"Look," I said. "I'll let you stay the evening if you promise one thing. No questions. For once, let's just be like normal human beings. Can you do that? Just for tonight?"

"Are you holding anything back from me?"

I looked him straight in the eye. "Yes."

He smiled slowly. "Well, looks like we've made some progress here. At least you're telling the truth now. Okay, just for tonight then. I think it would be wiser if you told me what you're hiding, but I'll try not to mention it again."

So for three hours we ate pizza, drank Cokes and laughed at the similarities of growing up in small towns in Kansas and California.

At one point, I asked him something that had been bugging me since this whole thing started.

"How did you know I was at Trigger's the day after Marla's murder?"

"Very complex police procedure. I had you tailed."

"I didn't see anyone following me," I said in amazement.

"Good, that means it was done right. Now, I have a question for you."

I looked at him suspiciously.

"Not about the case," he said. "Tell me, did you really castrate a bull when you were ten?"

I couldn't help but laugh. "Oh, that. It didn't seem to impress you much when I said it."

"Cops learn early to hide their true feelings." He picked an olive off his slice of pizza and popped it in his mouth. "I won't tell you what went through my mind. Did you, or was that a lot of hot air?"

"In a manner of speaking. Actually, it was a calf, and my dad did help me. It was part of a 4-H project, so I had to do it rather than the ranch hands who usually castrated our calves. It's not as hard as it sounds. You take this thing called an elastrator and fit them around the scrotum of the calf. Then when both testicles are through the rubber rings, you release the pressure and the ring constricts. It cuts off the blood supply and the testicles eventually fall off. Easy as pie. Doesn't hurt except for the first hour or two."

"Easy for you to say." His face held a slightly pained look.

I laughed and picked up another piece of pizza. "C'mon, Friday. I thought you said you spent every summer at your grandfather's farm."

"Wheat farm. Big difference. No blood and guts there unless you fall in front of a combine."

"Why philosophy?" I asked at one time during the evening. "I'd expect a cop to get a degree in criminal justice or torture techniques or something."

"Aaron—Chief Davidson—talked me into it. We were partners when I was going for my bachelor's. I talked so much about this philosophy class I was taking, he said I'd be stupid not to keep studying something that excited me so much."

A flicker of some emotion crossed his face and I wondered just how sick his friend was. "He was right," he said. "Being a cop is tough. There's only so much crap you can see without it affecting how you view life. Those classes saved my life. Now, tell me about you. Why do you call your grandmother Dove?"

"Well, the family story goes that my dad didn't talk until he was almost three years old and when he did, the first word he said was 'Dove' because that was what my grandfather always called her. Since Daddy is the oldest of six kids, it just set a precedent. No one's ever called her anything else."

By the time he stood up to leave at ten o'clock, I was almost sorry to see him go. But my mind was already on my trip to Salinas.

"This is my unlisted number." He jotted it down on the back of a business card as I walked him to the door. "Call me if you need me."

I turned the card over and read it. "Aaron Davidson—Chief of Police."

"They plan on him coming back," he said lightly. "Why don't you come by the station tomorrow and we'll have lunch?"

I continued staring at the card, afraid to look up, afraid he'd somehow read in my face what my plans were for tomorrow. But if I said no, he'd be suspicious. He might even have me followed.

"Sure," I said, feeling sad and angry at the same time. It was much easier being deceitful to someone you didn't like. "How about one o'clock?"

"That's fine."

After he left, I leaned against the front door, scratching my cheek with the edge of his business card. Any semblance of friendship started tonight would be over when I didn't show up for lunch tomorrow. A part of me felt regretful, but not enough to cancel my plans.

The tule fog was heavy when I left the next morning at five o'clock with a small overnight bag holding a change of clothes. At the last minute, I stuck Jack's pistol in my purse. The road to Salinas was desolate in spots, and after the incident with the pickup truck, I felt better about having it with me. I'd left a message with Constance's housekeeper that I was going to Santa Barbara to check on a couple of used pottery wheels and a kiln that a community college was selling. If nothing else, I was getting adept at lying. A useful skill if I ever wanted to sell used cars or vacation time-shares, two distinct career probabilities if Constance actually noticed how much work I'd been missing lately.

I stopped for gas in the town of Gonzales and ate at the first open cafe. A hand-printed sign peeking out from behind pink gingham curtains promised the best *huevos rancheros* in town. From the number of people, mostly Spanish, crowded in the small dining room, it must have been the truth. I sat down at the gray Formica counter and spun the aluminum creamer as I waited for my order. The buzz of mixed English-Spanish conversations reminded me of weekends at Elvia's house when I was a girl. A Spanish-music station played a song I remember Elvia's mother singing. The Aragon brothers, children of rock-and-roll, made fun of the Spanish folk music Sẽnora Aragon loved, though one of them, Rafael, did his master's thesis on it, and in the process, began to listen to it on the sly. Whether you want it or not, your upbringing can sneak up on you when you're not looking.

The spicy, meaty smell of the eggs and salsa was more appealing when they weren't actually sitting in front of me. The closer Salinas loomed, the more my stomach churned worrying about what I would find out from Suzanne Hart. I couldn't help but wonder if I was delving into this deeper than I should. Was knowledge always better than ignorance? That was a philosophical question that probably had no answer, or maybe too many. I thought about Ortiz. It was probably just the kind of question he'd love to debate or, more likely, lecture on.

"No like?" my chubby, coronet-braided waitress asked as she refilled my coffee cup.

"*Si*," I said, and smiled apologetically. "Not hungry. *No hambre*." I patted my stomach and tried to remember the Spanish word for sick.

"Ah." She rubbed her own stomach and I noticed for the first time she wasn't chubby, she was pregnant. Her face held a question.

"No." I shook my head and sighed. "*Corazón*." I lay my hand across the front of my flannel shirt, over my heart.

She touched a small brown hand to her smooth cheek. "Men," she said, nodding her head in sympathy.

"Yeah," I agreed, thinking about Jack and Wade, and with some reluctance, Ortiz. "Men."

I stopped at a Unocal gas station just outside of Salinas to check the phone book. I looked under "Hart" and found four listings. None of them knew a Suzanne. That left the bars. There were no listings under "Bar" and an unbelievable number under "Restaurants." I tried

"Nightclubs" and found a list that seemed manageable and probable. She might have gotten a job doing something else, but it seemed unlikely. The money made by cocktail waitressing was good, and people usually stayed with what they knew. For two tens and an extra five, the young gas station attendant sold me his last two rolls of quarters. I checked my watch—eleven-thirty—most of the bars should be open. I leaned against the glass wall of the phone booth and started dialing.

A little over an hour later, I had three possibilities—two Suzannes and a Susan. None of them with the last name Hart. But then, there was no guarantee that she was using that name. Susan was working now, but the two Suzannes worked the evening shift and wouldn't be on until six o'clock.

The Susan ended up being, as I expected, a washout. She'd lived in Salinas her whole life, had never been to San Celina and was married with twins, a Ford Explorer and a new guinea pig. All of this was told to me in less than five minutes. I would have known more if I hadn't insisted that I had a pressing engagement across town in fifteen minutes.

The next six hours dragged like one of Garnet's family stories. I walked for hours, stopping every so often for coffee or a Coke, too nervous to eat or sit anywhere for long. By the time I drove to the first bar, a long, narrow stucco building painted red and called the Short Branch Saloon, the caffeine had me as jumpy as a cat during an earthquake.

The Suzanne who worked there arrived a half hour late for her shift. I drank another Coke, fended off two cowboys wanting to two-step and tried to still my nervous foot. By the time she came in, I almost pounced on her. I followed her into the tiny, rose-scented bathroom and questioned her while she slipped into her short denim skirt and satiny Western shirt. In the dingy mirror she applied a thick layer of peach base on her pale, middle-aged face.

"I don't think I'm the gal you're looking for, hon." She took a rat-tailed brush and teased the crown of her white-blond hair, then smoothed a thin layer of hair over it. I hadn't seen anyone do that to their hair in twenty-five years. "I don't know any Marla, and I sure as heck never worked in San Celina. Dated a guy from there once. Rodney Joe Barnett. Know him?"

"No," I said, leaning against the sink, feeling like I wanted to throw up.

"You okay, hon?" She looked at me, concerned. "You look awful pale. You want some of my Max Factor here?" She held out the liquid makeup bottle.

"I'm fine, thanks." I bent over and splashed cold water on my face. "Too much caffeine, I think."

"We just can't handle it like we used to, can we?" she said with a final jab to her hair.

My last chance was a large, splashy country-western bar called Aunt Sudie's Goodtime Emporium and Drinking Establishment. The sign had enough neon in it to make the grade in Vegas. It attracted a crowd younger than most country-western bars and there was a six-dollar cover charge. I went up to the crowded horseshoe-shaped bar in the middle and asked for Suzanne.

"Called in sick," the thin, gauzy-haired bartender said, laying a red napkin down in front of me. "What'll it be?"

My heart dropped into my stomach. I ordered a Coke and tried to think of what to do.

"If her real name is Suzanne Hart, I need to talk to her," I blurted out when he set the drink in front of me. My voice sounded more desperate than I intended.

He gave me a curious but guarded look. "What about?"

"It's personal."

He looked at me and shrugged.

"Were you the guy I talked to earlier?"

"I don't know. When was that?"

"I called earlier and asked if there was a Suzanne working here. You, or somebody, said yes. Was that you?"

"Could be." He wiped the counter in front of me. I started to speak again, but he held up a finger and took an order from three giggling girls wearing almost identical outfits of short black denim skirts, fringed Western shirts and large Hopi-style silver earrings.

"What do you want her for?" He turned back to me, his pale green eyes mild and watchful.

"I have some information she might want," I said.

"You tell me the information," he said. "And maybe I'll pass it on to her."

"I told you. It's personal."

With an indifferent look he started mixing the drink orders of a tired-looking waitress in silver boots. The house band struck up "Mama, Don't Let Your Babies Grow Up to be Cowboys." He hummed along with the song, his eyes shifting over to me every so often.

"What makes you think she's the Suzanne you're looking for?" he asked about ten minutes later. He folded his towel and hooked it to his belt.

"Tell her Marla's dead, and we'll see if she's the right Suzanne."

That got a reaction.

"I'll be right back."

He called the other bartender over, whispered in his ear and then headed for the back of the bar, skirting the large dance floor filled with two-stepping bodies. I contemplated following, afraid he might take off and spirit her away before I could talk with her, but he was gone before I could get out of my seat. I poked at my ice and prayed he wasn't lying.

A few minutes later he came back, an angry look on his face.

"She'll see you," he said, coming back behind the bar. "But not without me there and I don't get off until midnight."

"But . . ." I started.

"Take it or leave it."

"Fine," I snapped. "I'll be waiting back there." I pointed to a small round table as far away from the dance floor and band as possible. Even so, I fought off dance requests all night, my refusals becoming more irritable as the night dragged on and the rhinestone cowboys got more obnoxious. After five hours of the house band's repertoire of twenty country songs, I could have played lead guitar on any of them.

"Brown Jeep's mine," the bartender said as we walked out into the clear, cold night shortly after midnight.

I followed him to a neighborhood of inexpensive tract homes a few miles away. He pulled up in the driveway behind a light-colored Dodge Charger and waited for me to park in front and walk across the wet, nubby grass.

He opened the door with a key from a ring attached to a long chain on his belt and stepped in ahead of me.

"Suzanne, it's Nick."

I stepped inside the small, overheated living room. A redheaded woman, thick through the middle, with spindly legs in black stretch pants and a billowing zebra-print top rose from the green plaid sofa.

"What happened to Marla?" she asked in a low, grating voice.

I inhaled unevenly and told her about Marla and Eric. Her face paled when I finished. The tattooed dagger over her right thumb seemed to lengthen as her fingers danced with an unlit cigarette.

"I don't want to cause any trouble for you," I said. "Just tell me if any of this has to do with my husband."

"Who's your husband?" she asked.

"John Harper. Jack. He was killed in a car accident on old Highway One about nine months ago."

"Oh, no." She bent over and held her head in her hands.

"What?" I asked in a desperate voice, my pulse racing.

She sat up, gestured for a light from Nick, who shook his head.

"Just give it," she said. "I'll quit some other time. "I worked with Marla at Trigger's, but I guess you know that already."

I nodded and she continued.

"One night we closed the place like we usually did, pushing the drunks out the door, counting the till. Then we decided to take a six-pack and a pizza and go down to the beach. Marla was having some man problems and we were going to talk."

She inhaled deeply on her cigarette and gave a tiny, cat cough. "She knew of a beach where you could drive right out on the sand. We were going to watch the sunrise. On the way we passed someone stumbling along the road. It was the strangest thing. Not a car anywhere. Just this guy tripping on his own feet along this little road. All dirty and bloody. Big gash on his arm."

"Who was he?" I asked.

She shrugged. "Some guy Marla knew from the bar. I only worked there a couple of months, so I didn't get to know them like she did."

"Why was he there?"

"I guess his car had broke down or something. We figured he probably wrecked it. I don't know. The guy was drunk as a pig. Marla hauled him into the back of her van and we drove to some ranch house outside San Celina. He could barely walk, but she helped him up to the front door and went inside. She wasn't in there but five minutes and then she took me home. The pizza was cold and the beer hot by then. Fool ruined our night." She took another long drag off her cigarette.

"Go on," I said harshly.

Suzanne eyed me coldly. "Hold your horses. Look, all I know is the next day she was reading the paper at the bar and told me she'd found a sure thing. I thought she was talking about a racehorse or something. A couple a days later she gave me five hundred bucks and told me not to tell anyone about what I saw that night. When I moved up here to be near my sister, she just kept sending money to me. Said she might need me to tell what I saw someday. It was no skin off my back. I took the money."

"Why did you conceal where you were, change your name?"

"She just thought it was a good idea. This was like cops and robbers to her. I didn't care. Just went back to my maiden name. Hart was my second husband's name."

"Could you find this ranch again?"

"It was past three in the morning after an eight-hour shift and four beers. I didn't know my name, much less where we dropped that guy off at."

"What did he look like?" I pressed.

"I don't know. Like a guy. Middle-ageish. Good-looking. I don't really remember."

"Did he have a mustache?" Wade? Ray? I didn't want to consider it, but I had to.

She thought for a moment, pulling absently at a strand of her thin red hair. "No, I don't think so. Seems to me he was clean-shaven. Looked like something the cat coughed up, but he was a pretty good looking guy. That, I remember."

"What did he look like?" I asked again, feeling desperate. This was all so ambiguous, like no real information at all. "Did Marla say his name at all? Did she talk to him at all?"

"Look, all's I remember is when she helped him out of the van, she made some kind of joke, called him something that made him laugh."

"What?" I said, my voice frantic. "What did she say? What did she call him?"

"Jimmy Olsen." Suzanne gave a wet cough. "She called him Jimmy Olsen. Now, what do you think she meant by that?"

18

I WANTED TO drive. Anywhere. Coming to the freeway on-ramp, north and south beckoned with conflicting arms, like divorcing parents with an only child. I pictured myself speeding north through the pastel housing tracts of San Jose, the pumpkin patches of Half Moon Bay, over the Golden Gate Bridge, up the long cold northern coast of Calfornia, Oregon, Washington, to Canada; changing my name, my citizenship, dyeing my hair black.

I drove south. The shock of finding out Carl was in the jeep with Jack the night he died finally caused an uncontrollable trembling in me that made it impossible to drive. Outside Paso Robles, I pulled over and parked in a scenic turnout overlooking a dark field where a farmer was night plowing, the headlights of his tractor a long silver knife in the blackness. Unusual for this time of year. I wondered what problems drove him out of his warm bed to carve the long, even furrows. I sympathized with him. At least plowing a field was something you could control.

I climbed up on the hood of the truck, leaned back

against the windshield, and stared up at the sky.

"Feelin' restless," Jack would have said on a night like this, stars like white stitches in a navy quilt sky. We'd ride across cattle-cropped pastures, miles from the ranch, tie the horses to an oak tree, spread out an old wool blanket and look for planets.

"Like playing connect the dots with God," he'd say, then turn to me and we'd make slow love, the lemony taste of his tongue, the husky rake of his calloused fingers on my neck, the sound of the horses blowing watery sighs in and out; nowhere to go, they seemed to say, all the time in the world.

I never knew myself capable of the kind of hatred I felt at that moment.

It became finally, as the dark sky faded into the gray-orange of morning, a blind, raging fury that threatened to explode like a dandelion at a child's puff.

As the sun came up, I started toward San Celina. I had no idea what I was going to say to Carl. It never occurred to me to be afraid, even though he'd probably killed two people. I only knew that I had to hear the truth of what happened the night Jack died.

I stopped by his dad's ranch first. The housekeeper informed me that both Carl and J.D. had been at the *Tribune* since three A.M. The computer had gone down and things were a mess. When I reached the newspaper, I used the employees entrance in back, walked through the empty lunchroom, past the unoccupied desks. The scent of a working office lingered: the crispy smell of old french fries, a mixture of sweet perfumes, the undeniable scent of a forbidden cigarette.

Carl sat in his office, his back facing the door as he talked on the telephone. I stood for a few minutes looking at him through the glass windows. The shininess of his blond hair, the very aliveness of it, angered me as he leaned back in his chair and laughed at something his caller said.

I paced in front of his office, not knowing how to start. Somewhere, a radio played softly. An oldies station. "Do you believe in magic?" the radio sang.

You remember the oddest things those moments in your life that are pivotal points of change.

I had been asleep in my childhood bed when Dove woke me that early morning nine months ago. For a split second, her hand on my shoulder, her voice sharp in my ear, I was a little girl again, time to get up, do my chores, run for the school bus, braids flying. My bare feet stung with cold as I stood in the kitchen where Wade told me, his voice tight with grief, choking out the words. The kitchen smelled of strawberries, onions and the steaks Dove had fried for dinner. I ignored Dove's arms, backed up against the refrigerator, shivering as if I would never be warm again. The refrigerator cycled, a mechanical insect in my ear; Daddy cursed softly in the background. "Benni, Benni," Wade had said.

I opened the office door.

"Benni," Carl said. He turned his chair around and hung up the phone. He gestured to the brown office chair in front of his desk. "What's wrong?" he asked when I remained standing. "You look like death microwaved." He laughed at his own joke, then stopped when I didn't respond.

"I've been up all night," I said. "Driving."

He furrowed his brows in concern. "Having trouble sleeping?"

"I went to Salinas. To find Suzanne Hart." I waited for his reaction.

"Oh?" he said, his face blank. "Who's Suzanne Hart?" He had to be the best actor in the world.

"A woman with a very interesting story."

"Concerning what?"

I set my purse down on one of the chairs in front of his desk. "I wish you'd just tell me," I said.

"Tell you what?" He tilted his head, perplexed.

"About Jack. Suzanne told me everything. Why keep pretending?"

He looked at me, his handsome features liquid with confusion. "Benni, I have no idea what you're rambling on about."

I started to cry. I couldn't help it. At a time when I most wanted to stay in control, be strong, my emotions sold me out. The tears came in great torrents down my cheeks, wet, salty, hot. Losing control made me angry, which made me cry even more.

"Oh, honey," Carl said. He stood up and came around the desk, holding out his arms.

"Get back," I said, my voice soggy from tears.

"All right," he said, his voice slightly hurt. He pulled some tissue out of the box sitting on his desk and held them out to me.

"No." I reached into my purse to search for some. I didn't want to take anything from him. My hands touched Jack's pistol. I didn't even think twice about pulling it out. I pointed it at Carl.

"Tell me about the night Jack died," I said.

"That isn't funny, Benni," he said.

"It isn't meant to be."

He glanced up as the door of his office opened. Julio, the night supervisor, started to talk, then stopped cold when he glanced over in my direction and saw the gun.

"It's okay, Julio," Carl said in an easy voice. "Just a joke Mrs. Harper is playing. Go back to work."

Julio gave him a nervous glance and backed out slowly.

"Now look what you've done," Carl said. "You've gone and scared Julio. Honey, why don't you just put the gun away and we'll talk about this rationally."

"Don't call me that," I said coldly. "And I'm not putting it away until you tell me what happened the night Jack died."

"What are you talking about?" His voice became irritated.

"Look, Carl, I know you were with him. I talked to Suzanne Hart. She told me everything."

"Who is this Suzanne Hart you keep talking about?"

I felt the gun tremble in my throbbing hand. Stop it, I commanded myself. Hold on.

"How could you? He laid there for hours before anyone found him. What if he was alive, Carl? What if he was alive?"

"I have no idea what you're talking about."

I felt the tears start again. "Don't lie to me, Carl. Not now. I swear, I'll use this gun if you lie anymore." For the first time, a look of fear came over his face.

"Honestly, Benni, I don't know what you're talking about," he said. "I admit, I don't remember him leaving but . . ."

"Don't give me that."

"I swear on my mother's grave, I didn't know about Jack's death until the next day."

"Who was driving? Is that why you killed Marla and Eric? Were they blackmailing you because they knew you were driving?"

He looked at me in confusion. "You mean the Chenier and Griffin murders? What have they got to do with all this?"

"What's going on here?" J.D. slammed the door open and stood, a big silver bull, in the middle of the room. "Young lady, I didn't believe it when Julio told me. You'd better give me that gun right now."

"Tell him," I said to Carl. "Tell your dad what a fine, upstanding citizen you are. What a good *friend* you are."

"What's she talking about?" J.D. asked.

Carl glanced at his dad and held out his hands, a dumbfounded look on his face.

"Girl, what would your daddy think?" J.D. said.

"He'd probably tell me to pull the trigger," I said. "He taught me that friendship meant something. You don't walk out on a friend. You don't leave friends to die alone."

"Give me the gun, Benni," J.D. said. "You're upset. You don't know what you're saying. Give me the gun and we'll just pretend like this never happened. Come on now."

"You just don't get it, do you? He's a murderer, J.D.," I said. "He left Jack to die and then killed Marla and Eric because they were blackmailing him. You raised yourself a fine boy here. You ought to be proud." Tears flowed freely down my cheeks again. The gun trembled in my hand. I wasn't sure what to do now.

I turned back to Carl. "I ought to shoot you. Let you lie there and feel your life drain out of you, inch by inch, like the way you did Jack."

"I don't remember," Carl said, his voice almost a whisper. "Benni, I never wanted you to know this but I don't remember a lot of what happened the night Jack died. Dad told me about Jack's accident the next day when I woke up."

"I don't believe you."

"I've had about all I'm going to take from you, young lady," J.D. said. He pulled a small pearl-handled pistol from his pocket and pointed it at me. "Now, give me that gun right now."

"Dad!" Carl exclaimed. "Put that away. It's bad enough Benni's gone nuts. This is getting ridiculous."

"I mean it, girl." J.D. gestured with his gun. "Give it to me now."

"How can you protect him, J.D.?" I said. "He killed two people. He left Jack to die. Don't you think he should have to pay for what he did?"

"I didn't—" Carl started.

"He didn't know about Jack until the next day," J.D. interrupted. "It was a dumbass thing, but he didn't do it on purpose. Jack was his best friend. Jack wouldn't have wanted him to have his life ruined over a stupid mistake."

"What are you saying?" I looked at him, confused.

"You heard me. You heard him. He didn't know what he was doing."

A thick, hoarse groan, like that of an injured dog, came from Carl. J.D. and I turned to look at him. His mouth worked but no sound came out. The look on his face was like someone who'd seen a ghost, or reality for the first time.

"You mean, oh shit, I didn't . . . I'm sorry. . . ." The words spilled out in a torrent, his face contorted in a horrible mask of realization and remorse.

"It wasn't your fault, son," J.D. said in a soft voice that sounded strange coming from him. He walked toward his son. "No one blames you." His face was full of some emotion, though I couldn't tell what—love, pity, regret.

"Wait," I said, the gun still trembling in my hand. "If he didn't even know about any of this, then he couldn't have killed Marla and Eric. Who else . . ." Then it dawned on me. But by that time, J.D. had already pointed the gun back at me.

"You never did know when to give up, Benni Harper," J.D. said. "You just couldn't let well enough alone."

"J.D." All I could whisper was his name. It had taken me hours to get used to the idea that Carl was a killer. That it was really J.D. seemed too shocking to even contemplate.

"Dad?" Carl looked unbelieving at J.D. His face was wet with tears. Even so, I couldn't help but feel disgust. He might not have killed Marla and Eric, but he'd still left Jack alone to die. Drunk or not, I didn't know if I could ever forgive him for that.

"I'll take care of it, Carl. You just go on to my office and wait for me." J.D. gestured with his gun for Carl to leave.

Carl looked at me, at the gun I had pointed at him, and gave a small, bitter laugh. "You'd be better off shooting me now, Benni. Dad's obviously not going to let you out of here, so you might as well perform one last community service before you die. Then we'll all be where we want. You'll be with Jack, and I'll be in hell where I belong."

"Carl," J.D. said. "Quit talking foolish."

He turned to his dad, a look close to amusement on his face. "Give it up, old man. You never did know when to quit helping, did you? You can't buy or manipulate your way out of this one. Why did you have to kill those people? Why?"

"Because we made a deal, a little every month. But that wasn't good enough for her. She wanted more, a lot more. Then that little wimp thought he'd take over when I got rid of her." J.D. shook his head. "Fixed his wagon. Kid was sitting there counting his money when I met him at the museum. He honestly thought we could work something out. As if J.D. Freedman would be held hostage by some little twerp like him." He gave a low chuckle.

Carl laughed. It was a creepy, disjointed laughter that

made me feel as if someone had dropped an ice cube down my back. J.D. laughed with him until, after a moment, he realized his son wasn't laughing with him, but at him. J.D.'s face became as still as a buck hearing a leaf crunch.

Carl picked up the phone.

"What are you doing?" J.D. said.

"Calling the police."

"Have you gone loco?" he said. "Put that phone down now."

"Or what? You'll shoot me? You should have done that the night Jack died; then none of this would have happened."

He dialed 911 and spoke evenly to the dispatcher. He was smiling when he hung up. "Someone's already called."

"That stupid Julio," J.D. said. "I told him not to call the police."

"Guess he thought he was protecting you," Carl said, laughing that crazy laugh again.

Out of the corner of my eye, through the glass windows of Carl's office, I could see the police moving cautiously through the outer room, guns drawn. Miguel's face stood out from the rest. It held a slightly sick look as he watched me hold the gun on Carl. I concentrated on the throbbing in my hand, trying to decide what to do. I held my breath and waited.

"Put the gun down, Benni," Miguel called out. From where he was standing, he could only see J.D.'s back. He didn't realize he had a gun.

"I can't," I called back, my voice high and wavering. More activity in the outer office. I glanced over and saw Ortiz's black hair among the uniforms—messy, uncombed, as if he'd just crawled out of bed.

"Give it up, Dad," Carl said in a voice as gentle as

a mother's with a sick child. "There's nothing else you can do. It's over."

J.D. stared at his son for a moment. A look passed between them, and for a moment, it was hard to tell who was the parent, who was the child. Years appeared on J.D.'s face, like one of those high-speed camera tricks that show a flower blooming and dying in the course of seconds. He slowly placed the gun on the desk in front of his son as if giving him a precious gift.

I lowered my gun and in seconds the room was full of police. Miguel gently pried the gun out of my hand.

"Are you okay?" he asked, laying a hand on my shoulder.

"I think so." It was too much to comprehend right then. Someone I'd known since I was a little girl had killed two people, was willing to kill me. For what? To protect his son? His reputation? Sheer ego? I stood over in a corner of the office while the police tried to sort out what had happened.

Ortiz walked over to where I was standing. I hugged my jacket close around me. All I could think was home—I want to go home.

"What happened?" he asked, his stern, cop voice like a splash of cold water. In a voice that broke every so often, I told him everything.

"Why didn't you come to me?" he said, gripping my shoulder so tight I could almost feel the bruise starting. I tried to pull away, but he wouldn't let go. "Do you realize what could have happened? Someone could have been hurt. You could have been killed."

At least I got separate billing.

"I ought to arrest you," he said.

"Arrest me? After I solved your case? Why would you arrest me?"

"I could fill five reports with the laws you've broken.

And bringing a gun into a situation like this. That's about the stupidest . . ."

"It doesn't matter," I interrupted. "I never intended on hurting him. I just wanted to . . ." I stopped, not sure about what I had wanted to do. "I just wanted the truth," I finally said.

He exploded into a barrage of Spanish. Something he said caused Miguel's eyes to widen in surprise. It was probably better I didn't know what it was. The other cops in the room inspected the shine on their shoes as his voice grew louder and more angry.

Oh, c'mon, I thought, when he didn't stop after a few minutes. I'm tired of this.

"Look, Ortiz," I said, attempting a calm, even tone. "Now, whatever it is you're saying, none of it happened, did it? I found your murderer for you. Case solved. All's well and all that." I gave my perkiest smile, fighting the urge to burst into tears.

He stopped dead and gave me a look that said he and I were back to square one.

"Book her," he said from behind clenched teeth to a shocked Miguel. "Assault with a deadly weapon."

19

"I DON'T CARE if he fires me, I'm not cuffing you," Miguel said in the same stubborn voice he'd had at six years old. He walked me to the patrol car and opened the front passenger door. "He's nuts."

I just laughed and patted his arm. Though, as Dove would say, I'd tied myself up tighter than Hogan's goat, I never felt less worried in my life. I knew somewhere down the road it was all going to cave in on me, but right at that moment, all I felt was an odd sort of giddy relief. Something had changed in me in the last two weeks. At that moment I felt like I could face anything.

"C'mon, Miguel," I said. "The worst that could happen is I spend a couple of years in the slammer. I'll write a book about it. Get rich and famous. Go on Oprah."

"That's not funny," he said, giving me a baleful look. He led me to the one cell at the end of the block reserved for women and juveniles. I was the sole resident. He left the door to the cell unlocked and brought me coffee and cups of water until I thought I was going to float away. He told me J.D. was upstairs being questioned and that he'd demanded his lawyer. They were working on obtaining a search warrant for his house. Apparently, Ortiz knew his job better than I thought. J.D. had been one of the suspects all along. I had just brought things to a head sooner than expected.

Ortiz must have cooled off slightly, because a couple of hours later, word came from up top no charges were being filed against me. After giving my statement, I was free to go.

Miguel dropped me off at the *Tribune*, where I picked up my truck. I gave enough of a statement to the reporters to appease them, then drove to my house, packed a bag, and left a message with Constance's housekeeper informing her I was taking a week off. Let her worry about the museum for a while. On the way home to Dove and Daddy, I swung by the mall. At eleven A.M. on a weekday morning, I was the shop's only customer.

"Are you sure?" The skinny girl with the platinum crew cut looked at me nervously in the mirror.

"Absolutely," I said and told her to get on with it.

"For the love of Mike," Dove said when she saw me. She ran her fingers through my newly shorn neck-length hair. "You look like one of them fashion models in the magazines." We walked out to the barn so Dove could feed an orphan calf whose mother had died while giving birth.

"Slow down, you greedy little thing," she said as she held the bottle up and the calf eagerly drank.

"What happened to the cow?" I asked as I perched on the side of the stall.

"She was just too weak to make it," Dove said. "And we don't have any spare mamas to graft it to, so I guess I'll be its mama." She looked up at me and smiled.

I smiled back. "Like with me."

"That's right. Only I'll bet you dollars to doughnuts

this one will probably be a mite easier to raise than you were."

"I was a good kid," I protested, kicking the side of the stall with the back of my boot.

"When you were sleeping."

"Dove?"

"Yes, honeybun."

"Did Mama ever talk about me to you? I mean, before she died. Was there anything she ever told you to tell me?" I don't know what I was searching for, some words of wisdom maybe, something to tell me how to make it through the rest of my life.

Dove thought for a moment. "Not really," she said. "She talked a lot about you, but it was always the things she was going to do for you. She even talked about what colors your bridesmaids' dresses were going to be. That was when you were insisting on everything you got being pink." Dove looked at me, her face still and sad. "I don't think she thought she was really going to die. Just couldn't imagine not seeing you grow up."

As we walked back to the house, she stuck her cool, dry hand on the back of my neck, then stroked my hair.

"Feels nice," she said. "Maybe I should go for it too. Garnet's going to snap a garter next time she sees you."

"It just seemed like it was time," I said, grabbing her hand and squeezing. "Where is Aunt Garnet, by the way?"

"That's right." She gave a rusty cackle. "In all *your* excitement you didn't hear the latest. Rita called."

"She did?"

"From Las Vegas."

"What's she doing there? Wait, maybe I don't want to know." I opened the back door and we went into the kitchen.

"She got married, the little fool."

"I don't believe it." I went to grab my braid and caught empty air. This new hairstyle was going to take some getting use to.

"Believe it. Garnet was so upset she went straight home to consult with the clan. Your cousin Remar's youngest son, Lyle, is doing pre-law down at the university in Little Rock. They're talking annulment."

"That's going to be a bit difficult. She's over twenty-one and I'm willing to bet the ranch *that* marriage has been more than adequately consummated."

"That's what I told Garnet, but you know her, nobody can tell her nothing. They're still hoping to get their hands on that money Rita was going to marry into."

The thought of Rita and Skeeter and the hullabaloo their marriage was causing made me smile more than once over the next few days. I helped Dove get all her pots and pans back in proper order, watched Daddy work with his latest love, a sorrel mare named Reba, and rode miles and miles over trails Jack and I had ridden together.

One day I stuck a jar of strawberry preserves in my saddlebag. As I stood on the edge of a deep ravine with the intentions of throwing it, in some great symbolic gesture, Jack's voice seemed to speak to me.

"Now, honey," he said. "There you go making something fancy out of nothing but plain old strawberries. Wouldn't they do a whole lot more good on a nice piece of toast?"

And I laughed. Maybe it was his voice in my head, or Dove's, or my own. It didn't matter. Because the whole point is, we're all a part of the people we love and they're a part of us and that never changes; it's a whole long chain, not held together by genetics but by something we can't see or measure.

I cradled the jar in my lap, sat on the edge of the ravine and watched a hawk cruise for its supper. It wasn't the last time I cried for Jack, but it would be a long time before I cried again.

"You're lucky the police didn't shoot you," Dove said on the fourth morning as she poured me a cup of coffee. She'd had me replay the scenario at least a dozen times, frustrated she missed out on the excitement.

"Believe me, I had their attention." I picked at the coffee cake she set in front of me. This was the first morning I'd slept in; the first night of good, dreamless sleep I'd had in a long time.

"Bet you scared the tar outta them," she said, the deep lines in her peachy-brown face moving upward in a grin. "All those big ole tough cops."

I grinned back. "I do believe I did."

"Good." Her braid swung around like a monkey's tail as she turned back to the turkey she was basting.

"Heard from your policeman?" She pronounced it pole-leece and she knew the answer; she was just digging at me.

"No," I said in a casual voice. He was the one thing I had purposely avoided thinking about the last four days. "Doesn't matter."

She turned, gave me a knowing look and gestured at the coffee cake.

"Eat up. You're too skinny. Most men like a little something to hold onto."

"I'll pretend you didn't say that." I pushed up the sleeves of my red sweatshirt and took a small bite, letting the brown sugar dissolve on my tongue. "Where's Daddy?"

"Outside someplace, and don't change the subject. You're too young to be alone."

"You weren't much older than me when Grampa died,"

I said. "You've been alone all this time."

"Honeybun." She pointed the dripping baster at me. "What with raising six kids and then you, I haven't been alone in over fifty years."

I rolled my eyes and played with the crumbly topping on the coffee cake.

"Elvia called earlier this morning," she said, closing the door to the oven.

"Why didn't you wake me?"

"She said she'd call back. She talked to Miguel. They got the tests back from the gun they found in J.D.'s collection. It was the one that killed the boy who worked with you. Stupid old fool. Doesn't he even watch TV? I would of got rid of it."

"Did she say anything about Carl?"

She looked at me with troubled eyes. "They can't do nothing to him, baby. There's just no proof he was driving. If they can get that Suzanne character to talk, the most he'd be charged with would be leaving the scene of an accident." She wiped her hands on her jeans, never taking her eyes off my face.

"I still can't believe J.D. would kill two people just to . . ." I couldn't think about what he really did. "To protect Carl's reputation, his own? I don't understand it."

"Habit," Dove said. "He's been bailing Carl out since that boy could walk. Some parents just don't know when to draw the line."

"But murder?"

"He probably thought it was the only way to protect his child. When we love someone, we don't always know when to quit."

"I can't believe you're defending his actions."

"I'm not, honeybun. I'm just telling you what he probably felt." She picked up a knife and whacked the head off a stalk of celery. "It's just a shame he never thought about those two kids he killed. That they were someone's children, too."

Outside, a car door slammed. Dove walked over to the large picture window in the living room and peered out.

"Who is it?" I asked after she stood there for a minute or so.

"Can't really tell from this angle, but it appears to be for you."

"What?" I walked over to the window. The hood of my Chevy was up and a long pair of legs in washed-out Levi's pulled tight across the thighs was bent over the engine while Daddy stood talking and gesturing with his coffee cup.

"I can see what attracted you to him," Dove said with a snicker.

"Dove!" I gently slapped her shoulder. "You're seventy-five years old. You're a great-grandmother, for Pete's sake."

"Which makes me more qualified than you to judge the quality of a man's butt." She looked back outside. "Looks pretty good. He must be one of them fellas who likes to exercise. Probably has lots of staying power."

"You are unbelievable. You sound like a teenager."

She patted my arm. "Best not let him get too close to me today. I might just give it a little pinch."

I groaned and shook my head.

She placed a hand between my shoulder blades and shoved me toward the door. "You'd better get out there before your daddy puts him to work shoveling crap in the barn."

As I walked down the porch steps, Daddy passed me, empty coffee cup in hand.

"Nice boy," was all he said.

Ortiz leaned against the white rail fence that lined our long gravel driveway. A smudge of grease from the Chevy's engine streaked the front of his white tee shirt.

"What are you doing to my truck?" I asked.

"Just checking it out." His eyes widened a bit when he saw me, but he didn't mention my hair. He gestured to a small pasteboard box sitting on the ground next to the truck. "Brought you something." I opened it with the toe of my boot and peered in at some mechanical contraption.

"What is it?"

"A new starter. I'm tired of worrying about you breaking down somewhere. It'll only take an hour or two to put it in."

"Oh." I didn't know what else to say. In my family, when a man started feeling proprietary about a woman's vehicle, that meant he had intentions. I wasn't sure what it meant to Ortiz. I stared at the ground and waited.

"You're welcome," he said in a wry voice.

We were silent for a moment.

"You have a heck of a lot of nerve showing up here after how you treated me," I blurted out.

"I am not going to talk about any of that with you. Every time I think about it, I have this uncontrollable urge to wring your neck."

"You!" I said. "What about me? You treated me like a common criminal. And I want to know why you didn't tell me you suspected J.D. all along? I can't believe you kept that from me."

"Why, so you could go running to Carl or J.D. and screw things up worse than you already did? It was a lucky break for us J.D. was stupid enough to keep the gun he killed the Griffin kid with, or we'd have squat to charge him with."

"Screw things up? I solved this case, Friday. You'd still

be out asking questions and writing things in your little notebook if it wasn't for me. Besides, that was *my* life you were putting on the line by not telling me what you suspected."

He moved forward and put his hand over my mouth. "I'm sick of arguing about this. I've followed you around like a friggin' puppy dog the last week and a half trying to keep you out of trouble. You know, you are the most pig-headed . . ."

I pushed his hand away. "Besides your obvious enjoyment at lecturing me and your peculiar interest in my motor vehicle, just *why* are you here, Ortiz?"

"Actually, your grandmother called me."

"What?"

"She said that if it was of any interest to me, you were probably ready."

"Ready for what?"

"She didn't say, but it was too intriguing to pass up."

I groaned. I was going to take that braid of hers, wrap it around her neck and pull. Better yet, I'd buy Aunt Garnet a one-way ticket back to San Celina.

"Don't be too hard on her. I'm sure she meant well." He reached over and pulled at a strand of my hair. "So, what happened here?"

I shrugged. "It seemed like something to do at the time."

"Psychologists say that men assert their freedom from authority by growing their hair long and that women show their independence by cutting theirs."

"You're always just crammed full of interesting facts, aren't you?"

He smiled. "It's cute. I like it."

"Believe it or not, that really wasn't one of my considerations when I had it done."

"New hair," he said, running his hand gently through

it. "Hair grown in the last nine months."

A part of me wanted to push his hand away, but a bigger part of me didn't. "Not much gets by you, does it, Sergeant Friday?" I said softly.

"Not the important stuff, *querida*."

"Okay," I said, deciding to get to the point. "This thing between you and me. What is it anyway?"

"What do you want it to be?"

"A question for a question. Is that what life with a cop is like?"

"I'm warning you, it isn't easy. Interrupted meals, interrupted holidays, interrupted . . . well, you get the drift. It's what broke up my marriage."

"Just how long are you going to be around these parts?" I asked. I climbed up and sat on the top rail of the fence so we were equal eye level.

He was silent for a moment. "Does it matter?"

I considered his question, then decided to tell the truth. "Yes, it does. I don't like to start things I can't see to some sort of finish."

"So I noticed." He grabbed the fence on both sides of me and leaned close.

"I have three months left, and they've asked me to stay six more. Aaron isn't getting better as quickly as anticipated." His face grew pensive for a moment, then he smiled. "After that, who knows? Is that long enough?"

I placed my hands on his shoulders and looked into his crazy gray-blue eyes. "I guess if we can't figure out something in nine months, then we're pretty stupid."

"Sounds about right to me."

"We're really different, you know."

"Yes. I, for example, have some sense."

I punched him in the chest. "You have a terrible temper. You really need to work on that. And I bet you can't even ride."

"I never had a problem with it before I came here. And I rode a horse once. Wasn't that hard."

"You are so incredibly arrogant."

"And that smartass mouth of yours is going to get you in real trouble someday."

"Oh, this is going to be great fun," I said.

"Sure is," he replied and grinned.

"We'll be in a fishbowl. No privacy whatsoever."

"Guess I'll have to get used to it." He kissed me quickly on the lips, then started to back away. "I'd better get cracking on that starter."

"Just a minute, Chief Ortiz," I said. Hooking my boots around his waist, I pulled him back and gave him a kiss he wouldn't forget anytime soon.

"What are you thinking about?" I asked some time later. I was off the fence and pressed against his clean, sweet-smelling shirt, his chin resting on the top of my head.

"About what I'd get if I rebuilt your carburetor."

I laughed and kissed the bottom of his chin.

"Could you do one thing for me?" he asked.

"Depends."

"My name's Gabe."

I laughed again. "I've grown kind of fond of Friday, but I'll try."

At that moment, Dove came out and rang the dinner bell.

"Bring the boy in for coffee," she called.

"She's enjoying this immensely," I said as we walked toward the house. "Be prepared to tell your goriest stories. Feel free to be as graphic as you like. Knowing the chief of police on a personal basis will be quite a feather in her hat with the historical society. All those old ladies are a bunch of bloodthirsty ghouls."

"She sounds like a pistol," he said, throwing his arm

around my shoulder as casually as if we'd known each other for years. "But then, I'm not surprised. Any last piece of advice before I meet her?"

"Yeah," I said, fitting my arm around his waist and slipping my left hand in the back pocket of his Levi's. Felt fine, real fine. "Whatever you do, don't turn your back on her."